# Death's Honesty

## by

## Brian Anderson

*The Lyle Dahms Mysteries*

The Wild Rose Press, Inc.
PO Box 708
Adams Basin, NY 14410-0708
Visit us at www.thewildrosepress.com

Publishing History
First Edition, 2025
Trade Paperback ISBN 978-1-5092-6189-5
Digital ISBN 978-1-5092-6190-1

*The Lyle Dahms Mysteries*
Published in the United States of America

## Dedication

To all of those who have supported me on this writer's journey—my family, my friends, my critique partners, and most of all, my readers.

Chapter One

From the earliest, my memories of my father are tinted blue. As a child I'd climb out of my bed in the morning, go into the kitchen, and find him hunched over the table drinking coffee, the creases of his dark blue uniform perfectly pressed and starched as stiff as razor blades. In my little boy mind, he loomed less a real person than a fairy tale giant, the coffee cup comically small, swallowed up by his massive hand. Quite simply, he filled up my world, dwarfing all around him—a veritable mountain of blue. Now, a pale blue hospital gown had replaced the uniform, and his once impressive frame was a frail cage riddled with cancer.

The television was on in the sickroom. Some daytime TV "doctor" was badgering a no-account, would-be ladies' man into taking some responsibility for the mess he'd made of his life. The studio audience seemed solidly behind the good doctor. Every time he made a point, the folks in the gallery would shout their encouragement, like good Baptists urging on their preacher when the Spirit is truly upon him. My mom was nodding right along, sitting near the foot of Dad's bed, staring up at the television set, distracted only occasionally by a beep from the IV or the quiet hum of a pump that came on automatically every so often to check his blood pressure. Mom had the only padded chair. I sat in a metal folding chair that screeched ominously each time I crossed my legs. My butt had long since gone numb. Sometimes I looked at the TV. Mostly, I stared at my dad.

A nurse came in. There must have been a shift change; it wasn't the same one we'd had earlier. Both Mom and I watched silently as the nurse checked the electronic regulator on the IV pole next to the bed, nodding as she stared at the readout. The scent of soap lingered about her, floral and clean, though ultimately overpowered by the harsh antiseptic tang that pervaded the room. The nurse laid her hand briefly on Dad's head before rearranging the bed linens and then checking the tape that secured a needle protruding from his hand. She glanced at me before bending down to check a tube that emerged out from under the covers. She followed the tube down to a square plastic receptacle half-filled with cloudy yellow urine.

"Have to change that before the end of the shift," she said, as if talking to herself.

Mom had been monitoring each of the nurse's movements minutely. When she finished, the nurse took another quick look at the chart by Dad's bed, then turned to Mom and smiled pleasantly. "Your husband seems to be resting comfortably, Mrs. Dahms."

Mom stood, her lips tightening into a grim little smile. "He hasn't opened his eyes or said anything in a couple of days now. Do you think he's—"

"Has Dr. Rudin been in to see you today?" the nurse interrupted.

"Not today."

"I'm sure he'll be in later," she said, patting Mom's hand. Then, glancing briefly at me, she asked, "Is this your son?"

"Yes," Mom replied. "My oldest. Lyle."

"It's nice that he could be with you," the nurse said, nodding in my direction.

"Oh, I couldn't get through this without Lyle," Mom confided, smiling at me.

The nurse patted Mom's hand again. "Take care of your mom, now," she told me before leaving.

"I will," I promised.

"We'll take care of each other," Mom murmured.

We watched the nurse leave. Mom stood by the bed for a long time staring out the open door into the empty hallway. Finally, she sighed and then ran her hand across her skirt, smoothing wrinkles only she could see. It was a dark skirt with horizontal lines that weren't entirely flattering to a woman of her build. Keeping her weight down had always been a struggle for Mom. Not so for Dad. Before his illness, my dad could brag that he weighed the same as he did as a defensive lineman in high school.

Me? I largely took after Mom. Dad, who was unfailingly complementary to my mother, rarely missed an opportunity to needle me about my extra pounds. Though tall as my father and similarly broad-shouldered, I'd always been considerably wider. As for my brother Chuck, a former model turned executive at a Wall Street brokerage house, neither excess pounds nor my dad's hectoring had ever been an issue.

Mom resumed her seat, returning her attention to the television set and inching up the volume. I went back to staring at Dad.

I'd never stopped seeing him as a cop. He'd retired some years before, but as a thirty-year veteran of the Burnsville, Minnesota police department, the job seemed to define him completely. His wasn't the most illustrious of careers. He'd never moved out of the patrol car, had never made plainclothes, or carried a gold shield. When asked about it, he'd shake his head, maintaining that it didn't matter, that the real work was on the street. Naturally, he complained about being on the low end of the pay scale, but even during hard times, he'd always provided for his family, sometimes even surprising us with vacations and other extravagances that you'd have figured were beyond his means. In the end, he'd insist, money wasn't what was important. That's not why he became a cop. What was important was enforcing the law. That and respect. He was big on respect. He'd put on that blue uniform in the morning, strap on his holster, climb behind the wheel of his patrol car, and drive out into the suburban Minneapolis streets to get his respect.

I glanced over at Mom. Dad had always been the strong one, striding purposefully through life while she kind of waddled along behind. I'd often wondered how Mom would get on without Dad around to call the shots. But she'd been holding together remarkably well, offering steady and uncomplaining support throughout his illness, making sure he was on time to his appointments and was honest with his doctors. Now, she was the one that seemed to radiate strength while Dad continued to shrink away from the drugs and the cancer.

He hadn't been conscious for two days. Mostly, he slept, but there were times when he'd become agitated, not opening his eyes, but tossing fitfully and kicking his legs convulsively, as though something were pressing down on him and he was trying to throw it off.

Even when he was peaceful, it was disturbing for me to look at him. He'd always been an imposing man—trim and strong, with steely gray-black hair and blue-gray eyes that seemed to take in everything. Cop's eyes. Now, only wisps of hair remained, and the last time I'd seen his eyes was when a nurse had pulled back his eyelids to check his pupils. So much for respect.

I had to give the old guy one thing, though. In a twisted sort of way, it was fitting that a man who had so long prided himself on being able to meet any challenge, to vanquish any foe, would finally be felled by rebellious cells from within his own body. It was as if the universe agreed that the only thing that could bring Ray Dahms down was Ray Dahms himself.

A commercial came on and Mom turned from the television to look at me. I smiled, then got up off the chair and crossed to the window. Mom had insisted that the blinds be closed so that Dad wouldn't be disturbed by light coming in from the outside. I'd restrained myself from pointing out that the fluorescent light fixture above his bed glared with the blue-white brilliance of a team of arc welders. Still, I didn't raise the blinds, instead merely peering through the blades out into a cloudy September afternoon.

"Marjorie, you there?" My dad's frail voice in the room startled me. Whirling around, I banged into the blinds. The rattle made him flinch.

Mom lowered the volume on the television and was on her feet. "Ray?" she asked. "Ray, can you hear me?"

He didn't reply.

She bent down close to him. "I'm here, Ray. I'm here. Chuck will be here soon. He's coming in tonight. Lyle's here, though. We're both here."

Dad shook his head slowly but with great determination, letting it roll completely from side to side.

"I gotta talk to Donnie," he insisted. "Where's Donnie?"

He hadn't spoken that name in nearly twenty years. Hearing it, I felt the color drain from my face. Mom cast me a concerned glance. I shook my head at her.

"*Lyle's* here, Ray," she repeated. "Been right here with me the whole time. He's been—"

Dad's eyes flashed open. There didn't seem to be recognition in them. It wasn't clear that he could really even see us. Instead, his eyes were wild, crackling with a frantic plea that contrasted unnervingly with his somnolent, immobile face. I'd seen him upset before, angry, but this was different. "I need to talk to Donnie," he said, intending to shout but managing only a harsh croak. "Donnie Murdoch. It's important."

"Donnie Murdoch?" Mom repeated. "The boy whose parents…" She stopped herself before she said it. "From back when Lyle and Chuck were still in school? The boy who stayed with us a while?"

Mom glanced at me uncertainly. "You remember Donnie Murdoch, don't you, honey?"

"I remember," I told her.

There was something in my tone that Mom didn't like, and she scowled at me. "We don't need to go into that now, Lyle," she said stiffly.

Dad winced as if stabbed suddenly. "What happened to that kid is my fault," he said. His voice, though barely audible, was shot through with dread.

Alarm crackled in Mom's eyes. "Don't talk nonsense, Ray," she told him. "You did everything you could for Donnie Murdoch."

"More than you should have," I added.

Mom ignored me. "The mess that Donnie made for himself didn't have anything to with you, Ray."

"They investigated us, you know," Dad said in a feathery whisper. "After his parents were killed. Knuck Fullmer, my old partner, he and I got the call. We were first on the scene."

"Yes, but I don't see—"

"They put us on restricted duty for a while," Dad interrupted, the gravel in his voice increasing. "They rooted around like rats sniffing after cheese. Didn't find nothing. But still—"

"It's okay, Ray," Mom assured him. "Everything's okay. You relax now. You must be so tired. You need your rest."

Dad didn't seem to hear her. "I tried to make up for it after. You remember. I tried. But I gave up. I quit trying after Donnie...after he..." Dad paused. "I gotta face that now," he said. "I'm fucking dying here, and I got this shit barking at my heels."

Dad fell silent, exhausted. He exhaled deeply and lay very still, his chest rising only slightly as he drew in shallow breaths. Mom, her face fixed with apprehension, leaned even closer to him.

"Maybe it's not too late," Dad said, rousing himself. "Maybe I can make it right. Maybe..."

He had to stop again to catch his breath. Then, eerily, he tried to laugh, managing only a cough. "Who am I kidding?" he asked. "You'll have to do it for me, son."

I hadn't even been sure that he knew I was in the room. "Do what, Dad?" I asked. "What do I have to do?"

It took a while for him to answer. "See about Donnie."

"What about him?" I wasn't able to hide the angry little quaver in my voice. Then again, maybe I didn't want to. "Why are you worried about Donnie?" I continued. "Are you forgetting what he did?" The quaver got stronger. "I haven't forgotten," I told him. "If I close my eyes, I can see it like it was yesterday. You weren't there. I was. Close enough to catch the splatter. You didn't spend months afterward reliving it every night in your dreams."

Dad opened his eyes again, raising a bony hand, not really reaching out but rather merely letting it float before him. "We gotta make things right," he implored. "I can't do it, Lyle. I'm not going to be here. I can't do it, and your brother Chuck…Well, he's not like us. Don't get me wrong. I love Chuck. More than anything. But it takes a certain kind, you know. Chuck's not the kind."

"But I am?"

Dad nodded feebly. "Yeah. You and me."

It was the only time I'd ever heard my father admit that I was like him in anything. He was staring at me, but his eyes were unfocused. If I'd have left the room, I don't think he'd have noticed. It was several seconds before I was able to reply. "I'll see what I can do."

Dad smiled. It was little more than a twitch at the corner of his mouth, but I'm sure it was a smile. He lowered his hand, closed his eyes, and seemed to sink into the bed as though, once again, a weight had descended, a weight against which he no longer had the energy to struggle. Before long, his breathing took on the rhythm of sleep. We listened to him breathe for several minutes before Mom motioned for me to follow her out into the hall.

I found it difficult to meet her eyes. One of us seemed to always be looking away. "Do you know what brought that on?" I asked at last.

She lowered her head thoughtfully. "No," she said. "Not really. Your dad's always been…I don't know, he's always been funny when it comes to that Murdoch boy."

"You're telling me," I said.

"I know this brings back terrible memories for you, Lyle. I'm sorry about that."

"I'm fine with it, Mom."

She stared at me for several seconds. "Your father always loved you, Lyle. You know that."

I smirked. "Well, I know he loves Chuck. He just said so. 'More than anything,' he said. And he's still thinking about Donnie Murdoch after all these years."

"Like I said, your dad's always been…I don't know, *peculiar* you might say when it comes to what happened to the Murdochs."

I nodded. "I got that impression back when he tried to replace me with Donnie."

Mom glared. "He never tried to replace you," she insisted. "He was trying to do the right thing, is all. He still is."

She paused, sniffed, and wiped at her eyes with a balled hand. Tears edged her now red-rimmed eyes. "When people get close to the…you know, close to the end, they can settle on the darndest things. You know, things they aren't happy about. Things they wish they could put right."

"Something about the Murdoch shooting that Dad wishes he could put right?" I asked. "He do something he regrets?"

"Of course not," she snapped. "Your dad would never, uh…He'd never…He's not…" She sniffed again. "He's not thinking clearly, is all. There were some questions raised back then is all. Nothing to it, but it

Brian Anderson

might have made your dad think some folks didn't trust him." She glanced back at the open door to Dad's room. "As if all his years on the force hadn't earned him enough trust."

"But he said what happened to Donnie was his fault," I pressed. "Why would he say that if there wasn't something—"

"There *is* nothing!" she exclaimed. There was a finality in her voice that startled me. It must have startled her a little as well. She backed up a step, then turned abruptly away. "Oh, Lyle," she said, her voice cracking, "I just can't take this right now. Can't we just—"

"Just ignore it?" I asked as calmly as I could. "Dad won't be with us much longer. We both know that. This is probably his last request. That's a pretty hard thing to ignore."

Mom turned away. "I know, Lyle. I know. I know. But…but it's been so many years. Too many. What good can come of this? I mean, even if you decided to…I mean, do you think you'd even be able to find him? By now, he's probably—"

"I'm a private investigator, Mom," I reminded her. "I'm pretty sure I could find him."

She managed a smile. "You really do take after your dad, Lyle." Her eyes were moist and reassuring. "You followed him into law enforcement. He knows he can count on you."

I chuckled. "Dad's never considered what I do to be law enforcement."

"I know he wanted you on the police force. But that's all water under the bridge now. It's just that he was such a…such a…"

"Dad was a good cop," I said.

"And a good man. And he tried to be a good father."
I nodded.

Mom grew quiet again. "Maybe you shouldn't, Lyle," she said at last. "Maybe we should just—"

"He asked me, Mom," I said. "Do you honestly think I could simply let it go?

Mom took a deep breath, then let the air out slowly through slightly pursed lips as though she were blowing out birthday candles. "No," she said, patting me awkwardly on the arm. "I don't suppose you could."

We returned to Dad's room. He seemed to sleep more peacefully after that. Mom and I watched television together until my brother Chuck arrived around midnight. Then the four of us, the whole family together for the first time in years, sat vigil, neither speaking nor touching, our silence made even more conspicuous by the soft murmuring of the television set.

When I glanced at the clock on the wall, it was nearly six in the morning. I stood up, easing the stiffness from my joints, and crossed the room to the window again. Peering through the slats, I watched as the horizon began to lighten, the darkness slipping away into a warm, pre-dawn blue. Within the hour, my father slipped into it, too.

Chapter Two

The woman at the end of the bar was young and trim with light brown hair worn well off her shoulders that flared outward like the bell of a trumpet. She had on a pair of tight blue jeans and a clingy, low-cut, yellow blouse stippled with blue flowers, a little ruffle edging its short sleeves. It looked like something Elly Mae Clampett would have worn. She accepted her drink order—a glass of house burgundy—from Skip, the bartender, with a grateful smile before returning to join her friends at a nearby table. I drained the last of my beer and signaled Skip for a fresh one.

"You know what's always bothered me?" I asked as he set the beer on the bar in front of me.

Skip, a deceptively slight-looking African American, glanced down at me indifferently. "I can't imagine."

"The kinfolk," I told him.

"The kinfolk?"

"Yeah, the kinfolk. You know, the part where 'the kinfolk said, *Jed, move away from there?*'"

Skip raised one eyebrow, which I took to signal his interest, but since half of his face was paralyzed and thus remained grimly fixed, I could never be sure I was reading him correctly. "Jed?" he asked.

"Yeah, you know, from the TV show *The Beverly Hillbillies*. The patriarch? Jed Clampett?"

Skip lowered the eyebrow. "I'm not having this conversation with you, Dahms."

"Come on," I urged him. "Are you telling me you didn't watch *The Beverly Hillbillies* when you were growing up?"

"Oh yeah," he answered, both sides of his face now equally expressionless. "That's what all us Black kids watched. Shows about white Southerners with guns out coon hunting."

I smiled. "So, you did watch it."

"I'll be going back to work now, Dahms," he replied, turning away.

I raised my glass at him. "Y'all come back now, hear."

I had returned my attention to my beer and was thinking about ordering an early dinner when Stephen Edgerton came into the pub. The ceilings in McCauley's were quite low, so low that customers tended to stoop warily as they entered. Stephen—my best friend and a fellow denizen of The Bijou, our nearby rooming house—elected to dip slightly at the knees instead of bowing his head. Taking long strides, he bobbed across the darkened room like a fleet-footed pigeon. He stopped at the bar alongside of me but barely glanced in my direction. Instead, he waved to Skip with a broad smile.

Skip gave Edgerton a curious half-smile in return. "Beer?" he asked.

"You know it."

Skip filled a glass and set it in front of Edgerton. "You might want to take that to a booth," Skip cautioned.

"Why's that?"

Skip nodded at me. "You sit there and Dahms is liable to gripe to you about the kinfolk."

"The kinfolk?"

Skip gave his head a doleful shake. "Don't say I didn't warn you."

He picked up a white terrycloth bar rag, turned, and worked his way down to the other end of the bar. Edgerton sipped at his beer, pushed his cascading red hair away from his face, ran a palm over his trim mustache and beard, and finally faced me. "The kinfolk?" he repeated.

"It's been bugging me, is all," I told him. "I mean, here's this guy out hunting, you know. Like the song says, 'shooting at some food...'"

"Wait a minute," Edgerton interrupted. Then he blinked and nodded decisively. "Okay, I'm with you," he said. "'An' up from the ground come a bubblin' crude.'"

"So, you watched the show growing up?"

"Sure. Everybody did. *The Beverly Hillbillies, Gilligan's Island, Hogan's Heroes*. They're our shared history. They're the lingua franca of our generation."

"Okay, so anyway," I continued, "Jed's out hunting and through an unbelievable act of providence comes into this whopping pile of cash—"

"Actually," Edgerton broke in, "it would be more accurate to say, 'pool of oil.' You know, 'Black gold. Texas tea.'"

"Yeah, yeah," I said, waving dismissively, "but here's my point. This local guy makes good beyond the dreams of avarice, right? But the good citizens of Bug Tussle, do they ask Jed to stick around, maybe reinvest some of those millions into the local economy? Shit no. Instead, as the song makes clear, 'the kinfolk said, *Jed, move away from there.*' Now, my question is, why were they so all-fired anxious to have this guy leave town? I mean, what dark secret made Jed such a pariah in his own community?"

Edgerton paused thoughtfully. "Maybe it wasn't Jed they were trying to get rid of," he ventured. "Maybe it was Granny. Or Jethro. Hey, maybe it was Elly Mae. Maybe her affection for all those 'critters' manifested itself in some deeply disturbing manner."

"Hoo doggies," I said.

"Hoo doggies, indeed."

We fell silent and Edgerton wrapped both hands around his beer glass and began to studiously examine the bubbles as they rose and popped on the surface. I tried not to be too obvious as I craned my neck in an attempt to steal another look at the woman in the yellow blouse.

"It's good to see you getting out more," Edgerton said.

"What do you mean? I've been getting out."

"No," he said, still staring intently at his beer glass. "Not so much."

I frowned.

"I haven't seen Naomi around lately," he observed.

"She went to my dad's funeral with us the other day," I reminded him.

"Since then, I mean."

I shrugged. "Well, you know."

Edgerton raised his glass to his lips.

Naomi Miller and I had been together for two years. The relationship had started out great if you didn't count the part about somebody trying to kill her. But after we straightened that out, she stuck around, and although we had to work at it a bit, we seemed to have something genuine together. But things started to go downhill big time nearly a year ago when she admitted that although she enjoyed being with me, she didn't think I was the kind of guy she could ever settle down with. I pointed out that neither of us wanted to settle down just then anyway, and we agreed to simply wait and see what would happen. What happened was that several months later, she sat me down and told me that she thought we should start seeing other people. She then went on to tearfully insist that she would always look upon me as her best and truest friend. Naturally, there isn't a guy on earth who wouldn't recognize this as the brush-off, and any self-respecting man would have run, not walked, away from the relationship. But that night, Naomi had managed to whip her conflicted emotions into something of a frenzy, which culminated in her taking her best and truest friend to bed with her. After that, neither of us seemed to be able to do the sensible thing and just break it off. But we had been seeing quite a bit less of one another since then.

"Pity," Edgerton said, still staring at his beer. "I like her."

I didn't say anything.

Skip came by and wordlessly dropped a red plastic basket of free popcorn in front of us. Edgerton ate a few handfuls before again turning toward me, his eyes crinkled with concern. "You doing okay, Lyle?"

"What do you mean?"

"I mean with Naomi and…you know, your dad?"

"I'm fine."

Edgerton nodded. "Can't be easy, though."

I sighed. "I'm going to miss them both more than I'd like to admit."

Edgerton smiled. "Ah, go ahead. Admit it."

I shook my head. "I'm a professional tough guy, remember? What if word got out?"

Edgerton chuckled but immediately went serious again. "It just seems so…" He searched for the word. "…so *synchronous*. You getting tighter with your dad toward the end. Naomi backing off because she doesn't think you'd make a good father. Then you losing your father. It's all so—"

"Naomi didn't say she thought I'd be a bad father," I interrupted.

"Yes, she did."

"How do you know?"

"You told me."

"You must not have heard me correctly."

"Yeah, that's it," he deadpanned. "I'm just saying it's funny is all."

"Uh huh. I'm in stitches."

"You know what I mean."

I drained the last of my beer. "I do. Now let it go."

Edgerton persisted. "You think Naomi's worried about the kind of dad you'd make 'cause she'd seen how you and your dad used to get along? From what you told me, the guy was never up for any awards."

"He did all right."

"Yeah?"

"Yeah. I mean, it's possible that, in retrospect, he'd admit that announcing, 'That's a good one,' every time Chuck or I farted in the living room may have been a bad strategy, but the guy did his best."

"Okay, but how good was his best?"

"Can we drop this?" I asked.

Edgerton smiled wanly. "Talking's good," he said. "You've been so mopey lately. I thought it was time

17

somebody—"

"I appreciate the thought. I really do. But the thing with my dad is…it's just complicated, you know. I'm not saying we didn't have our differences. But he got along with Chuck fine. Shit, how bad could he have been? There were kids in our neighborhood just itching to join our family. We even took one on once."

Edgerton stared at me for a moment. "Tell me about that."

I shrugged again. "There was this kid," I began, "Donnie. Donnie Murdoch. We went to the same high school. I didn't really know him very well. He was a couple of years older than me, and, in keeping with the pecking order, we rarely spoke."

Edgerton nodded.

"Anyway, Donnie was a big kid…not big like me, but tall and strong. He had this shock of unruly, dark hair and dark eyes that seemed perpetually cast downward. He was fond of flannel shirts and Levi's with shredded knees. In the yearbook his senior year, he said he hoped to become a mechanic. He was a pretty normal kid, I guess. A little shy. And he seemed to have trouble making friends, but…You know how it is. Other kids can be put off by shyness. It's like an obstacle, an extra little burden they can't be bothered to shoulder."

"It's not just this Donnie had that problem," Edgerton said, nodding.

"Kids don't like anybody different," I agreed. "And Donnie's folks didn't help things much. The elder Murdochs kept mostly to themselves. Oh, you'd see Donnie's mother out tending her garden. Or his dad driving off to work in the mornings in this aging Ford pickup. But Pam Murdoch never waved, never smiled, never stopped by for coffee and casual conversation with the other Burnsville womenfolk. And there was a gun rack in the cab of Vernon Murdoch's truck, and the stuff he hauled in the truck bed was usually covered—suspiciously, we thought—by a heavily stained canvas tarp. And while most Burnsville kids, me included, lived in standard issue 1960s era ramblers and split-levels, on third-of-an-acre lots, with dads, for the most part, obsessively devoted to lawn care, the Murdochs lived in a decrepit-looking, gray, two-story farmhouse on some five acres left untouched by developers. Instead of an over-watered, over-fertilized carpet of Kentucky bluegrass and creeping red fescue, the Murdochs mostly used their acreage to showcase a half dozen or so rusting cars and trucks that formed a kind of rustic sculpture garden."

"I know the kind of place you mean," Edgerton said.

I grinned. "All in all, though, they were pretty ordinary. I mean, nobody thought much about them. Then *it* happened. Fact is, I was down at the library earlier today rereading the newspaper accounts. It's incredible the kind of detail they released. Donnie wasn't home that evening. He had a job moving stock around the old Dayton's department store. But both Vernon and Pam were home. Pam was in the garden tending her carrots, radishes, and a few Early Girl tomato plants. Vernon had been in the garage working on a beat-up '68 Dodge he hoped to get running for Donnie. The killer got Pam first. She was shot in the upper torso. Killer used a shotgun. Like to have torn her in half. Vernon must have heard the blast and came running into the house. The killer was waiting there for him. He took his time with Vernon. They had quite a little set-to. Vernon was pretty badly knocked around before he, too, was shot. He got his in the kitchen. In the back. Cops figured he was making a break for it. But old Vern was still alive when the first patrol car pulled up. By then, the killer was long gone." I paused. "The first patrol car? It was my dad. Him and his partner, Johnny Fullmer. The guys used to call him *Knuck*. Short for *Knuckles*, Dad told me. And this is where the story takes a bit of a turn."

"Yeah?"

"Yeah. According to their report, my dad and Fullmer entered the house together. They called for an ambulance and immediate backup, then made certain that the shooter was no longer on the premises. My dad went outside to check the perimeter while Fullmer stayed inside with Vernon Murdoch. Fullmer said he thought he heard something in the basement of the house, so he left Murdoch lying on the kitchen floor while he went to check it out. Then a shot rang out. Fullmer races back up into the kitchen and finds Murdoch dead, a .38 revolver in his hand. My dad comes in and sees the same thing. They don't know where the gun came from. They don't know how a man in such bad shape could have found the energy to get up, find a gun, return to the exact same spot in the kitchen where he'd been lying before, and then put a round in his own brain. But that's how they wrote it up. Both Fullmer and my dad got modified duty for a couple of weeks while the department ran an official investigation. In the end, they let it drop. There were no other witnesses. The killer never surfaced. They couldn't prove that things didn't happen just like Dad and Knuck said they did. But it didn't smell too good, you know?"

"I guess not," Edgerton said. "Anybody ever figure out why they were shot?"

"That's one detail that never made the papers. There was lots of speculation, but nothing was ever substantiated. Dad never talked about it. We could tell the investigation was getting to him, but there was no way he was going to admit that he was worried or in over his head or anything. Fact is, I think it bothered him so much that it caused him to do just about the strangest thing he ever did."

"Which was?"

"One afternoon a couple of weeks after the Murdoch killings, I'm sitting in the living room, probably watching *Beverly Hillbillies* reruns, and in walks my dad. Trailing after him, holding onto a suitcase, is Donnie Murdoch. Dad tells him to stow his gear in the basement. We had an extra bed down there in case of company. Then he turns and tells me that Donnie will be staying with us. When I ask how long, Dad smiles and says, 'Long as he wants.' And that's it. No other explanation. Nothing."

"Must have felt sorry for the kid," Edgerton suggested.

"That's what my mom said. She said that Donnie was only a couple of months shy of graduation, that he'd lost his family, and just needed someplace normal to finish up school and sort his life out. I asked her why he had to stay with us. She said what she always said. 'Dad wanted it that way.'"

"Sounds like you were less than thrilled."

"I was pissed. Looking back, it seems kind of harsh, the kid having just lost both parents and all, but…but…You gotta realize my dad and I were going through a pretty bad patch just then. No matter what I did, it wasn't good enough. And when I fucked up, he'd shake his head and make some crack about how maybe there was a mix-up at the hospital, and I wasn't really his son. Stuff like that. It wasn't easy to hear."

"I don't suppose."

"The thing is…about Donnie. The thing is, I couldn't shake the feeling that Dad brought Donnie home to…I don't know, to replace me, I guess. It was like he was throwing up his hands and starting over. You know?"

"You think that's what he was doing?"

"I don't know. No. Maybe. I don't know."

Edgerton nodded. "So, how long did this Donnie stay with you?"

"Not long. He went away the next summer. After he graduated. And thereby hangs another tale."

"Yeah?"

"Oh, yeah."

I picked up my beer glass. It was long empty, but I stared into it anyway.

"You going to tell me?" Edgerton prompted.

I sighed. "Back then, every summer, I'd go to this festival called Racing Days that was held in Hamilton. The next town over. Back at the turn of the twentieth century, it had been a center for horse racing. The famous pacer, the Great Dan Patch, used to be stabled there. I started off going with my folks, but by the time I was in high school I'd go with my friends. On the surface, this thing was like every other small-town civic celebration. You know, an excuse for the town to indulge in a little self-promotion by marking off a summer weekend, blocking off a street or two, and bringing in kiddy rides, food booths, and a beer garden. But there was something about Racing Days—something that was disturbing to my young mind. A hidden yet palpable something that seemed to bubble beneath the veneer of wholesomeness. Something dangerous."

I wanted another beer and tried to get Skip's attention. No luck.

"Anyway, this summer celebration started off as a fun way for the town to celebrate its heritage. But by the time I was in high school, things had begun to change. At first, it was just some rowdiness in the beer garden. A rock thrown through the display window of a local car dealership. Motorcycles screaming through the usually quiet streets at night. Each year, the town fathers promised a more sedate, family-friendly event. Each year, there were more fistfights, more property damage, and more arrests. Then came Donnie Murdoch.

"That day, I'd driven over to Racing Days with a couple of friends—a fun-loving, basketball-player-tall kid with a loopy grin called Sticks and a guy named Jimmy Dolan who was old enough to buy beer and didn't mind carting us around in his red and black Chevy pickup truck. It was mid-afternoon, hot as hell, and despite a wishful feeling that somehow there was danger in the air, we were starting to get a little bored. I remember we were standing on the curb outside the Knights of Columbus burger stand. We were talking about leaving, maybe heading out to a movie or something, when I spotted Donnie coming down the sidewalk toward us. He'd probably have just passed on by if it hadn't have been for the fight. Two guys in their mid-twenties had done a little too much early afternoon beer gardening, and suddenly, they're shouting at each other in the middle of the blocked-off street. Donnie stops alongside us to watch as these two square off, lobbing epithets at one another. Just as it looked like things were about to blow over, the bigger of the two threw a punch. Instantly, they're round-housing on each other. The smaller guy finally clamps the bigger guy off in an impressive headlock, and they both tumble to the pavement. They're rolling, cursing, throwing punches, occasionally connecting. I turned to Jimmy and Sticks and said something like, somebody should do something about this. I was just making conversation, you know. Anyway, Donnie looks at me."

I swallowed. "It was there in his eyes. I mean, they were so focused, so intense. It was like something inside him had clicked. Like everything in his universe had lined up and this was his defining moment. 'Okay,' he says. And he steps off the curb.

"He never looked back. Instead, he walks over to these two guys. Donnie's some three or four feet away from them, and he reaches into the pocket of this blue windbreaker he's wearing and pulls out a shiny silver semi-automatic. When he reaches them, he places the barrel of the gun against the temple of the bigger man and pulls the trigger."

I shuddered. "I'll never forget the sound, the spray of blood and bone, the way the man tried to stand, and the slow crumble of his body back down to the pavement."

Edgerton moved his mouth as though to say something but instead simply exhaled loudly.

"Donnie ran," I continued, "but he turned himself in later that day. I had to testify at the hearing. I remember that pretty clearly, too. I wore a brown plaid suit, a beige dress shirt, and a dun-colored knit tie wide enough to serve as a lobster bib. I'd been well coached by my dad, but I was still scared. I didn't want to talk in front of all those people. And Donnie sitting right there in front, listening…" I shook my head.

"But it wasn't any big deal. That's what my dad told me anyway. He told me that over and over. No big deal. Just the first time I'd seen somebody die. Just the first time I had to point a finger and hold someone accountable."

I tried to smile, but I think it came out crooked. "Donnie was put away with a recommendation that he receive psychiatric counseling," I concluded. "Dad was on his deathbed before he mentioned Donnie again. Hamilton cancelled Racing Days. For a while, at least. I heard they started it up again a few years ago. I don't know for sure. I don't get down there anymore."

Edgerton turned away just long enough to signal Skip that we needed another round. "You said you were at the library today rereading newspaper clippings," he said. "Any special reason?"

"Yeah. When my dad was dying, he asked me to look up old Donnie. I figured maybe I'd find something that'd give me a place to start."

"I take it he's not in the book," Edgerton said. "You sure looking for this guy's a good idea? Sounds like you'll be stirring up old ghosts."

"Maybe," I told him, "But maybe you gotta do that before they'll crawl back into their graves."

Chapter Three

With counseling, Donnie had only done three years for the Racing Days shooting, and his probation had long since ended. I checked the computer in the lobby of the Bureau of Criminal Apprehension in St. Paul and found that he hadn't been convicted of another crime in Minnesota since the one that had sent him to jail. Of course, this could have meant that he left the state, but even if he'd stayed local, it didn't give me his full criminal history—the database wouldn't include things like whether he'd been arrested or if the authorities were currently looking at him for anything. If I wanted to know that, I'd have to ask a cop.

I thought about maybe pestering my old pal, Minneapolis Homicide Detective Augustus Tarkof, for the information, but reflecting on our history, I concluded that Augie would sooner have his hemorrhoids banded than do me this favor. I considered asking Johnny Fullmer, Dad's old partner. He was retired, but old cops always know someone on the force willing to help a former colleague. But ultimately, I decided against it. Finding Donnie Murdoch was between my father and me. No sense riling up bad memories for Knuck.

I checked the Internet but also came up empty. Nothing current on Donnie Murdoch. At last, it occurred to me to call our old high school.

I gave them a story about wanting to reconnect with a long-lost buddy, and the lady in the office was sympathetic enough but didn't have an address for him. She suggested I get in touch with another member of Donnie's graduating class and gave me the name Marisa Algren.

Marisa Algren considered her best years to have been those she spent back at dear old Burnsville High. As senior class treasurer, cheerleader, and one-time princess of the annual Snow Ball, she felt that she'd made her most important contributions to the world before she'd reached the age of majority. Her subsequent marriage to Billy "High-Steppin'" Randall, a former basketball standout, now owner of Randall's Comfort Shoes, had left her little to do besides raise the kids and reflect on her glory days at BHS. In her need to maintain some kind of relationship with the high school, Marisa volunteered to continue her service to her classmates by maintaining updated information on all of them. Think of the scandal if lax record keeping led to their failure to invite a former classmate to the next big reunion.

It turns out her devotion to this undertaking bordered on the obsessive. During our none-too-brief telephone conversation, she demonstrated the range of her scholarship by detailing for me what seemed like every marriage, birth, or mention in the local newspaper that could be counted among her beloved fellow alumni. Suffice it to say that Marisa had an address for each of them, including Donnie Murdoch. Anything less would have been unthinkable.

Donnie hadn't left the state. According to Marisa, he was living nearby in North Minneapolis.

I checked my watch. It was still early afternoon, and

although I spent several minutes vainly trying to think of an excuse I could use to put off the meeting, I finally decided to take a run up there and get it over with. I climbed into my Ford and, so the trip wouldn't be entirely unpleasant, I popped a cassette recording of a November 1941 *Fibber McGee and Molly* show into the tape deck. Fibber somehow gets it in his head that movie star Ronald Coleman is coming to visit. For all I know, he did. I made it to the North Side before the show was over.

It wasn't a bad neighborhood. I didn't see any Bentleys or Rolls-Royces parked nearby, but it wasn't Fallujah. The housing stock consisted mostly of densely packed, one-and-a-half-story houses that dated from the 1930s and '40s. Most of them were fronted with three-season porches; most were in adequate repair. I parked my car on the street in front of a dark blue-gray house with black trim that matched the address that Marisa had given me. There were several fast-food wrappers strewn along the street, some of which had blown up into the yard, but the grass had been recently mown, and the paint on the house flaked only in a couple of places. The front porch had some problems. It had sunken about three inches since the house had been originally built, pulling away from the foundation and forming a crevasse at the base of the front door. If you dropped your keys down there, you'd be a long time getting in.

I glanced around the inside of the porch before ringing the doorbell. It was mostly empty, although a ratty armchair squatted in the far corner. Upholstered in brown corduroy, it was positioned next to a round side table that supported one of the biggest ashtrays I'd ever seen. Good thing, too. There had to be a hundred cigarette butts in there.

Whoever lived inside was security conscious, I thought, pressing the doorbell. The front door was a windowless fiberglass fronted with a steel mesh outer door. Both were secured with deadbolts. The windows that looked out onto the porch were all covered with brown paper. I held my breath and listened but heard no sound within. I rang the doorbell several times before giving up.

I went back outside and stood for a moment, staring. The sidewalk curved along the side of the house, and I followed it back to where a gate barred access to the backyard. I tried the latch but found it locked. The gate tied into a seven-foot-tall privacy fence, so even on my tiptoes, I wasn't really able to get a look on the other side. There was nothing unusual in any of that. Lots of people have privacy fences. The only thing that really struck me was the smell. There was a harsh, ammonia-like odor wafting from back there, like every cat in the neighborhood used this backyard as its litter box.

Although it was fall, the day was sunny and warm. I went back to my car and rolled down the window. With nothing to do, I lapsed into daydream, for the thousandth time fervently wishing that I hadn't quit smoking. Naomi hadn't exactly made me quit. She'd just mentioned several times how bad it was for me and how disappointed she sometimes was that I wasn't taking better care of myself.

They tell you that you can't quit smoking for someone else, that the decision to quit has to be made for yourself alone. They're full of shit.

I sat there for about ten minutes tapping the dashboard and rearranging the mirrors before a young guy in a shiny new sedan pulled up in back of me. He got out of his car and glanced briefly in my direction before approaching Donnie's house. If my presence there bothered him, he didn't show it. He was inside the porch for several minutes but didn't have any more luck getting in than I'd had. After the sedan pulled away, I spent another forty-five minutes or so sitting in front of the house, drinking in the sunshine, humming to myself, and watching as, one by one, a half dozen other cars pulled up, their occupants getting out, approaching the house, then leaving with disappointed looks on their faces.

After a while, I got bored just sitting there and decided to take a walk. I went down to the end of the block and found the entrance to an alley that ran behind the house. The stench of cat urine was stronger back there. A detached garage faced the alley, the door closed and locked. A series of windows were laid out over the door, just above eye level, each square of glass covered from the inside by what first looked like a picture of a bell drawn atop a rectangular grid. When I got closer, I saw that the bell was a stylized human figure and that there was a small, jagged hole in the head of each of the little men. Shooting targets, I realized. Someone's idea of a subtle warning.

It must have been trash day because two large brown plastic garbage cans were sitting just outside the closed garage door. I peeked inside. In addition to white plastic bags of household refuse, both cans also contained a couple of empty bottles of acetone. I tore open one of the plastic bags and found it filled with dozens of punched-out foil pill cards, the kind you get with cold medicine. Judging from the number, somebody in the house had quite the runny nose.

I returned to my car. Unfortunately, sitting there, waiting for something to happen, afforded me too much time to think about what it would be like seeing Donnie again. I didn't like to admit it, but over the years, I'd never quite been able to shake a feeling of unease, even dread, whenever I thought about Donnie. When he first came to live with us all those years ago, I'd viewed Donnie, not so much as a real person than as an intrusion, an unwelcome stranger who'd come between my father and me. Then, after witnessing so "up close and personal" the calm, even matter-of-fact way he took the life of that guy at Racing Days, Donnie became an even more unreal figure to me, no longer an intruder, but a specter, a phantom that lurked at the edge of my dreams. From that moment, my image of evil—sudden, capricious, and unfeeling—became tied to my image of Donnie Murdoch.

I was looking at my watch, thinking about an early dinner, when I glanced up and spotted a tall man who looked to be in his early forties coming down the sidewalk. He walked with his head lowered, a slight breeze rustling through his dark hair. It took a moment before I was sure it was Donnie.

I was carrying a .38 revolver under my jacket, and I patted it as I got out of the car. He looked right at me as he turned to go up to the house but apparently didn't recognize me. I swallowed hard, then let him get both doors unlocked before I followed him into the porch.

"Donnie," I said.

He turned. He really didn't look all that different from the last time I'd seen him. He was older, of course. A triangle of wrinkles radiated from the outer corner of both eyes. He was tanned, as though he spent a lot of time outside, and he had a scar maybe a half an inch long on his left cheekbone that was considerably lighter than the rest of his face. His hands were grimy. Grease caked the wrinkles around his knuckles and was embedded under his nails. It was his eyes that had changed the most. I remembered his eyes as dark, but now they were twin chasms, his dilated pupils forcing back the brown of his irises until they were each little more than a thin corona.

"Donnie," I repeated. "It's Lyle Dahms."

"They're not here," Donnie insisted, his voice tight and much reedier than I'd remembered. He moved in front of the door as though to block my passage, pulling absently at the skin of his hands, his eyes darting about the porch. "Come back later."

"I came to see *you*, Donnie," I told him. "Don't you remember? It's me. Lyle. Lyle Dahms. You know, Ray Dahms' kid. You stayed with us that summer. You know, before you—"

Donnie backed up suddenly. If possible, his eyes went even wider. "What are *you* doing here?" he exclaimed. "I didn't hurt you. You've no call to be coming 'round here."

I stepped forward, my hand outstretched. Donnie backed up still further, only stopping when he found himself straddling the threshold of the open door. I put both my palms up as though surrendering. "Jeez. Relax, Donnie," I told him. "I'm not coming after you. Nothing like that. My dad asked me to see you."

"What's he want with me?" Donnie demanded. "I never did anything to your old man. Why can't you leave me alone?"

"Christ, Donnie, take it easy, okay?" I said. "Nobody wants to do anything to you. I just...I just..."

Seeing Donnie's disturbance, even fear, at my appearance went a long way toward shoring up my dwindling confidence, but nonetheless, words weren't coming any too easy to me. "My dad," I began, "he…he was wondering, is all. It's been a lot of years, and he…He was wondering how things were with you. How you're doing. That kind of thing."

Donnie stared at me. His huge pupils made his eyes expressionless, unfocused. He stood there a long time before he finally exhaled very slowly, and the muscles of his face relaxed perceptively. He took several carefully measured breaths. "I'm fine," he said at last. "Just tell your dad I'm doing fine."

I smiled grimly. "I can't actually do that, Donnie. I wish I could. He, uh…he died the other day."

Donnie tensed back up immediately. "But you said—"

"He asked me to look you up before he died. He was thinking about you. Thinking about you while he was…" I let my voice trail off.

Donnie stared some more. Then he nodded as though he understood. "That was nice of him," he said. "Your dad thinking about me, that's nice. Took a while. But it's nice just the same."

I shrugged. "You know how it is. A guy facing the end. He was looking back, is all." I paused. "He did say a curious thing. He said he owed you. He said what happened to you was partly his fault. I got no idea what he meant by that. I mean, he wasn't even around when you…when you did what you did. Maybe it had something to do with what happened to your folks. I'm not sure. Maybe he was…I don't know, feeling guilty about you losing them or something. I don't know.

He..."

Donnie shook his head. Although most of his panic had left him, he still seemed as tightly coiled as the spring of a bear trap. But his strained voice was now edged with sympathy. "Your dad didn't have nothing to feel guilty about, I'll tell you that. I'm the one that screwed up. Them doctors? The ones that I saw back then? They helped me with that stuff. It took a while. You and your family taking me in? I should have been grateful for that. Sometimes you gotta learn the hard way, I guess."

"I guess," I agreed. "Even so, Dad was just wondering about you, you know."

Donnie eyes suddenly lit up. "He didn't leave me any money, did he?"

I shook my head. "'Fraid not."

"That's okay," Donnie said, unable to keep the disappointment out of his voice. "He just wanted you to come by and let me know he was thinking 'bout me, huh?"

"Yeah." I paused, apprehensive about my next question. "That and see if maybe there was anything I could do to help you. You uh...Can you think of anything I can do to help you out?"

"Not if it don't involve money. Nice of you to ask though. I mean, it says a lot about you and your old man, I guess. After all, you and I never did get along real well. Even before the...you know."

"No," I admitted, "we never did. That wasn't about you, though. That was mostly about my dad and me. We were—"

Someone shouted suddenly from within the house— loud, grating, and unexpected, like a chainsaw at a prayer vigil. "Why the hell's the door open? God dammit!"

Donnie whirled around, cringing with such intensity that he nearly doubled over.

"Tooz!" he implored to the unseen man. "I'm sorry. I didn't know you were home. I…I…" He couldn't finish the thought. The fear in his voice was palpable. Unexpectedly, I felt an immediate need to protect him.

"Is that you, Donnie?" came the reply. "For chrissakes! Close the fuckin' door, ya goddamned nimrod."

Donnie turned back to me, ducking down turtle-like, his head nodding up and down rapidly. He lowered his voice. "I gotta g…g…go," he stammered. His words came out more rasp than whisper.

"Who the hell—" I began.

"Jesus! Can't a guy take a day off?" the man inside hollered down to us. "I'm trying to get some rest, and the goddamned doorbell doesn't stop ringing. Christ! Just tell whoever that fat fuck is to get his ass out of here."

Donnie glanced at me with alarm, clearly hoping that I'd take this as my cue to leave. I could do that, I thought. The way I saw it, I had two options. My business with Donnie seemed at an end. I could simply turn and go home. Confronting the guy inside the house not only would serve no good purpose but would prove once and for all that I possessed all the self-control of a petulant fourth grader. I smiled and pushed gently past Donnie into the house.

It took a moment for my eyes to adjust to the dim light inside. I was standing in a small entryway looking up at an open staircase that led upstairs. I glanced to my right. An expanse of hardwood floor opened up into a living room sparsely furnished with a tattered sofa, a lime green bean bag chair, and a huge flat-screen TV teetering atop a wobbly stand. I turned, and near the top of the stairs, I could just make out the vague outline of a medium-sized man.

I smiled up at him. "The trouble with taking on strangers, pal," I said in an even voice to the mostly hidden figure, "is you can never be quite sure what you'll be facing."

The man took a few steps down the stairs. As he did, he moved into the light streaming in through the still-open door. He looked to be pushing sixty, maybe older, not very tall, but hard, with sinewy muscles and prominent veins that bulged under the skin of his forearms like earthworms engorged after a rain. He was wearing jeans and a white pocket T-shirt that very nearly managed to hide a round little belly. He had a shiny pate encircled by curly, gray-salted, brown hair badly in need of a trim. It made him appear vaguely clown-like. But there was nothing funny about what he was cradling in his arms. Sunlight glinted off the barrel of a twelve-gauge shotgun.

I kept my smile in place as I pulled back my jacket to reveal the .38 in my shoulder holster. He smiled back at me as he slowly pumped a shell from the gun's magazine into the chamber. "I might tell you the same thing."

I nodded at his shotgun, smirked, and shook my head dramatically. *"They got guns. We got guns. All God's chillun got guns."* I quoted cheerfully.

The man's brow furrowed. "What'dya say?"

"It's from a Marx Brothers movie," I told him.

"What's it mean?"

I shrugged. "Got something to do with the absurdity

of armed conflict, I suppose."

We stared at each other for very long time. Finally, my adversary lowered the shotgun with a chuckle.

"You come to see me?" he asked.

I squinted at him. "Now, why would I do that?"

He chuckled again, I thought a bit nervously. "You're an indirect bastard, aren't ya?"

"Positively oblique."

He gazed at me for another moment before shifting the shotgun to the crook of his arm and extending his hand.

I slowly made my way up the stairs to where he was standing. I made him wait a moment before taking his heavily callused hand, affecting diffidence as he pumped mine firmly. "Name's Tousignant," he said. "Willard Tousignant. My friends call me Willie Tooz."

"They would, wouldn't they?"

He blinked at me a couple of times. "You got a name?" he asked.

"Uh huh. Dahms. Lyle Dahms. Came here to see Donnie. That okay with you?"

Tousignant grinned broadly, turning toward Donnie, who was still cowering out on the porch. "Shit yeah. It's okay. It's a free fuckin' country, isn't it?"

I shrugged again. "*Hail, Hail, Freedonia*," I said

The furrow returned to Tousignant's brow. "What's that you said?"

"The Marx Brothers again," I explained.

He nodded thoughtfully as though I'd said something useful. We continued to stare at one another.

"Anyway," I said after another uncomfortable moment, "I gotta be going. Donnie and I were just finishing up when you, uh…joined us. You didn't have anything to add, did you, Donnie?"

He shook his head determinedly.

"Guess we're done, then," I said, grinning. "Nice to meet you, Mr. Tousignant."

He smiled. "Like I said, my friends call me Willie Tooz."

"I heard you," I told him.

An unpleasant shiver ran the length of my back as I turned away from Tousignant and the shotgun. I descended the stairs. He let me get all the way into the porch.

"Where ya know Donnie from?" he called after me.

I turned around, stepping back into the entryway. "High school."

"Just getting reacquainted then?"

"Something like that."

"Got no real business here then?"

"Not your kind of business, Mr. Tousignant," I told him.

He cocked his head theatrically as though listening to distant voices. "Just what do you know about my business?" He paused. "Uh...*Lenny*, is it?"

"It's Lyle," I said. "And as for your business, if you expect to keep it secret, you're gonna have to be a little less obvious about it."

He cocked his head some more, pointing to his chest awkwardly with the fingers of a cupped hand. "Less obvious? What's that supposed to mean?"

"You're a crank dealer, Mr. Tousignant," I said. "You're cooking methamphetamines out back in the garage. The smell? The empty cold medicine packages? You don't need Scotland Yard to figure it out."

Tousignant shook his head. "That's a

whatchacallit…that's a slanderous thing to say about a fella, friend. You should be glad my lawyer ain't here."

"Uh-huh," I said.

He couldn't let it go. He glanced briefly toward the living room before returning his attention to me. "What made you say that about me anyway? You know me? We meet before?"

I turned to the door.

"You know, it's not nice coming into a guy's house, making accusations, making fun," he continued loudly. "That kind of thing can be bad for your health."

"I'll take my chances," I replied, this time not bothering to look back.

Donnie, still positioned beside the door in front of me, suddenly stiffened, his eyes darting toward the living room. I was nearly able to turn around before something slammed hard against my temple. There was no pain at first. Rather, a comforting darkness seemed to settle down around me, a darkness broken only by a dim blue glow, like the flame of a pilot light flickering in the distance.

I focused on the light, a tongue of flame dancing impossibly far away. Then came a flash as though the inside of my head suddenly ignited. It brought crippling pain. I felt myself tumbling forward, my forehead bouncing against the unforgiving floor. I tried to open my eyes. I may well have. I couldn't be certain. A searing wall of pain blocked out my sight.

I struggled to my knees, then heard a cracking sound. Immediately, a sharp ache in my side competed for my attention, momentarily distracting me from my splitting head. Hands were tearing roughly at my jacket. I realized with a jolt that someone was after my gun.

Galvanized by fear, my vision began to clear, and, like a drowning man, I flailed wildly until I was able to hook onto something. An arm. I clamped down hard, pulling my attacker close to me. Holding him, I remember thinking that Tousignant seemed bulkier than he'd appeared originally. But when it came to bulk, he had nothing on me.

I rolled, using the advantage of my greater weight to help me build momentum. All at once, I was on top, my opponent pinned beneath me. I reared back and rammed my elbow viciously into his belly, just below his ribcage. His breath exploded from him like a burst air tank. I pivoted and clocked him just under his left eye with a hard right hand. He moaned as I scrambled to my feet, pulled the revolver from my holster, and took a step backward.

"Good," Tousignant's voice echoed loudly in the otherwise soundless room, "now I got a clear shot."

I looked up. Tousignant was still standing on the stairs, his shotgun leveled at me. I looked down to the floor. The man I'd been struggling with was tall, heavier than Tousignant, with a full head of stringy black hair. He also had a slapper sticking out of his closed right fist. About eight inches long, composed of poured lead covered with supple black leather, I realized that if his aim hadn't been off, he'd have finished me with the first blow. The man on the floor began to wheeze and splutter, desperately drawing in breath, a string of spittle hanging from his slack lips. He groaned and tried to stand. His legs buckled, sending him back to the floor.

On the stairs above us, Tousignant let loose an evil-sounding cackle. "Not bad," he said. "You took that smack and still got the drop on my buddy there. But I damn sure got you nailed if you commence to shooting."

I was still a little woozy. I had to plant my feet unnaturally far apart and stoop slightly to keep my balance. My head throbbed and, intermittently, it seemed as though I was viewing the dim room through a lens covered in gauze. Although I was careful to keep my revolver trained on the prostrate figure at my feet, the barrel swayed unsteadily, like the prow of a ship pitching in the sea.

"You won't have this guy for a buddy much longer if you don't drop that scattergun of yours," I shouted up at Tousignant. I steadied my gun, drawing a tight circle, like a target, in the air with the barrel of .38.

Tousignant grunted softly. "Oh, don't ya be tempting me there, friend," he cautioned me lightly. "Fact is, my housemate there is mostly a pain in the ass."

By now, the man on the floor had pushed himself up into a sitting position just inside the door, resting in the scimitar of light that sliced into the room. He wiped his mouth, then gingerly touched the contusion that was blossoming on the side of his face. Like Tousignant, he was no spring chicken, probably in his late fifties. He wore a gray tweed jacket over an azure dress shirt that, although he wore no tie, he had buttoned to the collar. Gray hairs nearly outnumbered the black in his mustache, but the hair on his head was pure ebony, as though he set aside a sizeable chunk of his monthly income for hair dye. His face was deeply lined and olive complexioned, with acne scars and a prominent Adam's apple made even more noticeable by a growth alongside it—too big to be a pimple—that was covered with unsightly mottles of purple and strawberry. His eyes, fixed on me, burned with hatred.

For several tense seconds, no one made a sound or a movement of any kind. Then, issuing something that was half cough, half painful sigh, Tousignant lowered his weapon. He stared at it wistfully before leaning it against the wall beside him.

"You're lucky, friend," he told me, smiling slightly. "Breaking in a new roommate would just be too big a hassle."

I let my gun, still clutched in my hand, fall to my side. I nodded. "Better the devil you know," I said.

The man at my feet rose slowly. He took a moment to adjust his clothing, rather daintily I thought for someone who carried a blackjack. "If we chance to meet again, sir," he smoldered politely, "I will kill you twice." His words came out leisurely, sheathed in a nearly impenetrable Eastern European accent. Like Bela Lugosi, I thought.

I forced a smile and glanced up at Tousignant. "So, who is this guy?" I asked. "Count Scrofula?"

Tousignant let out a raspy chuckle, like the call of a crow defending a piece of carrion. "No," he said. "His name's Janos Bollok. Lives here with me and Donnie." Tousignant grinned. "It's like that old TV show. We got us a regular *Three's Company* 'round here, don't we Donnie? 'Cept there ain't no broads." He laughed at his joke.

I smiled crookedly at Bollok. "My pleasure."

Bollok made a slight bow, slipping his sap into the pocket of his jacket and studying my face minutely, committing it to memory. His eyes shimmered as though brimming with acid.

"I don't think he likes you, friend," Tousignant said. "If I were you, I'd be thinking about leaving. I don't know if maybe this is the first time I seen Janos on his butt. He's a cranky devil. Might be looking to even the score."

I let my hand stray toward my still throbbing head. "The score *is* even," I said.

"Still," Tousignant replied, "this might be a good time for you to hightail it out of here."

"That sounds like sage advice, Mr. Tousignant,"

I tried not to appear nervous as I turned and walked toward the door. As I passed him, Donnie followed me out onto the porch and then down the front steps. He cleared his throat and looked up at me with soft, hollow eyes.

"So," he said, "you're a tough guy now."

There was something indescribably mournful about the way he said it, as though I'd betrayed him.

I sighed resignedly, then pulled my wallet from my back pocket, removing one of my business cards. "Donnie," I said, "if you ever decide you want to get straight, if you ever get tired of hanging out with trash like that," I nodded toward the house, "I might be able to help you out. I know some folks. It wouldn't be easy, but…" I paused. "If you ever decide is all."

I handed him the card.

Donnie took it, staring at me, the lines at the corners of his eyes deepening. It took a while for him to respond. "This is where I belong," he said.

I shook my head. "If you ever decide different," I repeated before leaving him standing in the yard.

Pulled up at a stop sign some three blocks away, I reached up from the steering wheel and gently probed my scalp with my fingertips. A knot the size of a tangelo bulged painfully on the left side of my head, but I didn't appear to be bleeding. I stomped down a little too hard on the gas pedal, and my wheels spun noisily on the pavement.

I shook my head and reached down to reload the cassette in the tape player. But I thought better of it, deciding that I preferred the quiet. I'd done what was asked of me, I reminded myself. I'd carried out his last request without complaint. I even got roughed up doing it. No doubt Dad was out there somewhere shaking his head over that. But the job was done. I'd made the offer, was rebuffed, and even promised to help if Donnie changed his mind. Of course, I knew that he wouldn't. That's not what mattered. What mattered was that I'd offered. And any debt that my father imagined he owed Donnie Murdoch was now paid.

Chapter Four

"I couldn't believe it," I told Naomi as we neared my old neighborhood in Burnsville. "You should have seen them. Without their hair, they looked like overgrown rats."

I paused, tapping my fingers lightly against the steering wheel. "I used to be able to take the moral high ground when it came to pets," I continued. "I mean, dogs and cats are all right, but I used to scoff at anyone stooping so low as to keep vermin. Now look at me. I've got two rodents sharing my bedroom."

A tangle of orange-red hair had fallen across Naomi's face, and she swept it out of her way—not with a finger, but with her entire arm, the way a magician might cast a spell. A smile played at the corners of her mouth.

"Here we go," she said. "You spend weeks complaining that those dogs of yours need grooming, and when Stephen finally does something about it, you become…" She paused briefly, searching for the correct word. "…you become overwrought."

"I'm not overwrought!" I insisted, working hard to maintain a straight face. "And, for the record, they're not my dogs. Just because Edgerton insists on claiming that they are in our joint custody does not make them mine."

"You sound overwrought," Naomi noted.

"Not in the least. I was just…just taken aback, is all.

I'd gotten used to them as…I don't know, as yipping little dust mops. Then I come home and find them completely shorn, all scrawny with pointy snouts, beady eyes, and these icky, clicky toenails. And worse. They've got these horrible little bows on their heads. I mean, first, Edgerton makes me get them neutered, and now he's got them visiting this doggy beauty salon. When will the emasculation end? He'll be dressing them in frilly little underthings next."

"I'm sure they looked adorable," Naomi said.

"Just darling," I huffed. As I turned the car onto the street where my boyhood home stands, my stomach sank precipitously. I had an impulse to turn the car around and race back to the city. Instead, I forced a grin. "It wasn't so bad for Nigel," I continued, tamping down the emptiness that had opened within me. "He's generally pretty clueless anyway. But you could tell Basil was embarrassed by the bows. He'd paw at them, occasionally looking up at me with these huge soulful eyes, blaming me."

"Now, Lyle," Naomi said gently. "How bad could it be? It's not like they're Rottweilers or Great Danes. Basil's a cockapoo, for god's sake. The dog can only look so butch. And Nigel, he's a…he's a…"

"He's a Lhasapoo," I reminded her.

Naomi shrugged. "I think if you're any member of the Poo family, you're pretty much gonna have to rule out any pretense of machismo."

"You calling my boys wimps?"

Her eyes twinkled. "Yes."

I pulled my aging Ford into the driveway and, without thinking, ran a hand over my head to check that my hair was relatively presentable. As I did, I put a little too much pressure on the still somewhat pulpy contusion on the side of my skull. I winced and let out a small groan.

The twinkle abruptly faded from Naomi's eyes. "How's your head?" she asked, her tone anything but comforting.

"It hurts," I admitted.

Naomi nodded. "That'll happen when you insist on playing the bully."

"You don't know that I was playing the bully."

Her eyes flashed with challenge. "I would if you told me what happened."

I shook my head. "It's just the job," I told her. "Don't worry about it."

Naomi stared for a moment, then turned away.

I switched off the car's ignition and looked up at the lights burning brightly inside my parents' house. It was the first time I'd been back since I'd driven Mom home from the funeral. Oh, I'd called nearly every day, but each time she'd invited me to come out and visit, I'd found some excuse to decline. After a few times, Mom got wise. She invited Naomi instead.

Naomi was still giving me the silent treatment as we stepped from the car. I knew that I should have told her about the whole Murdoch business. In the past, I would have. But lately, the more I told her, the more she seemed to turn things back upon me. Nothing I did seemed to quite measure up. I guess I hoped that silence would be a safer strategy. Silly boy.

The exterior of the house had been spruced up considerably since the funeral. The leaves had been raked, the lawn was newly mown, and the small shed where my dad kept his yard implements had a fresh coat of paint. Chuck, I thought. Chuck had stayed with Mom for a week or so afterward. He'd had plenty of time to get the work done around the house since he was minus the distractions of his wife and kids. They hadn't made the trip. Something about shielding the kids from the ugly reality of death until they were older.

Mom was excited to see us. When she opened the door, she beamed so brightly I wished I'd worn sunglasses. "It's sooo nice of you to come," she cooed.

I glanced at Naomi. Her mouth was set in a soft smile, but a noticeable flintiness lingered about her eyes.

Mom was wearing a lacy apron over a cream-colored turtleneck and matching slacks. Dad had always preferred her in dresses, but as his illness progressed, I'd noticed that she'd taken to wearing slacks. Of course, she had every right to dress the way she wanted, but I had to agree with Dad that dresses were, perhaps, more flattering to a, shall we say, "big-boned" woman like her.

Mom took our coats and ushered us into the living room, sighing contentedly as she pointed to the hors d'oeuvres that she'd laid out on the coffee table. Naomi handed Mom a bottle of white zinfandel that she'd insisted we bring. Mom glanced at it with approval. "How lovely. I'll get us down some glasses. We can have some wine while we're waiting for dinner."

"Uh. You two go ahead," I said.

Mom chuckled knowingly. "I'm pretty sure there's still some beer in the fridge."

I took my time in the kitchen, poking about in the cupboards and glancing through a pile of mail—mostly bills—that lay on the counter before finally opening the refrigerator door. On the bottom shelf, just where they'd always been, roughly half a case of longnecks lay on their sides, stacked to form a kind of pyramid. I grabbed one, opened it, and then returned to the living room to find Mom and Naomi sitting together on the sofa, sipping the rosy wine while giving each other tight little smiles.

Mom looked up as I entered the room. "It's sooo nice of you to come," she repeated.

Next to the sofa was the faux-leather recliner that, for as long as I could remember, had been the seat of power in the house. Dad's chair. On the little round end table beside his chair, Dad had kept everything he'd be likely to want or need. Still sitting there, as if waiting for his hand, were the TV remote control, the TV guide, and a coaster for his beer. The table was also a thicket of photographs—reminders of the life that he'd built for himself. Most prominent was a wedding shot of Dad and Mom, surrounded by several pictures of Chuck and his family, a photograph of Dad in uniform, and, if you hunted hard enough, even a small picture of me. It was not my favorite picture. Taken for the high school yearbook, it showed me with shoulder-length hair, my head cocked at an odd angle, my mouth fixed in a sloppy grin, and a truly goofy look in my eyes. I don't know how he'd managed it, but the photographer made it appear that not only was I drunk at the sitting but had also just discovered the comic possibilities of the whoopie cushion. I'd offered to replace the photo many times, but Dad wouldn't hear of it. "Looks just like you," he'd say.

As I neared them, Mom reached over and cheerfully patted the arm of Dad's chair, indicating that I should take a seat. I shook my head, crossing over to the loveseat on the opposite side.

From my outpost on the loveseat, it was a bit of a

reach to get at the hors d'oeuvres—wheat thins, squares of Bongards medium cheddar, and tiny triangles of sliced olive loaf—but I like a challenge. Unfortunately, the olive loaf had a metallic tang and smelled vaguely like a petroleum refinery. I resolved to have only a couple of pieces.

"Lyle tells me that you're still taking computer courses at the community college," Mom said enthusiastically, turning back to Naomi. "Are you thinking of that as a career?"

Naomi shrugged. "I'd rather not waitress all my life. A little computer literacy can't hurt when I go looking for an office job somewhere."

"Anyone would be glad to have you," Mom said in her sweetly singsong voice. "Why the neighbor girl? Heather? Her mom tells me she started in the mailroom in one of those insurance companies out there on Interstate 394. You know, out there in St. Louis Park, Golden Valley, wherever. Well, she wasn't there two weeks before they started talking about training her for a position in the claims department. And I don't want to talk out of turn, but Ray used to say that Heather's not got the brains God gave an artichoke. I can't imagine what they'd do if they got their hands on you. Probably make you vice president."

"That's very kind of you to say, Marjorie," Naomi said.

"Well, I mean every word of it. You have a future ahead of you. You can count on that." She paused. "You both do." Mom didn't actually come out and say that she expected that Naomi and I would spend this future together, but it was clearly implied.

Naomi smiled and slowly raised her eyes to look at

me. I was far enough away that I don't think she could tell I was blushing.

Mom sighed abruptly, then drew herself up, swiveling her head and peering about the room nervously, like a mother hen surveying her brood. "I'm looking to the future, too."

"Yeah?" I asked.

She folded her hands in her lap. "Yes. I've been wondering if I should keep the house. I've got a friend. Carla Haberman? When her Wes died, she'd moved into a condo over in Edina. Lovely place. It overlooks a pond, and she gets sparrows and nuthatches coming right to her balcony. It has a pool, and the best part is she never has to do any yard work. It's all paid for by the association dues."

It took me a moment to respond. I was suddenly keenly aware of the sound of my breathing and the ticking of the mantel clock on the other side of the room. "I uh...I can help you out here with the yard work," I said at last. "You don't need to move because of that."

Mom leaned forward. "Oh, Lyle. I wouldn't want you coming all the way down here just to do yard work."

Her tone was dismissive, but I couldn't let it go. "It's only forty-five minutes," I insisted. "I think I could manage it."

"It might be nice to have closer neighbors," she said earnestly. "Sometimes I feel so isolated here."

"What about Mrs. Schlader next door?" I asked.

Mom put her wine glass down. "Lyle, she's ninety-three. I'm afraid she just doesn't get out like she used to." She paused. "Are you saying that you don't think I should move?"

I shook my head rather more vigorously than I'd

intended. "Not at all. No. You should do what you want. I'm just surprised, is all. I mean, we've been here so long."

"Actually, Lyle. *We* haven't. It's just me now."

I nodded.

"Chuck thinks it's a good idea," she said brightly.

"Probably is then," I agreed. "He's the one with the MBA." I paused. "He's the one you can count on."

Mom lowered her eyes. "I count on you both," she said quietly.

We sat in uneasy silence for a moment or so. I reached for a cracker and another wedge of olive loaf.

"Of course, if I do move," Mom ventured cautiously, "I'd have to downsize a bit. Chuck said there were one or two things that he'd want. Not the big stuff, of course. Just things he remembers from when you boys were younger. Sentimental stuff." She paused. "I was wondering, Lyle…I was wondering if maybe—"

"Really, Mom," I interrupted, "I appreciate it, but I don't have a lot of room at my place. Besides, I have everything I need."

"I was thinking about maybe…" She let her voice trail off, her eyes slowly traveling across the room. My eyes followed hers until they lighted on my Dad's gun cabinet standing sentinel by the front door.

The truth was Dad had a pretty nice collection of weaponry. Mom had never wanted guns in the house, especially when Chuck and I were younger, but you can't be married to a cop and expect the house to be gun-free. Of course, Dad had more than just a gun or two. In addition to the Remington 870 he used for his infrequent duck hunting expeditions, the Winchester Model 70 for his even less frequent deer hunting trips, and his trusty

.38 Smith and Wesson service revolver—the same type of gun I carried—there was the highlight of his collection. All by itself in a lower drawer, in a wooden case lined with silk, Dad kept a Mark XIX Desert Eagle—a .357 Magnum with a 6-inch barrel—one of the most powerful handguns made.

I admit I admired the gun. Adequate protection is important in my line of work, and I could foresee the Desert Eagle coming in handy in a variety of circumstances. For example, were I to be confronted by a rampaging elephant, the big gun might be a nice hedge. That is, if I could keep the recoil from knocking me on my ass.

Mom's eyes met mine.

"You asking if I want his guns?"

Mom shrugged. "You know I've never like having them in the house. They make me nervous."

I shook my head. "They won't suddenly go off by themselves, you know."

"I know. But your dad spent so much time cleaning them, taking care of them. I don't know how to do any of that. You could, though. I'd hate to see them just…I don't know, just waste away."

"I don't think Dad's .357 is going to just waste away, Mom. Besides, they belong here. They're a part of this place. As much as…"

"As much as he was," Mom said, finishing my thought for me. "Just you think about it, okay, honey? We don't have to decide tonight."

The kitchen timer rang, and Mom hurried to her feet. "Now you just sit there, you two," she insisted. "Just have to check the hot dish. I'll be right back."

After Mom had disappeared into the kitchen, Naomi

leaned toward me. "You could be a little more helpful, Lyle," she whispered.

"How am I not helpful?"

"She's looking at her options. You should encourage her."

"How am I not encouraging her?"

Naomi sighed. "It's obvious that you don't want her to leave this house."

"How is that obvious?"

Naomi started to tell me but then thought better of it. Instead, she sighed heavily, folded her arms across her chest, and set her jaw firmly. After that, she and I waited in silence. I avoided her eyes, afraid of what I'd find there.

Thankfully, soon afterward, Mom proudly placed her casserole in the middle of the dining table. "There's nothing like a one-dish meal."

I smiled. That had been something of a mantra around the Dahms house when I was growing up. Over the years, Mom had scoured dozens of cookbooks, had clipped countless recipes from the newspaper, and had sat through God knows how many hours of TV cooking shows. But at dinnertime, like as not, we'd hear the familiar refrain, "There's nothing like a one-dish meal."

Generally, this meant we were having either goulash—the very un-Hungarian, Midwest version that's basically a mélange of browned hamburger, tomato sauce, and elbow macaroni—or tuna noodle bake—a mélange of canned tuna, peas, cream of mushroom soup, and, of course, elbow macaroni. One or two zip codes in the Twin Cities area alone are enough to keep the local pasta manufacturing people in business indefinitely.

Mom sat, glancing only briefly at the empty chair at the head of the table, and prompted me to serve. I stood and picked up the silver serving spoon that she'd laid next to the scalloped casserole dish. Tonight, I noted, it was tuna.

Despite her devotion to recipe research, my mom wasn't exactly known for her skills in the kitchen. Still, it took rather more work than even I'd anticipated to get the spoon through the topping of crushed potato chips and even more to get it through the top layer of over-baked macaroni which were so dried and shriveled they resembled deep-fried wood shavings.

"Everything looks lovely, Mrs. Dahms," Naomi said. "I just wish you hadn't gone to so much trouble."

"It's no trouble to cook for the people you love," she said, glancing up at me.

Naomi noticed the glance, her eyes flickering momentarily in my direction, but otherwise, she remained impassive. I spooned a helping of the hot dish onto Mom's plate, noting that the middle layer of noodles was considerably moister than the top. Cooked until bloated and as soft as tapioca, they quivered obscenely on the plate.

As I turned to serve Naomi, Mom smiled up at me and gushed, "You two are just such a…such a healthy couple."

I winced. "Healthy" had been what she used to call me growing up. Dad had other names for it. Porky and Lard-Ass come to mind.

I spooned a none-too-generous portion of casserole onto Naomi's plate. I had to admit that Mom was right, though. Naomi did look healthy. One of the things that attracted me most to her was the fact that she was certainly no stick figure like the anorexic cover girls gracing the pages of magazines in the supermarket. Instead, Naomi was tall and round, yet oh so shapely, with full, womanly breasts and an unmistakable aura of strength that seemed even more potent the times she yielded to me. Her small mouth, now primly fixed, seemed to hold secrets. But there was light dancing in her blue eyes as if to say that those secrets were merry things eager to spill out. Her freckle-splashed cheeks were framed by marvelously long tangles of hair—the color of embers—that shone lustrously as though spun from the afterglow of a radiant sunset.

Despite our recent troubles, I was deeply aware of the hold that she had on my heart—a hold that I feared, once released, would leave me profoundly diminished. There was no question that I'd be a fool not to fight to hold on to her. And no question that fighting wouldn't be enough.

Although I hadn't told her, Mom seemed to know that our relationship was under some strain. Throughout the meal, she kept smiling at us, obviously relishing the opportunity to bring us together, perhaps even hoping that we'd come to our senses and plight our troth right there at the dinner table. Instead, Naomi talked briefly about her waitressing job, I brought up the dogs' recent grooming again, and Mom mostly fussed about—passing salad and rolls and asking if we were getting enough to eat.

When she'd cleared the plates, Mom asked if we'd like coffee and scurried into the kitchen to get dessert—milk chocolate Jell-O pudding. She mentioned that she had a can of whipped cream if we wanted it. She was still in the kitchen arranging the dessert tray when I called to her. "Oh, by the way, Mom. A couple of days ago I took care of that little errand that Dad mentioned."

Mom peered around the corner at me. "What errand is that?"

"The Donnie Murdoch thing."

Mom's face became expressionless. "Oh," she said and continued to stare.

"He's fine," I told her. "I asked him, and he said he didn't need anything. That we didn't need to worry about him."

Her eyes crinkled. She looked down and smoothed at her apron. "It wasn't too…too hard on you, was it? Seeing him, I mean."

"Not at all," I said. "I just wanted you to know it's all done now."

"Who's Donnie Murdoch?" Naomi asked.

"Just a guy we used to know. Dad was thinking about him. Asked me to look him up is all."

I was certain that there was nothing in my voice, nothing in my manner that in the least bit suggested there was anything in this for her to be concerned about. Naomi furrowed her brow. "If that's all, then why would it be hard on you?"

"It wasn't," I said.

The light in Naomi's eyes crystallized into prickly shards. "If you don't want to talk about, that's fine."

"There's nothing to talk about," I assured her.

"Uh-huh."

"Why *uh-huh*? I'm serious. It's nothing."

"Uh-huh."

I caught my mom looking at us. There was great disappointment in her eyes. She went back into the kitchen. After an eternity, she returned with the pudding.

She carefully placed a bowl in front of each of us, then sat, staring down at her dessert in uncomfortable silence. I'd had many such meals at this table, I reminded myself. Dining with Dad was rarely a lot of laughs. He had this way of making me feel like just another perp down at the station. He'd sit at the head of the table as Mom asked us boys about our day. He barely talked, only occasionally even looking at us, but of one thing I was certain. He was judging. Listening and judging. By high school, Mom could no longer get anything out of Chuck and me. If she wanted information from us, she'd have to catch us away from the dinner table. Away from Dad. There was simply too much pressure in the dining room. I glanced up at my dad's chair, slightly surprised to find it empty.

Finally, Mom broke the silence. "Donnie Murdoch was a boy who stayed with us briefly a long time ago," she said, though she didn't actually look up at Naomi.

"Oh?" Naomi said.

Mom raised her head, anxious eyes moving from me to Naomi. "Yes. His parents died when he was a senior in high school. Donnie had no one else. Ray thought Donnie needed a place, just until he got through school, you know. He stayed here."

Naomi smiled. "That was very nice of him. And not surprising. Mr. Dahms always impressed me as a man who…" She paused. "…who always tried to do the things he thought were right."

Mom relaxed visibly. "He was a man of conviction," she agreed.

Naomi turned to me. "Lyle's the same way. That's probably the first thing that attracted me to him. Once he's decided what has to be done, nothing seems to keep him from doing it."

I sighed gratefully.

"Of course," Naomi continued, "he's one of the most hardheaded, least compromising, most infuriating men I've ever known."

Mom chuckled nervously but with evident relief. "I had that problem with Ray, too," she noted. "On the whole, I'd say it balanced out nicely."

"I guess I could say the same," Naomi said. "Most of the time."

Naomi and Mom went on to talk briefly about desserts, even sharing a laugh when Mom told her about how when I was younger, I'd insist that she let my pudding sit in the refrigerator uncovered so that it would form a skin. As a kid, I'd been known to assert that pudding skin was "the best part." On the whole, the atmosphere became markedly less edgy, but still, I was thankful when the table was cleared, and Naomi and I were heading out the door.

As we took our leave, Naomi thanked Mom, again mentioning that she needn't have gone to so much trouble. We were out on the front walkway when Mom suddenly exclaimed, "Lyle! I just remembered! Johnny Fullmer called this morning." She lowered her head, then looked sheepishly up at me. "He asked for your office number. He didn't call you, did he?"

"No."

"Well, he might."

"Did he say what he wanted?"

"No. Just that he'd give you a call."

"How'd he sound? I mean, did he sound like he wanted to get together for a beer, or more like he wanted to poke me in the nose?"

Mom's expression clouded with puzzlement. "Why

would Johnny Fullmer want to poke you in the nose?"

"I'm just joking, Mom."

She pouted briefly, then, a smirk widening across her face, she said, "Watch out *I* don't poke you in the nose."

I feigned shock. "Why, Mother!"

She laughed. She was still laughing as she closed the door.

"I don't think I've ever heard her joke like that with you," Naomi said as I held the car door open for her.

"I don't think I have either."

It was a quiet ride, but not uncomfortably so. I turned the radio on softly and watched as the streetlamps drifted by. Naomi cuddled against the door, occasionally humming along with a song on the radio. When we reached her apartment, I leaned over, and she kissed me lightly. But when she opened the door and the overhead lamp came on, I saw that her bottom lip was trembling slightly.

"Why don't you want your mom to move?" she asked.

I started to say that I didn't care one way or another, but I suddenly realized that this wasn't true. I didn't want Mom to move.

"I don't know," I admitted. "Maybe it's all this change. I've never been real big on change. It's going to take me a while to get used to my old man being gone. I guess that's all the change I can take right now."

Naomi nodded but remained silent for some time. "Sometimes it's better when change just happens," she said at last. "It's harder when you know that you gotta do something, but you keep putting it off, worrying about how it's going to affect everyone else."

I swallowed hard. "I guess if it's the right thing, then you need to just do it and worry about the effects later."

Tears began to well in Naomi's eyes. "I'm not just talking about your mom moving," she told me.

"I know."

Chapter Five

I didn't make it into the office any too early the next day. After I dropped Naomi off at her place, I headed down to McCauley's for a nightcap. Dan Tompkins, a long-time waiter from the restaurant upstairs, was sitting alone at the bar sipping at a glass of the house Chablis, a libation that he affectionately referred to as "lighter fluid."

Joining him, it quickly became apparent that, like mine, Dan's mood was not one of sunshine and lilacs. He was staring morosely at the bottom of his second glass of wine when he revealed to me that the previous day he'd broken up with his boyfriend, a fellow that Dan had been living with for nearly two years. This breakup melded with my troubled relationship with Naomi, making Dan and I soul mates of a sort and I turned him a particularly sympathetic ear.

When Dan grew tired of unburdening his troubles and seemed in no greater spirits, I made what I thought was an inspired suggestion. I advanced—as a proposal for our mutual investigation—that we endeavor to discover just how much alcohol we'd need imbibe in order to take our minds off the current, miserable state of our separate love lives. I admit that as the drinking went on, the experiment became marred by faulty record-keeping. However, Dan and I did discover that we both knew the words to an extraordinary number of TV theme songs from the 1960s and 70s.

Alas, during our third run-through of the *Underdog* theme (God, I miss Wally Cox), I lost Dan. Skip, who'd been tending bar and had clearly had enough, fixed us with a stare hard enough to bore through steel.

Both Dan and I knew it wasn't just bad form but actually dangerous to get on the wrong side of Skip. Upon noticing the look, Dan—obviously the smarter of our duo—abruptly announced that it was time he be heading home. Stripped of my singing partner, I, too, soon sauntered off into the early hours of morning.

Thus, it was that, after catching up on my beauty rest, it was actually late afternoon the next day before I got myself into work.

Although it's a mere two blocks from my place in the Bijou, I usually drive over to the office. Who knows, I might be called upon to wheel into the mean streets at a moment's notice. That day, I had to circle the crowded lot a couple of times before finding a parking spot. I momentarily considered whether the large number of cars might portend a cluster of prospective clients waiting outside my office. But I knew better. Almost nobody who parked in our lot actually did business with anyone who worked in the building.

Located in Dinkytown, a Minneapolis neighborhood adjacent to the University of Minnesota and one of the toughest places in the free world to find affordable parking, the cars in the lot largely belonged to students willing to pay premium prices to park only a mere mile or so from that coveted late afternoon chem lab. Inside the building, the most conspicuous sound was not the clip-clop of eager clients streaming down the corridor to my office, but rather the low hum of florescent lights breaking a silence that could perhaps best be described as sepulchral.

I climbed up to the deserted second floor, unlocked my door, shuffled briefly through my mail, then crossed to the window to stare out at all those cars some more.

Before leaving the Bijou, I'd knocked at the door to Edgerton's room. He hadn't been home. Nothing unusual in that, I reminded myself. But I couldn't help noticing a certain hollowness within me as I stood there alone in the hallway waiting for someone I realized wasn't coming to the door. I put it down to the lingering ill effects of all that beer from the night before, but still, I could have used a little conversation. Not some daytime TV-style gabfest, mind you, but rather just a little something that might help fill in a bit of that emptiness. Now, in my office, staring out at the crowded parking lot, my insides seemed to yawn even wider.

I withdrew from the window, busied myself making a pot of coffee, then checked through the mail again. Finally, hoping to counteract the mausoleum-quality stillness of my tiny office, I switched on the radio. The gods smiled on me. The sullen silence of the room was replaced by the soul-stirring, heartbreaking, and ultimately life-affirming sound of Muddy Waters.

I dropped the mail on my desk, sat down, leaned way back in my chair, and let the music take me places. The hollowness in me remained, but on the honeyed strings of a guitar driven by a breezy harp, things didn't look so bad. I, too, was now heading out on the road. Muddy and I were leaving together, destined for Louisiana with the goal of showing all them good-looking women just how to treat your man. I was mentally packing my rucksack when Johnny Fullmer walked through the door.

For a time, growing up, I couldn't picture my father without seeing Knuck Fullmer standing beside him. At first sight, he and my dad seemed an odd pairing. Where Dad had been a towering presence—as if carved from a block of granite—his old partner, Knuck Fullmer, was a slight man, medium tall, with long limbs and sharp, angular features that made him seem slighter still—as though he'd been whittled from a sapling. Out of uniform, Dad was fond of blue jeans and flannel shirts. Knuck favored dress slacks, shirts with stiffly starched collars, and sports jackets.

But although Dad and Knuck were very different, they had that tight bond that so often develops between people who work closely with one another—a bond that is perhaps even stronger when the two people are in a business that involves riding around with firearms. Beyond their genial ribbing—privately Dad called his partner "Powder-puff" more than "Knuckles"—and occasional disagreements, they shared something that few of us will ever have—the secure knowledge that, if the situation arose, each would unhesitatingly risk his life for the other.

As a kid, I was convinced that they shared something else as well—disappointment with me. Of course, I'll admit that, like most kids, I tended toward the mistaken impression that the world revolved around me and that this occasionally led to my reaching erroneous conclusions. I'll even admit that it's possible that when they were together, Dad and Knuck had other things to do besides think about me. But more than once, when Knuck was over to the house, I'd pass through the living room, and they'd suddenly clam up, refusing to continue their conversation until I was out of earshot. Once, I doubled back to find them laughing. Laughing, I was sure, at me. This childhood certainty, even after all those years, made the sight of Knuck Fullmer standing in my doorway feel vaguely unsettling.

He seemed a bit discomposed himself. He stared at me, then glanced back at the nameplate on the door, his expression both puzzled and disdainful as though he couldn't quite bring himself to accept that this was what I was doing with my life. He had a fifty-dollar haircut and was dressed in a pair of black slacks and a blue blazer with shiny brass buttons over a pale blue dress shirt. A surprising amount of pure white chest hair, like strands of spun sugar, escaped through the open collar. The jacket was pretty well-tailored; it very nearly concealed the bulge of the handgun he carried underneath.

I reached over and clicked off the radio. "I'm goin' down to New Orleans," I told Knuck. "Get me a mojo hand."

If Knuck had been puzzled before, he was now positively bewildered. Twice he made as if to reply but couldn't find the words. "I have no idea what that means," he said at last.

"Me neither," I admitted. "But I gotta get me one."

I stood and extended my hand across the desk. Knuck, looking somewhat wary, took it and pumped it firmly. I pointed at the wooden client chair opposite the desk, and we both sat down.

"I didn't get much of a chance to talk to you the other day at the funeral," Knuck said, sitting very erect in the chair. "Sorry about that. You just don't know how much we're all going to miss your old man."

I nodded. "Thanks."

"Really makes you think, don't it? Something like that?"

I nodded again. "I really appreciate your coming by to tell me that, Mr. Fullmer."

"Call me Knuck."

I'd nodded enough. This time, I just smiled at him.

"Yes sir," Knuck continued, "your old man was somebody you could always count on. I'm certainly going to miss him, I'll tell you."

"You already have," I noted. "Twice. Not that I mind hearing it."

Knuck's eyes narrowed. "I should hope not."

I forced a broader smile and shrugged. "You didn't come all the way up here just to proffer your regrets for not talking with me at Dad's funeral. Did you, Mr. Fullmer? Sorry. I mean, Knuck."

He stared at me, his chin raised slightly, I thought, defiantly. After a moment, he lowered his chin, and a soft smile appeared on his face. "No," he admitted. "There's something else."

"Something about Donnie Murdoch?" I ventured.

Knuck blinked rapidly several times. "About who?" he asked. His voice was, I thought, a shade louder than it needed to be. "Donnie Murdoch? Why would I be thinking about him? Hell, I ain't thought of him in twenty years."

"It's been a while."

Knuck shook his head. "Hoo boy! I just don't know where you got the idea that I'd be here to talk about the Murdoch kid."

"*Hoo boy?*"

Knuck's brow crinkled with irritation. Before he

could reply, I stood up and slowly made my way out from behind the desk. "Just something Dad talked about before he passed," I said. "You want some coffee?"

"Uh, sure."

I poured us each a cup and placed his on the desk in front of him. "Dad didn't talk to you about Donnie?" I asked. "Recently, I mean."

Knuck shook his head and let his eyes wander around the room. "Nope," he assured me. "Your pop and I talked a lot the last few months. You know, while he was, uh, failing. But I don't recall us discussing Donnie Murdoch." He turned back to me. "I ain't thought about him since his trial."

"Okay," I said, retaking my seat. "So, what did you come to see me about?"

Knuck squirmed briefly in his chair. He ran the tips of his fingers carefully through his hair, plowing shallow furrows through his graying temples. "It's not a big deal," he told me. "But it seems like a two-man job. You remember Mindy?"

"Your daughter," I said.

Knuck's eyes brightened. "Yeah. My daughter. I got a little favor to ask. It has to do with her."

"Ask away."

Knuck frowned. Evidently, my response had been more noncommittal than he'd expected. "Mindy's really turned into quite a little gal," he said. He paused, swelling a bit. "She always seemed to know what she wanted out of life. You probably know that after high school, Mindy went off to culinary school in New York City. Place called the Culinary Institute of America. They call it the CIA for short." Knuck chuckled. "I'd tell folks that, and they'd think my kid had turned out some kind of spy."

"I've heard of it."

Knuck leaned back in his chair. "I'm not surprised. It's quite the prestigious place. Lots of famous chefs graduated from there. Quite a recognizable list of alumni. My little girl among them."

I sipped at my coffee.

"Mindy kicked around the Big Apple for a few years working in various hotel restaurants," Knuck continued. "Honing her craft, so to speak. A couple of years ago she surprised her mother and me by coming home, back to Minneapolis. She's done right well for herself here. So well, in fact, that in a couple of days' time, she's set to open her own restaurant. Over in the warehouse district."

"Trendy," I noted.

"And how. We couldn't be more excited for her. But…" he paused. "But there are one or two problems."

"What kind of problems?"

Knuck set his elbows on the desk, interlaced his fingers, and leaned forward. "It started off no big deal, you know. Some graffiti. A little garbage from the Dumpster out back strewn around in front. Little things. Then, a few days ago, somebody set a fire."

I set my coffee cup down.

"Wasn't much of a fire," Knuck said, shrugging. "Just some oily rags and damp cardboard piled up next to the wall out back. The wall's brick. There was a whole lot of smoke, but no real damage was done. Still…"

"You start to take notice," I said.

"That you do," Knuck agreed. "The kicker is, the day after the fire, a couple of guys come around. The place isn't open yet, but they come waltzing in through the back door while a delivery's coming in. All of sudden, they're standing in the kitchen. Pretty as you please. Young guys, early twenties, dressed like punks. Mindy asks 'em what they want, and they tell her they've heard about the trouble she's been having. About the graffiti. About the garbage. About the fire. Say they can help her with that sort of thing."

"But it will cost her," I said.

Knuck nodded.

"This restaurant? Has Mindy got partners or did she put up the money by herself?"

"Partners? Of course, she's got partners. She's backed by the same outfit financed Morey's downtown and a couple other places."

"Uh-huh. And what are the partners saying about this shakedown?"

Knuck crossed his legs and stared at his foot as he bobbed it up and down. "We haven't told them."

"No?"

"No. Mindy came to me first. I told her to sit on it. Told her to let me take care of it."

"Hmm," I said.

"What's that mean?"

"Just hmm. You got a plan?"

Knuck smiled unpleasantly. "I thought we'd talk to them."

Since he was doing the smiling, I went back to nodding. "*We*?"

"I could use the backup," he said.

I thought for a moment. "Why aren't the cops talking to them?"

"Never called 'em. Figured we could take care of it ourselves."

"Cops generally like to be let in on this sort of

thing," I said. "You know, that way they can keep track of the bad guys. Maybe keep them from doing this to some other business owner."

Knuck glared at me. "You forgetting *I* was a cop for over twenty-five years?"

"Not forgetting," I said, "just reminding. And you're evading the question."

Knuck abruptly stood up, his chair rolling back noisily from the desk, while he stood before me, his face fairly twitching with rage. I'm sure it was meant to be intimidating, but as skinny as he was, it was like being menaced by an angry beanpole.

Staring steadily down on me, he said, "For me, there is no question. My daughter needs my help. And she's gonna get it. *My* help. Not some beat cop so busy he ain't got the time to handle it right. You don't want to help me? Fine. But there ain't no way I'm handing this off. My daughter's counting on me."

I took a moment to respond. I didn't like it. I didn't like it at all. A couple of hoodlums clumsy and stupid enough to try this sort of thing on a high-end restaurant surely wouldn't present much of a challenge to even the most hard-pressed beat cop. It was just plain wrongheaded for Knuck to take it on himself. But Mindy was his daughter, and my experience with fathers was that they didn't always make good decisions when it came to their kids. And Knuck really wasn't taking it on by himself. He'd asked me to help. Maybe, if I went along, I'd be able to keep him from making any further bad decisions.

I stood up, and, for a moment, Knuck and I stared at one another. "You set up a meeting with these bozos?" I asked at last.

"Yep."

"Where and when?"

"Tomorrow afternoon. Mindy's restaurant. It's not open yet, but most of the work's done. Should be nice and quiet."

"We're just looking to scare them off, right?"

"You bet," Knuck assured me. "We'll just throw a scare into 'em."

I opened a desk drawer and pulled out a sheet of paper and a ballpoint pen. "Write it down," I told him. "I'll be there."

Knuck actually slapped the desk with glee. The sound seemed to ricochet from wall to wall like an errant bullet. "I knew I was right to come to you, boy!" he exclaimed. "Your father'd be proud."

I thought about that. He was right. He was, after all, Dad's best friend. More than that. His partner. Dad would have wanted me to help. But the fact remained that it would make a whole lot more sense to bring in the cops. Handling it ourselves simply didn't strike me as a smart move. And growing up, perhaps the thing my old man most warned me against was letting anyone, even a friend, play me for a fool.

Chapter Six

At the intersection of Third Street and Third Avenue North in Minneapolis stands the old National Biscuit Company bakery. Built in the nineteenth century—seven stories tall, square, solid, and orderly—its façade of light brown stone glowed rosy in the slanting rays of the afternoon sun. Years before, Nabisco, following their costly (and bloody) feud with rival snack cracker elves, had been forced to abandon the building. Like so many in the warehouse district, it had been ill-used in the ensuing decades.

But in the 1990s, the impressive structure was rehabbed by a local arts group as studio space for what their literature calls "mid-career artists." As the building was located smack dab in the middle of what was now Downtown's most highly touted restaurant district. I gather that, unlike entry-level artists, those awarded the "mid-career" designation are no longer required to starve. And these lucky aesthetes were about to get a whole new lunch option. On the northeast corner of the old bakery, tucked under a green awning, with a newly installed neon sign just itching to start buzzing, was Mindy Fullmer's new eating establishment. The sign, dark when I arrived, was a single, vaguely oriental, calligraphic letter "M."

I drove around until I spied a parking spot only a block or so distant and hoofed it lazily back to the restaurant. When I got there, I tried the front door but found it locked, and not a soul in sight when I peeked through the window. I then made my way around to the back of the building, where I found another door—this a banged-up, windowless metal—that, like the front door, was also locked. There was no sign of a bell, so I commenced to banging up the door some more, kicking loudly at it until someone opened it from the inside.

The someone was Knuck. He was dressed in brown slacks and a gray tweed jacket with brown suede patches on the elbows. The jacket hung heavily on his lanky frame and was unbuttoned to reveal a white dress shirt, a gold tie embossed with overlapping diamond shapes, and his .38.

Knuck glowered at me. "You mind not denting the door, Lyle? We'd at least like to get a couple weeks use out of the place before we have to start replacing things."

Glancing at my watch, I noted that it was shortly after five o'clock. "You said they'd be here at five-thirty?"

Knuck's scowl faded, and his mouth curled into a prideful smile. "Yeah, we got a couple minutes," he said. "Come on in. I'll show you around."

I hadn't exactly been angling for the grand tour, but I nodded my acquiescence and Knuck opened wide the door, motioning for me to enter. We stepped into a narrow kitchen gleaming with stainless steel. Coolers, countertops, a large mixer, and a particularly deadly-looking meat slicer—all were polished to a wince-inducing luster beneath rows of industrial wattage, florescent light fixtures. A gas range took up nearly half the room consisting of two huge, side-by-side ovens topped with six burners in the middle, a large grill area on the right, and on the left, what looked like two port holes punched into the range top with large woks perched over each one. More woks were piled haphazardly behind them. There didn't seem to be any food in the kitchen, nor any evidence that anyone had ever actually cooked in there. The air was harshly antiseptic; I had to pinch my nose lightly to ward off an approaching sneeze.

"You just can't freakin' believe how much that puppy set us back," Knuck said, pointing at the range.

"Looks like a good one," I said lamely. "So, you got money invested in the place?"

"Sure do."

"Just you and Mindy?"

"Nah," Knuck said. "I told you. We got partners."

I nodded. "I remember. The guys behind Morey's."

Knuck grinned. "Never thought I'd be in the restaurant business."

I grinned back. "And working with your daughter. That's gotta feel…"

"Like I hit the goddamn lottery, Lyle. Like I hit the lottery."

"So, where is Mindy?"

"In the office," Knuck told me. "Taking care of business. We open next Saturday." He rubbed his hands together. "There's a ton of things to do."

Next Knuck led me through the kitchen and out a set of double doors into the dining room, stepping aside to give me an unimpeded vantage point from whence to drink it all in. Taking my cue from the sign, I'd been expecting an oriental theme, but the place was decorated more like a traditional men's club. It was dimly lit; the walls were green—dark olive accented with a lighter avocado—that went nicely with the reddish-brown crown molding that edged the ceiling. Booths upholstered in leather the color of Pinot Noir lined both sides of the room, more tables between them. But instead of the fox hunting prints one might associate with a club, along the wall, tiny spotlights illuminated several black and white photographs of famous people, all of whom seemed to be eating. A supermodel whose name I forget, her sunken eyes peering vacantly out from an abyss of dark eye shadow, held aloft a forkful of impossibly long pasta. A young actor, whose name I couldn't bring to mind either, stood bathed in shadow. Shirtless and glistening, he smiled enigmatically at a brace of lobster tails on the table in front of him. But behind a small bar on the right side of the room, tough guy actor Lee Marvin, looking like he'd vastly prefer being somewhere else, was nursing a highball.

"What do you think?" asked a beaming Knuck.

"Spiffy," I told him.

Knuck was trying to decide how to respond to that when a door opened behind us, and I turned to find Mindy entering the dining room from behind the bar.

She was medium tall, trim, and pretty in an ordinary sort of way. She wore a white chef's jacket with that oriental "M" stitched in black thread over her left breast. Tied around her waist was a spotlessly clean, pure white apron. On her head, she wore a round, brimless, dark gray cap that formed to her head like an oversized yarmulke. The hair peeking out from under the cap was short and brown, with peroxide blonde tips that resembled spiky feathers. When she spotted me standing in the dining room with her father, she stopped and smiled warmly.

"Lyle!" she called out. "Dad said you'd be coming by today. It's great to see you. I'll bet it's been ten years."

Her eyes were set a little too close together, and as she approached, they narrowed as though I were an artifact requiring study. I extended my hand to her. "Longer," I said.

Mindy's eyes darted uncertainly to my outstretched hand before she wiped her own on her apron and placed it weakly in mine.

Although I'd known Mindy Fullmer since I was a kid, she wasn't someone I'd ever thought of as a friend. Her parents lived across town, so outside of the once-a-month or so that our families got together, we didn't see each other very much. When we did—our folks dragging us to each other's homes, forcing us together, and asking us to make nice while not disturbing their "adult time"—the atmosphere wasn't exactly conducive to breeding a lasting friendship. We didn't go to elementary school or junior high together, and although we both attended Burnsville High School, Mindy was a couple of years older, so we never had much to do with one another. She was in Donnie's class, I remembered.

"Nice place," I told her.

Mindy swiveled, surveying the room intently as though it were unfamiliar to her. "Things are coming along nicely," she said after a moment. "But there's still so much to do before Saturday's opening I can hardly believe we'll get to it all. Still…" She paused. "We'll be okay, though. We gotta be okay." She smiled. "No other option."

I returned her smile. "What's the menu like?" I asked.

"Eclectic," she said. "We're calling it

Midwest/Asian fusion."

"What? Like deep-fried cheese curds served with a side of wasabi?

Her eyes shone with patient bemusement. "Something like that."

"You think Lee Marvin would have eaten here?" I asked, pointing.

Mindy snorted softly. "Oh, that. We put that in for Dad." She smiled good-naturedly at Knuck, her eyes nearly disappearing.

"Hey," he replied, feigning anger, "the decorator signed off on it. Said it would help the room appeal to a…How'd she put it? An upscale, masculine demographic. Ask Lyle here. What do you think, Lyle?"

"I think it's uh…spiffy."

Knuck chuckled, Mindy joining him, but her smile quickly thinned. Then we stood, letting an awkward silence seep out between us.

Before it got too awkward, Mindy said, "It's nice of you to help Dad out with this thing. He tells me not to worry, but the truth is I'm a little nervous."

Knuck frowned. "We talked about this," he reminded her. "This is no big deal, sugar. You worry about the important stuff. Let me take care of this…this distraction. If things go the least bit screwy, Lyle's got my back."

"Screwy?" Mindy asked. There was a note of carefully controlled anxiety in her voice. "We open Saturday, Dad. I can't afford for things to go…screwy. Is there any risk that—"

Knuck cut her off, his mouth set in a somewhat condescending, definitely parental grin. "No risk at all, Mindy girl," he assured her. "No risk at all." He glanced at his wristwatch. "Those guys should be here any minute. Why don't you go back in the office? Just stay in there like I told you. This whole thing should only take a couple of minutes."

"But Dad—"

"No 'but Dads,' okay?" Let me do this for you."

Mindy stared at her father for a moment. She was clearly not happy, but she did as he asked. She left the room.

Mindy gone, Knuck poured us each a mug of coffee from a large torpedo-shaped urn, and we sat in a booth adjacent to the small front lobby with a clear view of the door and waited. "I do appreciate you coming, Lyle," Knuck told me. "I really do. But since we ain't never worked together, I'm thinking we better set some ground rules."

"Set away."

"First, since this is my place, or rather Mindy's, you're gonna want to let me do the talking. You can just kinda hang back and…and…"

"And look pretty," I said.

Knuck smirked. "Dare to dream, Lyle."

We'd both mostly drained our coffees when a couple of figures appeared at the door. One of them cupped his hands against the glass and peered inside. Knuck and I got to our feet. I let him get the door.

The first guy to come in was a white kid in his early twenties, wearing a purple Minnesota Vikings stocking cap complete with a gold pompom over closely shorn blond hair. His hands were thrust into the roomy pockets of a Vikings starter jacket, which he had zipped up to his prominent Adam's apple. He had a narrow beard that traced the line of his jaw, and his mouth was grimly set.

He entered slowly, his gait like a lazy camel—shoulders slumped, hips thrust slightly forward, and his long legs making loopy, angular strides. He nodded as he walked, his eyes mere slits, as if his eyelids were just too heavy to keep completely open.

I keep running into tough guy wannabes who think that squinting a lot somehow makes them appear more formidable. I think it makes them look like their mommies should tuck them in earlier at night.

"Yo," he said as he passed me.

"Yo?" I replied.

His eyes opened slightly, but he made no other response.

The second guy was also in his twenties, an African American, who in contrast to his partner, not only had his eyes wide open, but actually seemed pretty happy to be joining us. He was short, about five and a half feet tall, with a mobile countenance and a smile that slid about his face as though it was greased with petroleum jelly. As he approached me, it slipped from self-satisfied grin to great big howdy of a smile. A greeter at the local box store smile.

Knuck closed the door, turned to face our guests, and gestured toward the booth we'd been sitting in. The two young men looked at each other, then sat down as instructed, the friendly Black guy on the inside, the somnolent white guy on the outside. The sleepy guy stretched his long legs out into the aisle and dropped his head nearly to his chest. He kept his hands in his jacket pockets. Knuck took a seat across from them, tucking his long legs under the table. I remained standing, crossing my arms and briefly trying out that squinty eye thing. I had to stop. Things got all blurry.

Since Knuck had made it clear that this was *his* meeting, I waited for him to start things off. He did not, however, appear to be in much of a hurry. He glanced at our visitors in silence a couple of times but mostly kept his head down, rubbing his hands together, watching them intently, as though practicing for shadow puppets later.

Finally, the sleepy guy broke the silence. "Yo," he repeated, nudging his partner and nodding at Knuck. "This must be Daddy. The chef lady's daddy, I mean. The one who called us." He was so pleased with himself that he almost showed us his pupils.

"God damn, Knuck," I said. "We're gonna have to watch out for this guy. Kid's so perceptive it's spooky."

Knuck had no reaction whatsoever, but the sleepy guy mustered up enough energy to look up at me. It took him at least fifteen seconds before it occurred to him that I might be putting him on. When it did, he glared and, his hands still in his pockets, began to rise to his feet. His heart must not have been in it, however, because when his partner laid a hand on his arm, he immediately let himself sink back down into his seat.

"Gentlemen. Gentlemen," the friendlier of the pair intoned, "let's not get off to a bad start. Come now. Let's remember that we're all here for the same reason. Y'all got a restaurant to open. My boy here and me, we come to see about helping you out with that. Everybody's on the same side. We're all here to do business." He paused, his smile widening to gator-like proportions.

It was, I had to admit, a killer smile marred by only one small thing. Amid an expanse of sparkling white, one tooth in front was as gray as a cigarette ash. I wondered if it hurt him.

"You called us, hey?" Graytooth continued. "You said come in and talk. Let's us start talking."

Knuck nodded, drumming his fingers lightly on the table. He sighed, then lifted his eyes. In my experience, all cops have a vibe they like to give off in a situation like this—some guys like cocky, some thoughtful, some prefer scary. But ex-cop Knuck didn't seem to have made up his mind how he wanted to play it. Indecision flickered in his eyes like the wings of a tiny bird.

Knuck caught me staring and abruptly turned to our visitors. "You made my daughter a proposition," he said evenly. "I wasn't there, and I don't like getting things secondhand. I'm wondering if you can lay it out for me here in person. That way I'll understand all the particulars."

"*Particulars!*" Graytooth exclaimed. "I like that." He leaned in toward Knuck. "I'd be happy to give you the particulars. My friend and I represent a whatchacallit…a coalition of concerned citizens. That's right, we're awful concerned about the whole quality of life thing we got going down in this neighborhood. You know, the vandalism, the assaulting, and the general…uh…uh…" He screwed up his face theatrically as he searched for the word he wanted.

"Hooliganism," I offered helpfully.

Graytooth beamed. "*Hooliganism,*" he drawled, rolling the word around in his mouth like a gumball. "Exactly! We need to deal with this current spate of hooliganism."

"That there hooliganism sure is bad stuff," I agreed.

"So, what you're telling me," Knuck continued, "is that if we pay you, we won't have as many problems with this, uh…"

"Hooliganism!" Graytooth exclaimed brightly, finishing Knuck's sentence for him.

"Okay!" Knuck snapped. "Let's agree to knock off the goddamned vocabulary lesson. Just bottom line it for me, will ya? We pay you and you stop causing trouble for us. That about right?"

Graytooth's sunny expression dropped like a dowager's bust line. "Causing trouble?" he moaned. "We'd never cause you any trouble! Who said anything about us causing you trouble? I'm hurt. That's what I am. This was never about us causing trouble. You got that all wrong. See, we're the ones want to keep other folks from causing the trouble. That's the first thing we got to get clear. Now, it's true that if we expend our energies looking out for you, we won't have the energy to be doing something else. That happens, we might find ourselves, shall we say, out-of-pocket some. In that eventuality, our hope would be that you might want to show us your, uh…your gratefulness through some monetary appreciation. That's what we were thinking, anyway."

"It's not about the money, Knuck," I chided. "It's about the love."

Knuck ignored me. "How much money we talking about?" he asked.

"Well, now," Graytooth said, nudging his partner, who'd slumped even lower in the booth, "it is hard to put a price on love. I guess it would all depend on how much of our help you'll be needing. A fancy place like this could become a real popular target for those hooligans we been talking about." He put his fingers to his chin. "How about…um, I don't know. How about five every month?"

I slapped my hands together. "You'll do all that for us for only five dollars a month? Hot damn!" I reached for my wallet. "I probably got a half a year's worth on me right now."

Graytooth threw up both hands. "No! No! No!" he exclaimed. "Hold on there, big guy. You've made a bit of a mistake. Not five dollars. Five thousand dollars. Of course," he added, "that's just to start. If we need to bring in extra help, it could go higher."

"Oh dear!" I gasped. "And things were going so well, too."

Knuck wasn't enjoying the conversation anywhere near as much as I was. Leaning across the table, his face reddened, and his voice quavered with barely checked anger. "You're the one making the mistake, pal."

Graytooth leaned back but managed to hold on to his smile. "Mistake? No mistake. I'm just making a business proposition. Everything's open to negotiation."

"Well, negotiate this, Hoss," Knuck told him. "You're trying to shakedown a cop. A *cop*, you understand. That makes you some kind of world-class idiot, don't you think?"

Graytooth's smile still didn't waver. "I gotta tell you, officer," he replied, "we knew you used to be a cop before we came in here. But we decided not to let that…that accident of employment close off our opportunity to do business together. Besides, we figure a man was on the force as long as you was is sure to have put a little something extra aside for…what'cha call it…contingencies."

Knuck started to say something, but I couldn't help myself. "Did I hear you right?" I interrupted. "You knew he used to be a cop, and you decided to pull this anyway?"

Graytooth shrugged. "A man's past don't matter to me," he said. "It's the future we're concerned about."

"That's awfully magnanimous of you," I said. "I'd have thought—"

Graytooth, a triumphant smile sweeping across his face, didn't get to hear what I thought before Knuck exploded. "This matter to you, asshole," he shouted suddenly, lunging across the table and grabbing him by the shirt.

A stunned Graytooth frantically tried to squirm out of Knuck's grasp. "Hey now! Hey now!"

As Knuck pulled Graytooth across the table, his partner, the sleepy guy, finally seemed to wake up. His eyes widened, and he tried to push the table out of his way. But it was bolted to the floor, and he could only get about halfway to his feet before his thighs banged into it, rattling the empty coffee cups. As he struggled to get his feet under him, he dug furiously in the deep pockets of his jacket.

Unfortunately for him, before he could either get out from behind the table or remove whatever he was reaching for, I had the barrel of my .38 nuzzled against his temple. He froze immediately, his hands still hidden in his pockets.

Knuck continued to wrestle with Graytooth, rolling him from side to side atop the table. But he neither threw a punch nor went for his gun. To be honest, it looked more like an antagonistic tango than a brawl.

"Knuck!" I called out. "What do you say we quit fuckin' around and just shoot these guys?"

Graytooth stopped hollering. Knuck looked over at me, nodded, and let go of his shirt. Graytooth slumped back into the booth as Knuck reached into his sports jacket for his revolver.

My guy's hands stirred in his jacket pockets, so I pressed my gun barrel a little harder against his skull. Leaning in, I said, "I bet you got a nine in there, don't you? In your jacket pocket? I bettin' it's a nine."

He didn't reply.

"Yeah," I continued. "Everybody's got a nine nowadays. My grandma's got a nine. How 'bout you, Knuck? You think it's a nine?"

"Sure," Knuck replied, his voice a bit louder than it needed to be. "A nine."

"Golly," I said, "let's see if we're right."

As I took a step back, the young man went back to squinting at me. "Don't matter you taking my piece," he said. "No way I let some fat guy get away dissin' me like this. You're one dead motherfucker."

I grinned. Then, as quickly and as hard as I could, I hit him on the bridge of his nose with the butt of my gun. The impact was so loud that, for a moment, I thought I'd cracked the grip.

He doubled over, his hands racing from his pockets to his injured nose so fast I didn't actually see it happen. All at once, they were just there, blood seeping through his fingers. "I think you broke my nose, man!" he wailed.

"You think?" I asked. "You want me to hit you again to be sure?"

Saucer-eyed, he stared at me, then shook his head wildly.

"Still need to see what's in your pockets," I reminded him. "You too," I said, pointing at Graytooth. "On your feet."

Knuck got up first, coming to stand beside me as we

watched the two men ease slowly out of the booth.

"Well, I'm not carrying," Graytooth assured us, managing a fragile, china doll grin.

"Good," I told him. "Then I might not have to shoot you." I emphasized the "you" ever so slightly.

Our would-be business partners turned around and assumed spread-eagle positions like a couple of pros. While I patted them down, Knuck stood guard. He didn't look any too happy watching the guy whose nose I'd broken drip blood on the new carpet. I went through their pockets. True to his word, Graytooth had no weapon, but he did carry a worn black leather wallet, so stuffed with cash register receipts and credit cards that it flopped open by itself when I laid it on the table.

His partner had no wallet—in fact, he had no personal information on him of any kind. But I was right about the gun. It was a nine-millimeter semi-automatic. A bit showy if you ask me.

I slipped it, barrel first, into my belt at the small of my back and ordered the two men face down on the floor, warning them to keep their fingers interlaced behind their heads. Knuck continued to cover them while I searched through Graytooth's wallet.

The credit cards were under several different names, but his driver's license identified him as Latrine Hawkins. I read it twice to be sure I hadn't made a mistake. "Your name's Latrine?" I asked, staring down at him. "L-A-T-R-I-N-E."

He grinned sheepishly.

I shook my head. "I gotta know," I said. "What happened? I mean, was your mom trying for Latrell? Did someone write it down wrong? What?"

The embarrassed hoodlum lowered his eyes. "No,"

he said, letting out a nervous chuckle as he glanced at his bleeding partner. "It's a long story. I really wouldn't want to be wasting any more of your time."

"I got time," I told him. "You got time, Knuck?"

Knuck nodded but without apparent interest.

"Go ahead," I prompted. "Tell us all about it."

"Well," he began, "there's something you gotta understand. My mom…" He shook his head dejectedly. "Well, my mom is a strong-willed woman. Strong-willed. The day I was born, the nurse brought me in to Mama and asked what name they should write on the birth certificate for me. Mama says, 'Latrine.' The nurse asks her to spell it. Mama spells it. The nurse says you can't name a kid 'Latrine," and she explains to Mama that it's a…you know, another name for toilet. Mama says she thought the name up herself. Says through all those hours of labor she thought of only two things: a healthy baby and the name Latrine. Says she never heard of a toilet called latrine, and she didn't think anyone else in the neighborhood heard that neither. She wouldn't give in. Insisted the nurse write it down, So, Latrine I am."

"You graduate high school, Latrine?" I asked

"Sure did," he said, smiling. "Mama wouldn't have it no other way."

"You got all the way through high school with a name like 'Latrine?' My hat's off to you. You must have got beat up every day."

"I mostly went by my street name," Latrine admitted.

"What's that?"

Latrine mumbled something I couldn't make out.

I waved my gun around. "What's that?" I repeated.

"Booger," he said, just loud enough to be heard.

I didn't have the heart to laugh at him.

"And you?" I asked, turning to Latrine's partner.

Both of his eyes had darkened, and the blood flowing from his now pulpy nose had soaked through the front of his jacket. "Cleanhead," he told me.

"Not anymore," I said.

"So, uh, not to rush you fellas or anything," Latrine interjected, "but what you got in mind here? I mean, what are going to do with us?"

"Well, I don't rightly know, Latrine," I said. "I mean this asshole…" I pointed to Cleanhead. "This asshole, I gotta shoot." I shrugged. "He threatened me. Can't let that go."

"Come on, now," Latrine implored. "He was just mouthin' off. You don't have to—"

"Yes, Latrine," I interrupted, "I do. Those are the rules. Guy with a gun threatens you, you gotta take him out. I don't make up the rules."

"Yeah, but—"

"No buts, Latrine," I replied. "Ha! That's a pun, isn't it?"

Latrine forced a smile, but I was pretty sure he no longer found any of this funny.

"Okay, okay," Latrine said, staring up at my gun barrel, his breathing becoming more labored. "But I got no gun. I didn't threaten you."

"Good point, Latrine," I said. "But…you did try to shake us down. That wasn't very nice. I let you go, how am I supposed to know you won't come back here? You said it yourself. We got a business to run. Can't be having you guys barging in here disturbing the lunch rush."

"But I wouldn't—"

"Nope. It's no good, Latrine. Just no good. We're gonna have to clip you both. We got us a floor drain in the kitchen. And a whole bunch of really good cutlery. I figure we just haul you back there, hack up your carcasses, pack you in maybe two or three garbage bags apiece, and distribute you amongst the various Dumpsters out back. Kind of an ignoble end, but we all got to go sometime. Right Latrine?"

"He's just trying to scare you, Booger," Cleanhead piped up. "Fat fuck thinks he's tough."

Cleanhead saw me coming but just wasn't fast enough. I crossed the floor at a trot and drove the heel of my hiking boot into his skull. He bounced once against the floor, groaned softly, and curled up into a ball.

"This is your quiet time, son," I told him. I don't think he heard me.

I turned back to Latrine, grinning menacingly. "He's right, you know," I confided. "I am trying to scare you. How's it working so far?"

Latrine stared at the now motionless Cleanhead but didn't answer.

I turned to Knuck and winked. Then, stepping toward Latrine, I painted a tight circle in the air with my gun barrel. "Say goodnight, Latrine," I said.

Since we hadn't worked it out beforehand, I was a little surprised when Knuck picked up his cue. "Ah, hell, Lyle," he broke in. "Let him go. Let 'em both go."

I whirled around. "You're kidding me, right, Knuck?"

Knuck shrugged. "Nah. I mean, what the hell? They didn't do any real harm. And I damn sure ain't afraid of 'em coming back here. I mean, look what happened to 'em this time? They gotta know if they show back up here, they're Dumpster chow."

"No way," I said, shaking my head. "The one with the gun threatened me. He could come back here. Only sure way to stop that is by clipping him."

"We got their names," Knuck pointed out, a wonderfully genial quality to his voice. "I know a lot of guys on the force. I can always have somebody run them. We get their addresses. Their families' addresses. We change our minds, we can take 'em out anytime. Don't sweat it. Hacking 'em up here? Too messy if you ask me. We gotta open in couple days. I got other shit to do."

I paused, rubbing my chin. Latrine's eyes were fixed hopefully on me. "If it's the butchering that bothers you, Knuck, I don't mind doing it," I told him.

The hope in Latrine's eyes turned to horror.

"Ah, it's not just that," Knuck countered. "This is my daughter's place. We do it here, she's liable to tell her mother. I'll be hearing about it for weeks."

"I got my car out front. We could take them somewhere else," I suggested.

Knuck paused. "No," he said firmly. "We should just let them go."

"You sure?"

"I'm sure."

"Okay, it's your call. You change your mind, let me know, huh? Like you say, it won't be hard tracking them down."

"You'll be the first person I'll call," Knuck assured me. He turned to Latrine. "Looks like you can go," he said.

Latrine let out a sigh so big I think the windows bulged. "You uh…You won't regret it, gentlemen," he

91

insisted.

"Just get the hell out of my restaurant," Knuck told him.

Latrine scampered to his feet and started for the door.

"Wait a minute!" Knuck exclaimed. Pointing at the still-prostrate Cleanhead, he said, "Take that with you."

As Latrine bent over to help his fallen comrade, Knuck loped across the room and flung open the front door. The setting sun sent streaks of brilliant yellow-orange light, like fiery dragon's breath, onto the lobby floor. Latrine half-carried, half-dragged his partner through the door and into the street.

Knuck closed the door behind them.

"You think they'll be back?" I asked him.

"After the way you handled that one guy? Not likely."

I shook my head. "It's hard to be sure," I cautioned. "I mean, I'm not worried about Latrine, but that Cleanhead? He could be back. He gets the right combination of liquor and bad advice into him, he could do something stupid."

Knuck waved at me dismissively. "I'll be around. Either one of 'em comes back, I'll be ready."

I nodded. "Well," I said, "it was nice working with you. You were great there at the end. I particularly liked that 'Dumpster chow' line."

"It's a gift," Knuck joked. He stared at me briefly, a small, apologetic smile flashing across his face. "Took me a while to get going, though," he admitted. "Sorry about that. Retirement, huh? Been out of the game too long, I guess. Good thing you were here."

"You'd a been just fine without me," I told him.

"Still," Knuck said, "I owe you for this, Lyle. Least I can do is buy you a drink. What do ya say?"

I wouldn't have predicted it but having Dad's old partner offer to buy me a beer filled me with unexpected pride. Suddenly, I was downright flush with accomplishment. This time, I thought, I'd really come through. "A drink would be great," I told him.

Smiling, I slid my revolver back into the shoulder holster.

We were most of the way to the bar when Knuck suddenly stopped. "Shit!"

"What?"

Knuck turned back to the door. "That one guy left his billfold," Knuck said, pointing to the bulging wallet lying on the table.

"Yeah, so?"

Knuck went to the table and picked it up. Maybe I can catch him."

"Why would you do that?"

Knuck shrugged. "Guy's probably too stupid to know how to replace it. Anyway, I'll just see if they're out there."

I blinked. "You're kidding me, right?"

"Not at all. It'll only take a minute.

It finally struck me that he was serious. "Knuck," I warned, "that's really not a smart play."

"Quit being such a mother hen, Lyle. I'll be right back." He stepped toward the door.

I sighed. "Fine," I said, "but I'm coming with you."

Knuck was about to argue when a door opened behind us and Mindy reentered the dining room. "Is it all over?"

"Just about, sugar,' Knuck assured her, holding up

an open palm. "Just one last detail to take care of. You stay there. Lyle, stay with Mindy, huh? I won't be a minute."

"Knuck, I still don't think—"

He interrupted me. "Just stick, okay?" There was something in his voice that I found difficult to ignore. I stared at him. "Uh, um, okay," I stammered at last.

Concern crowding her already pinched-off features, Mindy hurried toward her father. Just as quickly, Knuck headed out the door, letting it close behind him.

Mindy twirled around slowly, wobbling like a top on its dying spin. "What's he doing?"

"I really don't know."

"Should he be—" Mindy began.

She was interrupted by a gunshot on the street outside. Her eyes went wide with alarm. Reflexively, I pushed Mindy back into the dining room away from the door. Snatching my gun from its holster, I shouted, "Stay here!" Mindy nodded unsteadily as I turned to race out onto the sidewalk. Another shot rang out.

Outside, I spotted Knuck, hunched over, standing about a half a block down the street. It wasn't until I'd nearly reached him that I saw Latrine lying on the concrete at Knuck's feet. Knuck's revolver was in his hand, a curl of smoke rising from its barrel.

"Where's the other one?" I yelled.

Knuck didn't look at me. Instead, he motioned toward an adjacent alley. I plunged into it, broken glass crunching under my feet. I didn't see anyone as I ran to the end of the alley. I surveyed the street beyond. There was no sign of Cleanhead. Cautiously, I made my way back to Knuck.

He was still standing over the fallen Latrine, still

clutching his revolver. There was a tiny puncture in Latrine's hockey jersey, just above the belt line, but a widening pool of blood was spreading out beneath him. He groaned softly. His eyes were open but rolled up inside his head, so there were two bleached white marbles where his pupils were supposed to be. Pain had twisted his mouth into a horrific parody of a smile.

"Knuck!" I demanded. "What happened?"

At first, I wondered if Knuck was in shock. He just stood there, unmoving, staring down at the dead hoodlum. But I'd seen shock before—the disbelief in the eyes, the slack-jawed absence of feeling. This wasn't that. This was a whole lot more casual.

Knuck faced me and shrugged. "Had to do it," he said simply, holstering his revolver. "I guess we'd better call the police after all.

## Chapter Seven

Homicide Detective Augustus Tarkof stared grimly at the plastic bottle of spring water in his hand. On our way to the interview room, we'd made a stop at the little alcove where the detective squad kept its coffee maker. Although it was late in the day, there was still plenty of coffee left in the carafe, and I'd offered to fill a cup for each of us. Tarkof paused thoughtfully but declined, instead bending down to pull the spring water from a small, dorm-style refrigerator that was tucked under the counter.

Tarkof watched with unusual scrutiny as I poured my coffee. His normally cold, gray eyes seemed edged with something almost warm. Certainly not joy in welcoming me back to his squad room. During our long acquaintanceship, Tarkof had made little secret that I'd never be on his Christmas list. But there was a softness, a wistfulness there that I hadn't remembered seeing before. Tarkof caught me staring and led me quickly away.

Inside the interview room, he motioned me toward one of two chairs situated on either side of a rectangular wooden table. The air was still and heavy. Tarkof closed the door and stripped off his dark gray suit jacket, revealing an ample waistline, a blue striped tie, and a white shirt with half-moon stains the pale yellow of a primrose under his arms. Again, he paused to stare at my coffee cup before setting some paperwork down on the table and taking the seat opposite me. "Okay, Dahms," he said at last, tugging open the spout of his water bottle. "Tell me again why you and this Fullmer were meeting with those guys."

"We've been over this, Augie," I reminded him. "First at the crime scene. Then, again on the ride over here. You could take better notes."

Tarkof tilted his head back and, positioning the tip of the bottle maybe three inches above it, attempted to direct a stream of water into his open mouth. "Indulge me," he said when he'd finished. Although he wiped at his chin, a large drop of water clung stubbornly to his ill-trimmed mustache.

"Like I told you. Fullmer is an old friend of the family. Those punks were hassling his daughter. He promised her that he'd handle it but thought it wise to bring me along as backup."

Tarkof set the water bottle down and opened a manila folder that lay before him. As he flipped through its contents, I looked up to check out my reflection in a mirror that took up nearly the entire wall behind him. Of course, I knew it wasn't just a mirror but a one-way window designed to allow others in the adjacent room to watch unseen during an interview. Even though I didn't think our little discussion would warrant eavesdroppers, I couldn't help but make faces while Tarkof wasn't looking.

At least, I didn't think he was looking. To my embarrassment, when he raised his head, there was a distinct note of patient exasperation in his expression. "So, you're saying these two were looking to collect protection from the daughter?"

I shrugged. "I'm saying that's what I was told. Basically, my job was to stand around and look intimidating while Knuck talked to perps. It was his show. I will tell you that the highlight of the conversation was when the Black guy, Latrine Hawkins, said that for five thousand a month they'd find it in their hearts to keep anything untoward from happening at the restaurant."

"That was the highlight?"

"Yeah. That and the explanation of how Hawkins came to be named after a toilet."

Tarkof narrowed his gaze. "So, Hawkins made the offer, and you two declined to give them the money?"

I smiled. "Didn't seem like a prudent investment."

Tarkof tapped the folder. "So, you shot them instead?"

My smile crooked into a smirk. "Nice try, Augie, but as you know—and ballistics will prove—I didn't shoot anyone. I wasn't even on the scene when the Hawkins kid got shot."

"So you say," Tarkof stressed.

I sighed. "You want to go over this again, that's fine with me. I heard two shots. I exited the building and saw Knuck standing over Latrine. Knuck said that Cleanhead—or whatever his real name is—took off down the alley. I followed after him, but he was gone."

"And you never discharged your weapon?"

"No."

"And your friend Fullmer? He fired twice?"

"I only heard two shots. Knuck told me he got a shot off at Cleanhead but missed. I didn't spot a blood trail when I checked out the alley, so I'm guessing you'll find Knuck's other bullet down there somewhere. If you look hard enough."

"Oh," Tarkof assured me, "we'll be looking hard enough." He paused. "Fullmer tell you why he shot at them?"

"No."

Tarkof nodded. "Hawkins died, by the way. You hear that?"

I hadn't. I glanced back up at the mirror. I could feel Tarkof's eyes on me. After a moment, I shook my head. "That sucks," I said. "I liked Latrine. I suppose now his bereaved family will haul Knuck into court on some wrongful death deal. Hawkins said he had a strong-willed mother. Might come after me, too, for all I know."

With a grunt, Tarkof pushed back from the table. "That's what happens when you start pulling guns on other citizens, Dahms. I hope you're not looking for sympathy from me."

"As I said before, I didn't actually pull my gun on Hawkins. I did pull it on his partner. Inside the restaurant. I didn't have much choice. Cleanhead was packing, and he went for it."

Tarkof frowned.

"What did you expect me to do, Augie? Just let him start shooting at us?"

Tarkof leaned forward. The drop of water finally fell from his mustache, landing on the table with a surprising splatter. "I expect the same thing from you that I'd expect from anyone else, pal. I expect you to let the cops handle this kind of thing. If you two hadn't gone all Lone Ranger on us, Hawkins would be alive right now."

"Batman and Robin," I corrected

"What?"

"You said 'Lone Ranger.' There were two of us. I

gotta think that Batman and Robin would be a better analogy."

"I gotta think you'll be looking at a collapsed lung if you don't quit squeezing my shoes," he warned.

"I'd be Robin," I insisted. "Still got my boyish good looks."

Tarkof closed his eyes for a moment.

"Headache?" I asked.

"Never mind," he said.

Tarkof closed the folder and pushed it aside to get at another seemingly identical folder beneath. He opened the second folder and studied it for a moment in silence. On top, I could see a mug shot of the man I knew as Cleanhead.

"The one you guys chased off," he said, pointing. "This guy. Looks like his real name is Mason Slidel. Anti-Crime's got a record of several skels going by the name Cleanhead, but this Slidel is the only one known to be an associate of the late Latrine Hawkins." Tarkof turned the file so I could get a better look at the photo.

"That's him," I confirmed.

"Slidel's got himself a reputation as a shooter. Never been convicted, but they're looking at him for a couple of drive-bys. Hawkins was primarily a drug dealer." Tarkof paused. "Neither of these guys has been known to pull anything like the scam you and Fullmer are trying to sell us."

"It's delightful to see young people branch out, isn't it?"

"Not so delightful to see them shot dead in the street,"

I lowered my eyes, remembering Latrine writhing on the pavement as he waited for the paramedics to start working on him. All at once, I didn't feel like joking. "I told you, Augie. I liked Hawkins. But the fact is his death just doesn't have a lot to do with me."

"You tell yourself whatever you need to, Dahms. I just got one question. What did this Fullmer do to piss you off?"

"What's that supposed to mean?"

Tarkof picked up the sports bottle, tilted his head, and sent another stream of spring water into his waiting yap. The spectacle was becoming more cringe-worthy each time he subjected me to it. Swallowing, he answered, "It means that I'm trying to understand this story you're telling about how Fullmer came to follow Hawkins and Slidel out into the street. You really sticking to that nonsense? You want me to believe that after a couple of hoods try to shake down his daughter, after one of them tries to pull a gun on you, Fullmer suddenly decides to rush out after them to return a lost wallet?"

Tarkof shook his head from side to side—slowly, as though something was loose in there, and he was trying to get it to fall back into place. "I just hope that if I ever ask you to cover for me, you'll come up with a better story than that. Either you're really as dense as I've suspected all these years, or you're mad at Fullmer and feeding us this crap as some kind of payback. Either way, I don't like having my time wasted."

"I know how it sounds, Augie," I insisted, "but it's true. There we were. I had Slidel's weapon. We'd tried to throw a scare into Hawkins. There wasn't anything left for us to do but let them go. So, we did. Then Knuck spots the wallet and heads out the door. I tried to warn him against it, but he went after them anyway."

"And you didn't follow him? I thought you were supposed to be backing him up."

I remembered how Knuck had insisted I wait inside the restaurant. "I was going to, but I, uh…I got distracted."

"Uh-huh." Tarkof closed Slidel's file. "That's convenient. For you. It pretty much puts all this on Fullmer. You know, if somebody's gonna take it in the shorts for this, it's going to be him. I wouldn't have thought you'd want that. Not with him being your dad's old partner and all."

A sudden flush warmed my cheeks. "Knuck mentioned he was my father's partner?"

Tarkof nodded. "Yeah, and we checked." He reached under the folders and drew out a couple of stapled sheets of paper. "Got this from the Burnsville PD." He paused, studying the document momentarily. "Fullmer had himself a nice career. Most of it spent with your dad." Tarkof looked up. "Sorry about that, by the way. You losing him, I mean." His tone softened ever so slightly as he said it.

I looked away. "Thanks."

Tarkof returned his attention to the document. "Only black mark I see here has to do with a couple that got murdered a while back. Pam and Vernon Murdoch. Says here Fullmer spent some time on restricted duty. Looks like he rode that out with your dad, too."

Tarkof ran his finger slowly down to the bottom of the page. "No real details. Just that Fullmer and your dad were reinstated." He paused. "Anything there you want to tell me about?"

Tarkof kept his eyes on the document, rolling a pen in his fingers. It bothered me that he didn't look up. "I was a kid at the time," I told him. "I remember Dad being around the house for a couple weeks. I think we picnicked once. That the kind of thing you're looking for? I'm pretty sure we had fried chicken. I could ask Mom if it's important."

"I can probably get by without knowing. But thanks for being so forthcoming."

I smiled. Tarkof finally raised his head and smiled. I leaned back in my chair and sipped at my coffee. It was not good coffee. In fact, it wasn't actually coffee so much as an inky black brew that had sat on the burner so long that I swear it was chunky. And that wasn't the worst of it. There was the smell. The one small cup seemed to fill the entire room with an acrid aroma that was simultaneously burnt and musty, as though a small, damp animal had gained entrance only to be flash fried by unfortunate contact with an electrical outlet. Even so, as he watched me sip at it, something pulsed in Tarkof's eyes.

I set down my cup. "Can I get you some coffee, Augie?"

"No thanks," he said. "I'm trying to cut down."

I stared at him. "Why would anyone do that?"

Tarkof glared back. "Doctor suggested it."

"What'cha do, stiff him on a bill?"

Tarkof waved a dismissive hand, then fiddled with the spout of his water bottle. "Too much caffeine isn't good for you."

"I don't have my morning coffee, I get headaches."

Tarkof closed his eyes tightly. His eyelids twitched. "This isn't about my caffeine intake, Dahms, he said, opening his eyes. "This is about you and Fullmer and what happened out on the street today."

"I told you. I don't know what happened on the street. I wasn't there. If you want to know more, you'll have to have to ask Knuck."

Tarkof glanced down at the folder again. "Oh, we have. Probably have to ask again. His story stinks. Yours, too."

"I don't know what to tell you. You don't like the story? Make up another one. After all, you and I both know that you're not really going after a nearly thirty-year veteran of the police force because he clipped some known felon who was threatening his daughter. I don't know what happened when Knuck went out to return that wallet. Maybe one of them made a move. Something made him pull his gun. The guy was a cop for a long time. He may be old, but that don't mean he's lost his instincts. He did what he thought he had to do. End of story. Now, if we're through here, I'd like to go home."

Tarkof turned his head, casting a deliberate gaze at the mirror behind him. He eased back from the table, neatly stacked his papers, slipped them back into the folder, and stood. Getting to my feet, I followed him to the door. Just before he opened it, Tarkof reminded me, "Slidel's still out there, you know."

"I know."

"That bother you? You're not worried he'll be looking to even things up a bit?"

I shrugged. "You guys are looking for him, right?"

Tarkof ran a hand over his mustache. "Right."

"I've got faith you'll pick him up."

"I'm not sure we have anything to hold him on. We know he wasn't armed when Fullmer followed him outside. I don't think we have a case against him for trying to shake down the daughter. We might have if you and Fullmer hadn't cut us out, but…" Tarkof spread his hands out in a gesture of helplessness.

"Oh, you'll think of something, Augie. Like I said, I got faith. And if you don't, the truth is it's not really *my* problem. Fullmer did the shooting. If Slidel's going to come after somebody, it'll likely be Knuck."

Tarkof grunted. "Sounds to me like you're breaking up the partnership. Fullmer know about this?"

The image of Knuck Fullmer standing over Latrine Hawkins swept into my mind—the absence of emotion in his eyes, the disinterested shrug as his victim writhed at his feet. I shook my head to dispel it, but the image stayed with me.

"Fullmer was my dad's partner," I said. "Not mine. Knuck asked me to do him a favor. I agreed. You gotta admit it didn't turn out very well. I don't see myself doing him another."

Tarkof grunted again and ushered me out of the interview room. I was nearly to the elevator when he asked, "Seen anything of Donnie Murdoch lately?"

I turned around slowly. "Why are you asking about him?"

Tarkof flashed a mirthless smile. "I don't know. Reading your old man's file got me interested, I guess." He tapped the folder he was holding against his leg. "So…" He paused. "You seen him?"

It took me a moment to answer. "As far as I know, Donnie Murdoch no longer exists."

Chapter Eight

I didn't sleep well that night. It could have been the coffee I'd had at the police station—I know I'm not supposed to have caffeine after five o'clock—but more likely it was the recurring memory of Latrine Hawkins bubbling and moaning on the sidewalk. That and a gnawing sense that Augie Tarkof wouldn't have asked me about Donnie Murdoch unless something was wrong.

The Donnie with whom I'd become reacquainted struck me as harmless—just another strung-out loser drifting along in a meth-induced haze, unlikely to have either the brains or the ambition to involve himself in the protection scheme that Hawkins and Slidel had tried to pull on Mindy Fullmer. Why was Tarkof so interested in him?

And what did Tarkof know that I didn't?

I went into the office late the next day, broke early for lunch, and instead of working on any of my open cases, spent the afternoon reading the newspaper. Knuck shooting Latrine made print, but it was a small story on page three. The reporter mentioned that the police were conducting an investigation but that preliminary findings were that Knuck had fired in self-defense. I was right. Despite their questions, Tarkof and company were taking pains to protect their fellow cop.

I moved on to the comics page, but my mind kept returning to Donnie Murdoch. Tarkof hadn't only asked about Donnie, he'd asked about Donnie's parents as well. Having his mother and father so violently taken from him had been devastating for Donnie, responsible for putting in motion whatever it was that led to his murderous catharsis at Racing Days. Was that the end of it for him? Was Donnie really the cowering, spaced-out addict that he seemed, or, underneath, was he still the killer he'd once proved himself to be? He'd had years with little else to do but think about the people and events that altered his life. He knew that there had been questions about how the investigation into his parents' murders had been conducted—specifically, how my father and Knuck Fullmer had performed their roles. Was it possible that Donnie harbored resentments? Could he have been behind Hawkins and Slidel's visit to Mindy Fullmer's restaurant?

You have to be a pretty good judge of character to survive in my line of work, and I truthfully didn't think that poor, drug-addled Donnie had enough left on the ball to successfully negotiate the intricacies of the extra value menu at the local burger joint, let alone concoct some plan of revenge. But even if Donnie didn't have it in him, what about his housemates, Tousignant and Bollok? Those two were considerably less hapless. And didn't Tarkof say that Hawkins was a drug dealer? Bollok and Tooz weren't just selling crank out of that house in North Minneapolis. They were into the production end of things. To make real money, they'd be moving it out on the street and would have a sales force. Was Hawkins working for them?

But the more I turned it over in my head, the less I made it work. Where was the connection between the Fullmers and Bollok and Tooz? Granted, Knuck Fullmer was one of the cops who found Donnie's parents dead, and Mindy had been in his class at dear old Burnsville High. But so what? How does the fact that they all knew Donnie at one time or another become Bollok and Tooz sending Hawkins and Slidel off to shake down Mindy? It didn't make sense.

About four o'clock in the afternoon, tired of doing nothing, I folded the paper away, locked up the office, and returned to the Bijou.

There are times I like the comradery that living in a rooming house affords, and there are times when I'd truly like to be left alone. The previous day's events had left me craving solitude, and I tried to enter the Bijou as stealthily as possible. I inserted my key in the lock carefully, turned it precisely, and opened the door slowly. I didn't want any of my housemates to hear me come in and mistake my return as an invitation to conversation. The only companionship I craved was the bottle of Summit Extra Pale Ale that was waiting for me in the refrigerator in my room.

I closed the door silently behind me and glanced down the hall toward the living room. Listening, the only sound I heard was the measured tick-tick of the distant mantel clock. I inched toward my room.

"Hey, Lyle, come in here!" Edgerton's voice, like the crack of a timber giving way, suddenly sounded from the living room. "You gotta see this!"

I thought about ignoring him, maybe sneaking back outside and, later, claiming it never happened. But instead, I padded off down the hallway toward him, mouthing curses, my footsteps heavy with resignation.

The Bijou was a large house, originally built as a single-family home at the turn of the twentieth century but subsequently reconfigured as a rooming house. Its proximity to the nearby University of Minnesota and its general state of ill repair—which served to keep the rents low—made a room at the Bijou highly sought after. To meet the demand, each successive owner had carved up more and more of the house into small bedrooms, leaving relatively little common space. The living room was a cramped afterthought situated at the end of the ground floor hallway, made even more crowded by the surprising amount of furniture squeezed into it. A big screen TV, a large coffee table, three mismatched armchairs, and a brown corduroy sofa—its torn and threadbare upholstery partially covered by a sheet imprinted with scenes from the first Star Wars movie.

"It's a collector's item," Edgerton was known to insist.

As I entered the room, Edgerton was sitting at the far end of the sofa. Little Nigel, our black Lhasapoo, sat on the carpet at Edgerton's feet, his head raised, peering upward. Basil, the buff-colored Cockapoo, was curled up serenely in Edgerton's lap. What made this scene of domestic tranquility noteworthy was that as he sat there, Basil's tongue repeatedly disappeared down the neck of a beer bottle that Edgerton held out for him.

Edgerton looked up at me and smiled. "I had no idea his tongue could be that long."

I watched slack-jawed as the edges of the dog's tongue curled to accommodate the relatively small diameter of the bottle's opening before plunging inside, reaching down the neck an incredible three to four inches before sliding back out with a noisy slurp.

I'll admit that I was unusually put off by the sight and it took a moment for me to find my voice. "I hate to tell you this," I said at last, "but most people don't share their drinks with their dogs. Setting aside for a moment the sanitary questions involved, don't you think you're risking the little guy's health? I mean, I have no idea how well the average mutt holds his liquor. Do you?"

"It's an empty bottle, Lyle."

I nodded. "I'm not surprised, judging by the way he's going at it."

"It was empty when I gave it to him," Edgerton assured me. His eyes brightened. "It was the damnedest thing. When I finished the beer, Basil here kept looking at me. He was staring at me with unnerving intensity. Then he crawled up into my lap. Finally, he started pawing at the bottle. It was either let him have it or risk being shredded."

"That or actually get up and put the bottle in the recycling bin."

"Don't talk crazy, Lyle. Anyway, I held it down where he could reach it and…Well, he's been doing this for like fifteen minutes. It's fascinating. I mean, just look at him."

I looked at him. "It's disgusting. Not only that, it's…it's just plain weird."

"What's weird about it? After all, every dog's gotta have a trick."

I sighed. "Yeah, but couldn't you teach him to fetch or play tug-of-war? You know, something dog-like." I wagged my finger at the bottle. "A thing like that's just gonna further alienate him from other dogs. Let's face it; Basil's never been the most well-adjusted little guy."

"What do you mean he's not well-adjusted?" Edgerton asked, indignation rising in his voice.

"Stephen," I reminded him, "we can't keep his food

in the kitchen because he's afraid of the vinyl flooring."

Edgerton paused. "Okay. I'll admit he has some issues. But that doesn't mean—"

"He's taken to hiding his kibble in my shoes."

Edgerton crinkled his brow. "Your shoes?"

I nodded. "I've been meaning to tell you. The other day, I went to put on my Rockports, the nice brown ones, the ones I never wear. The ones my mom bought me. Anyway, I go to put them on, and they're full of dog food."

Edgerton thought for a moment. "That could mean anything. It could mean mice. Maybe mice put dog food in your shoes."

I smiled patiently. "This place may not be the Ritz, Stephen, but you know perfectly well we've never been troubled by a mouse infestation."

"We don't have to be infested. Maybe it's only one mouse."

"Stephen, I've seen him. Basil sometimes carries his food around the house. He'll load his cheeks up like a chipmunk and take his meal on the road. I've seen him do it."

"So? He's social," Edgerton insisted. "Why would he want to eat all alone when he can eat where his family is?"

"How's that explain his loading up my Rockports?" I asked, rather more loudly than I'd intended.

Basil stopped his licking for a moment to stare at me. Edgerton rubbed Basil's ears briefly, then tapped his fingernail on the beer bottle. Basil returned to probing the neck with his tongue. Then Nigel stirred, craning his neck to look at me before standing up slowly. Then, as sprightly as a wood nymph, Nigel sprang onto the sofa.

He stared at Basil, then at Edgerton. Edgerton smirked knowingly and moved the bottle away from Basil, holding it toward Nigel. Nigel examined it quizzically, gave it a couple of unenthusiastic licks, and turned away. Edgerton gave the bottle back to Basil, who attacked it with renewed gusto.

"I really don't know why your knickers are in such a twist," Edgerton said. "It's like you're trying to stifle the dog's creativity. It's almost like you're..." He lowered his voice conspiratorially. "It's almost like you'd prefer him to be more like...like you know who."

"*You know who*?" I repeated. "You mean Nigel?"

At the sound of his name the black dog jumped down from the sofa and ran toward me, his mouth open, his head tilted, his eyes wide and vacuous.

"Shhh!" Edgerton whispered dramatically. "He'll know we're talking about him."

"What's wrong with that? And what's wrong with Basil being more like Nigel."

Nigel glanced toward Edgerton as though he, too, wanted an answer. Edgerton gave him a doleful little smile. "Don't get me wrong," he said. "I love Nigel. It's just that...that Nigel's never impressed me as much of an abstract thinker. Now Basil, on the other hand—"

"They're dogs, Stephen," I interrupted.

"And you're saying that means that they are incapable of higher reasoning? I never took you for such a speciesist."

"A what?"

"A speciesist. Someone so narrowly focused on the interest of his or her own species that he or she doesn't allow him or herself to even consider the interests of other species."

"Have you always talked like this?"

Edgerton ignored me. "Then again, maybe you're just jealous that I taught the dog a new trick. Maybe you could teach Nigel a trick. Maybe that would make you feel better."

I closed my eyes and rubbed my hand over my brow. "What would make me feel better is a beer. I'll leave you and the boys to your…your whatever the hell this is."

I turned.

"Where you going for this beer?" Edgerton asked.

"My room. Why?"

"You bring some home with you?"

"No," I replied cautiously. "But I've got one left from the other night."

"Well," Edgerton drawled. "You used to."

I turned back around. "What do you mean 'used to?'"

Edgerton lowered his head contritely, placing the bottle he'd been sharing with Basil on the coffee table, the label facing me. It was a Summit.

"You took my last beer?" I asked. There was a plaintiveness in my voice that surprised even me.

"Tell you what," Edgerton said, getting to his feet. "I'll spot you one at McCauley's." He glanced at the mantel clock. "Say, have you had dinner yet?"

"No."

"Great. We'll both eat. That is if you can lend me a couple of bucks. I'm pretty well tapped out."

I stared at him for a moment. "Sure," I said at last. "No problem."

Edgerton took the dogs out back so they could do their business while I went into my room for little other reason than to peek in my small refrigerator to make certain that Edgerton had indeed taken my last beer. Having satisfied myself that a walk to McCauley's couldn't be avoided, I crossed the room to my closet to grab a jacket. On the way, I spotted the photograph of my parents perched on my wall shelf. Mom beamed while Dad, his head slightly lowered, stared out at the unseen photographer with cool gray eyes that held a hint of restrained hostility. I'd tried not to think about my Dad much the past couple of days. It hadn't been easy, especially while working with his old partner, but each time my mind turned to memories of my dad, I'd managed to push them aside. Now, the specter of Donnie Murdoch and his murdered parents was shadowing me, and with them trailed the ghost of my father. I'd done my best, I reminded myself. I'd tried to fulfill his last request of me. There was nothing more I could do.

I slipped on my jacket, locked up, and when Edgerton came back in and had secured the dogs in his room, we left for McCauley's. I can't say that I really remember the walk over. Instead, all at once, there we were, looking for an open booth. We found one along the far wall between a group of well-scrubbed underclassmen and a booth occupied by the Pirate, a McCauley's regular so named for his eye patch and the ever-present leather cowboy hat that he wore turned up in the front, like the three-cornered headgear worn by movie matinee buccaneers. The group of students appeared relieved by our arrival if only because Edgerton and I would provide a buffer between their table and the Pirate, who was in loud voice and gesticulating wildly at his dinner companion—a companion that only he could see. Before sitting, I reached over and rapped my knuckles on the Pirate's table, put a finger to my lips, and shushed. The Pirate glared, but his volume dropped to a mumble.

Skip came by and, without prompting, dropped two dark beers and two menus on the table in front of us. As Skip drifted back toward the bar, Edgerton said, "You realize you haven't said a word since we left the house?"

The truth is, I hadn't noticed. "Sorry, Stephen. Got some things on my mind."

Edgerton flipped open a menu and settled back in the booth. "Care to unburden yourself?" he asked, surveying his dinner choices before casting a casual glance up at me.

I shook my head. "Nah. It's nothing really. Nothing to worry about anyway."

"I didn't say I was worried. I just find that it's usually a good idea to air things that are bothering you."

"I didn't say I was bothered."

Edgerton smiled. "No. You didn't. But you are."

I smirked at him. "You're an insufferable buttinsky, you know that, don't you?"

Edgerton's smile broadened. "You want to talk or not?"

"Hell no."

"You sure?"

I thought a moment. "No," I admitted.

Edgerton laughed. "So, what's bothering you?"

I gave him a nonchalant shrug but felt the right side of my face screw up involuntarily as though I were suddenly channeling Popeye. "Ah, it's nothing. It's just this damned business with my dad's old partner. That and the other thing I told you about. The Donnie Murdoch thing."

Edgerton nodded, then settled back in the booth.

"What business with your dad's old partner?"

It took me a while to lead him through it. I started with Knuck walking into my office, detailed the events at the restaurant, and ended with Latrine Hawkins dead and Augie Tarkof asking me about Donnie Murdoch. Edgerton listened without interruption, nodded at appropriate moments, and waited until he knew I was completely finished before saying anything.

Sighing, his face weighted with concern, he said, "Front me enough money for a meatball sub, willya?"

I stared at him. "I pour my guts out to you, and all you can think about is meatballs?"

"It comes with a pickle spear," he replied. "Big sucker. Nice and garlicky."

I scowled. "Were you even listening?"

Edgerton turned to signal to Skip that he was ready to make his dinner order. "Sure, I was listening. I just don't think you told me what's really bothering you."

"What's that supposed to mean?"

"Well, I couldn't help but notice you left something out."

"Left what out?"

He smiled a thin, even devilish smile, but his eyes were clear and kind. "You didn't mention your dad in all of this"

I shook my head. "What's my dad got to do with it?"

"I think we both know *that's* the question. Isn't that the real problem? Worrying about how your dad fits into all this?"

I laughed. "Well, thank you, Dr. Freud! It's not enough I get to see some guy bleed out in front of me. It's not enough that I get dragged off to the police station. No. It all has to lead back to my parents. You got any other big theories you want me to hear?"

"You about finished?" Edgerton asked me.

I snorted, then nodded.

"Lyle, it shouldn't take therapy to get you to see what's going on here. Your dad's on his deathbed. He's looking back on his life, asking himself what we'd all be asking—Is there anything I'd change if I had the time? He comes up with a name. Donnie Murdoch. Now, he doesn't come out and say it, but he's feeling guilty about something, and he asks you to check the guy out. 'To make things right,' didn't he say? So, you try to make things right. Then, almost immediately, your dad's old partner—the same guy who helped your dad investigate the murder of Donnie's parents—shows up and gets you involved in a shakedown-turned-street-killing. Then the cops join in, asking you about this Donnie. So, the logical question for you is this: What did you stir up, and what compelled your dad to ask you to do it in the first place?"

"That's two questions," I pointed out.

"You got me there. Do you have the answers?"

I stared at him. I'm not sure how long. I wasn't really looking at Edgerton. Instead, I was staring into the face of Knuck Fullmer after he'd shot Latrine Hawkins, his expression disinterested, as though he'd done no more than smack a mosquito that had landed on his arm at a Fourth of July picnic. Then I flashed on my father's face that last time we talked, on the desperation that shone in his eyes as the last moments of his life dwindled down, and all he could think of was some unfinished business that involved a kid he'd tried to help years before. I had to wonder, had he taken in Donnie simply because the orphan needed a home? Had it been to help make up for some of the disappointment he had in me? Or was there another reason? A darker reason. One so powerful, perhaps so shameful, that its memory consumed him in the last moments of his life.

I hated to admit it, but Edgerton was right. It all really did come back to my dad. Or rather, to my dad and me.

"So," Edgerton prompted, breaking my reverie. "*Do* you have the answers?"

"No," I admitted. "But I think you might have earned that meatball sub."

He smiled. "So, what's your next move?"

"We order," I told him. "But tomorrow, I gotta do something I never thought I'd be doing. Tomorrow, I start investigating my father."

Chapter Nine

When it came to looking into my father's relationship with Donnie Murdoch, the most obvious person to start with was my mom. If Dad had ever truly confided in anybody about why he asked Donnie to live with us and how he felt about the way Donnie had left, it would have been Mom. I'd talked with her about it a couple of times over the years. Even though my father hadn't been in the room, she'd stuck to the story that Dad had taken in Donnie because he felt bad about the way Donnie had lost his parents, because as one of the first people on the scene, he felt a sense of obligation to the newly orphaned boy, and because Donnie had been only some two months shy of high school graduation and thus the commitment would be blissfully short-lived.

I'd always had the impression that there were things that she wasn't telling me, details with which, for whatever reason, she didn't want to trust me. The one thing Mom made clear was that she wanted the whole question of the Murdochs to simply melt away. I couldn't blame her; I wanted the same thing.

After Edgerton and I returned from McCauley's that night, I resolved to get up the next morning, drive down to Burnsville, invite Mom out to coffee, and get her to open up to me about all things Donnie. But as I was setting the alarm, I found that, like the promise of youth, my resolve had evaporated. The fact is that I'm most successful getting information out of people by leaning on them. Although there was certainly no question of leaning on Mom, the idea of confronting her about Donnie made me uneasy to the point of nausea. I couldn't bring myself to bother her with it again. Not then, anyhow.

I'd already read and reread the newspaper accounts published at the time of the Murdoch tragedy, garnering, I thought, as much as I ever would from the publicly available versions. It was possible that Knuck might know something that didn't make the papers, but since by investigating my father's involvement in the case I was also investigating Knuck, I thought it best to wait before letting him know that I was looking into things. That, I reasoned, left asking Donnie himself.

If I wanted anything approaching the truth, I'd need to talk to Donnie alone, as far as possible from the chilling influence of Messrs. Tousignant and Bollok. The best way to do that, I thought, was to catch him at work. I would also need some kind of "in," something I could use to get him to open up to me. I figured I'd start where I'd left off, getting Donnie to believe that I was still trying to carry out my dad's wishes, still trying to help him. If that didn't work, I could always try a more threatening route.

As I didn't know where Donnie worked, I had to get creative. When I'd visited before, Donnie had arrived home on foot. It had been afternoon, about the time most people would be getting off work, especially if the job had an early start time. Most people aren't lucky enough to have jobs close enough to walk to from home, so I figured that Donnie must have taken the bus. So, the next morning, as dawn began to streak the eastern sky, I was sitting in my car, parked about three-quarters of a block down from the house that Donnie shared with his drug dealer roommates, sipping coffee and watching for signs of early risers. It wasn't long before I was rewarded. A faint light appeared in the window of one of the upstairs rooms, followed soon after by a brighter light shining from what I assumed was the bathroom. About fifteen minutes later, the front door swung open, and Donnie exited the house.

As I expected, he turned and walked down the street away from me, heading for a bus stop on West Broadway some three blocks distant. I held off a bit, then pulled away from the curb, moving the car to the parking lot of a convenience store with a mostly unobstructed view of the bus stop where Donnie waited. The early morning light was dim, but I could see him fairly clearly and I watched as a couple of different buses came and went before the one he wanted arrived. After he was aboard, I followed the bus onto the street.

I hate tailing buses. You wouldn't expect it to be all that difficult. I mean, they're too damn big to suddenly pull a fast one on you, squealing into a tight U-turn, darting through traffic, and disappearing down a side street. Hell, if you've got a schedule, you even know where the thing is going and which streets it will take to get there. No, the problem with tailing buses is that you look like such an idiot trying to stay behind one. They lumber along, repeatedly pulling over to the curb, while you creep behind trying to come up with plausible reasons not to do the logical thing and pass. Meanwhile, the drivers behind you are becoming increasingly frustrated, honking and cursing the blue from the sky.

Fortunately, people on buses are generally oblivious

to what is going on outside. With their eyes glued to their reading material, closed in restless slumber, or merely fixed in unseeing torpor as they anticipate the mind-numbing drudge of the coming workday, it tends to take more than a little honking to attract the average bus rider's notice.

Nevertheless, as I proceeded sluggard-paced behind Donnie's bus, one driver in a bright yellow Saab did his best to alert everyone within a quarter mile or so to his displeasure with the way I was driving. Leaning steadily on his horn, he sped up and came alongside of me with his window rolled down. "Get a hat!" he bellowed cryptically before racing ahead. I was still trying to figure out what he meant by that when the bus pulled over to the curb, and Donnie got out.

He walked down the sidewalk about a half-block before he turned toward a large, single-story warehouse that sat well back from the street. The front façade of the building was faux gray marble dividing large display windows that showcased pots, pans, barware, and an enormous stand mixer—the bowl of which appeared larger than my room back at the Bijou. I followed Donnie around back, directing my Ford into an adjacent parking lot. The rear of the building was no showcase. Instead, it was an expanse of white-washed cement block split by a cavernous loading dock. A sign next to the dock cautioned, "Drivers: Please Do Not Bump into Building."

I had to circle the parking lot a bit before I found an empty spot a couple of rows away from the rear employee's entrance. I got out of my car quickly, even breaking into a trot, in order to catch Donnie before he disappeared inside.

"Donnie!" I yelled. "Hey, Donnie! Wait up!"

He froze at the sound of my voice, his hand stretched out toward the doorknob.

"Donnie," I said, "it's me, Lyle."

He bowed his head submissively when I reached him. He didn't respond. Instead, he fixed his gaze intently on the ground, silent and radiating fear. "I know," he said at last.

"I have a couple of questions for you," I said, setting my mouth in a huge smile that I hoped he'd sense if not actually see. "Thought I'd catch you before work. Hope that's okay."

At least he didn't run away. Instead, Donnie bobbled, leaning first toward the door, then rocking back as though tugged by an invisible leash. "I got to go in now," he said so quietly I could barely hear him. "They'll be waiting for me."

I took a step toward him, raising a hand, thinking I'd pat him on the shoulder, but although he didn't actually move, Donnie seemed to shrink out of reach. I withdrew the hand and shrugged. "It'll only take a minute," I insisted, still trying to invest my voice with a palpable cheeriness. "It has to do with that favor I told you about. The one my dad asked me. The one where he asked me to check to see if you were doing all right."

Donnie continued to keep his head down, reaching up and smoothing at his dark hair, drawing it forward as though trying to hide his face. He had a band-aid just over his left eyebrow. It didn't quite cover a scabbed-over cut, maybe an inch and a half long that sliced diagonally down toward his temple. The skin around the cut was darker than the rest of his face. A bruise, partially faded.

"I gotta go in now," Donnie repeated. "I'm late."

I ignored him. "So, this is where you work?"

"Yeah."

There was a sign above the door that read, "Fauntleroy Restaurant Supply."

"Warehouse work?"

Donnie nodded.

"I remember you saying you wanted to be a mechanic," I recalled.

"This is the job I could get," Donnie said, a whiff of defensiveness in his nearly inaudible voice. "Something goes wrong with a loader they let me look at it sometimes."

"Cool," I said. "I've worked in a few warehouses. I used to work temp jobs. Got sent everywhere to do…God, I can't tell you all what. Damn glad to be done with that, man."

"You a cop?" Donnie asked abruptly.

I tilted my head, attempting to get a better look at his still averted face. "What makes you think that?"

"I meant to ask before. Last time. I meant to ask was you a cop."

"I'm not a cop, Donnie."

He nodded. "I thought maybe…you know, since your old man was one and all, and with you coming around asking questions."

"I've been coming around because I've been thinking about you. Because my dad asked me to. I'm not trying to roust you or cause you any trouble."

"What then?" Donnie asked. "What *are* you trying to do?" He attempted to hide it, to swallow it back, but his voice became tinged with irritation.

He finally raised his head.

"I told you I gotta work," he continued. "They don't like it if you're late. You think making me late ain't gonna cause me any trouble?"

I studied him for a moment. It was fairly clear that he'd had a little something that morning to take the edge off, but his eyes seemed more familiar than they had when last we'd met. His pupils, though still wider than they ought to have been, appeared more normal, as though the small amount of anger he was allowing himself was therapeutic, countering somewhat the effect of whatever drug he'd taken.

"Your boss won't give you a moment to talk to an old friend?" I asked. "Must be a tough guy. I'll tell you what, he gives you a problem about this morning, you talk to me. Like you said last time, I'm a tough guy now, too."

The anger in his voice faded, replaced by a plea. "What do you want from me? I don't know what you want from me. I don't know—"

"We got history, Donnie," I told him. "I haven't always been entirely comfortable with our history, but it's there, and it's something I can't ignore. Old memories keep nudging me, telling me I gotta look to you for answers. I've tried to ignore it, but you're a big part of my past. Too big for me not to be part of your future."

Donnie's breathing became more rapid. "That sounds like a threat," he said, his voice tightening. "Is that a threat?"

"No threat, Donnie," I assured him. "But I need a few minutes of your time. A few minutes and a little honesty. Give it to me, and I can move on. But I'm not going away until I get it."

The sun had crept higher, but the parking lot was still largely swathed in semidarkness. A pair of car headlights swept us, and soon after, I heard a car door close in the parking lot behind us. I turned to see a tall, young man dressed in blue jeans and a flannel shirt walking away from an ancient rust-pocked sedan. He stared steadily at us as he approached, his countenance narrow, sizing me up. He nodded at Donnie, then walked past us to the door. But something made him turn back around.

Carefully avoiding eye contact with me, he asked Donnie, "Everything all right?"

Donnie nodded back.

The young man flashed a wary smile. Holding the door open, he asked, "You coming in?"

It was his perfect opportunity, but to my surprise, Donnie didn't take it. Instead, he held up a hand saying, "Later, Stan. I'll just be a minute. Thanks."

The man nodded again and stepped forward to be swallowed up by the darkness inside.

Donnie spent several seconds looking hard at the closed door. Then he backed up slightly, sliding his feet across the pavement until he came to stand in a small dip in the asphalt where rainwater had swept a patch of pea gravel. Once again, he brought up a hand to smooth at his hair, his feet shuffling, rasping in the gravel. He then reached into his jacket pocket, his hands trembling slightly, and pulled out a pack of cigarettes. He put one in his mouth and fumbled a bit with his lighter but managed to get it glowing. Then, he held out the pack to me. "Want one?"

I shook my head. "No, thanks."

Donnie inhaled deeply on his cigarette. As he did,

the worried furrows in his brow smoothed as though he was drawing in confidence with the nicotine. He stood a little straighter, his previous fear and anger cooling to mere wisps that drifted deep in his eyes. "I remember you used to smoke."

"I gave it up. Not too long ago. My girlfriend made me."

"Girlfriend? So, you never married or anything?"

I shook my head. "Nah. Truth is, I'm not even sure I have a girlfriend anymore. We've been having some…uh, some difficulties." I paused. "You got anybody?"

Donnie smiled crookedly. "No," he said. "I mean, nobody steady." He shuffled in the gravel some more. "Haven't had a steady girlfriend since…I don't know, since high school, I guess." He paused. "It's not easy when you're a con."

"Not easy when you have a drug problem either," I said.

Donnie immediately stiffened. "What'cha wanna go and say a thing like that for?" he asked, panic snapping at his words. Whipping his head around to survey first the door to the warehouse, then the parking lot, he leaned forward, trying to whisper, but his voice actually growing louder. "They don't go for that sort of thing around here, man. And anyway, it's not true. It's…it's bullshit. What do you mean I got a—"

I held up a hand to cut him off. "Save it, Donnie," I said gently. "I've been to your house, remember? I've met your roommates."

With an effort, Donnie fell silent, dropping his cigarette to the asphalt and following it down with his eyes. Carefully grinding the smoldering butt out with the heel of his work boot, he said, "I better be going in now."

Again, I ignored him. "Speaking of your roommates, well, they're assholes. You know that. Palling around with them is only going to land you back in prison."

He flinched noticeably when I said "prison."

"You got that wrong," he countered weakly. "They take care of me. They're my friends."

I pointed at the band-aid on his forehead. "Your friends give you that?"

He cleared his throat, his eyes flitting uncertainly about the pavement. "No."

"That one asshole, that Bella Lugosi wannabe…What's his name?"

"Bollok," Donnie muttered.

"Yeah, Bollok. He wasn't exactly a happy camper when I left you last time. He blame you for my coming around?"

Donnie sighed, shrinking within himself once more. His head lowered as though overcome by gravity. But when he looked up, he was smiling. "I tell ya," he said, "I never thought I saw old Janos so angry as when you left that day. He was so mad he like to have busted something."

"He take some of that out on you?" I asked. "He seems the type"

"A little," Donnie admitted. "Not much, though. Tooz don't let him bat me around too much."

"Good thing you got Tooz."

"Yeah, good thing."

"You known him long?"

Donnie's expression brightened. "Tooz? Oh, I've known Tooz since forever. Since before my folks died."

He paused. "Tooz and my dad, they were tight. Tooz is the only friend of my dad's I remember from when I was young."

"Really? I don't remember him at all. He live near us back when we were in high school?"

Donnie shook his head. "No. Tooz never lived in Burnsville. Him and my father knew each other back in Baltimore. That's where we lived before Burnsville."

"They work together? Tooz and your dad?"

"No, they were friends is all. That was a long time ago, man." He glanced at his wristwatch. "I can't get into that now," he said. "I really gotta go. I can't...I can't afford to lose this job." He smiled again, but it was stiff and artificial, as though carved by a sculptor with an unsteady hand.

"I understand, Donnie," I told him. "I sure wouldn't want anything like that to happen. It's just that...I didn't really get a chance to ask you what I came here to ask. How 'bout we have dinner? After your shift? I'm buying. There's a Yippy's Burger just up the street. You could meet me there. We could get a burger. Talk. I could drive you home after, if you want. Whaddya say?"

"I don't know," he began. "I gotta—"

"What time do you get off?" I interrupted.

"Me. Uh...three-thirty. But—"

"Great!" I exclaimed. "I'll meet you at the Yippy's. Say, three forty-five?"

He stared at the door to the warehouse, but his eyes kept losing focus, as though the door was moving farther and farther away. "I guess I could...I mean—"

"Three forty-five, it is!" I interrupted happily. "I'm really looking forward to it, Donnie. I really am."

Donnie crossed to the door. I watched as he pulled

it open. From inside, the loud clack of a pallet jack dropping its load split the quiet of the parking lot. Before he disappeared into the warehouse, Donnie turned back around. "You know how it is sometimes, Lyle?" he asked. His voice was unsteady, but there was a clarity in his eyes that had been missing before.

"How what is sometimes, Donnie?"

"You know, how sometimes you start something rolling. You maybe didn't even mean to, but you start something rolling, and there just ain't no way to push it on back?"

"Yeah, that can happen," I agreed.

He nodded. "Been that way for me since that day in Hamilton. Like a brake snapped, and this big old steam engine started moving, rolling right over me. Like no matter which way I run, it's always there, ready to roll over me again."

Looking at him, his hand on the doorknob, half in the light of the steadily brightening parking lot, half wrapped in the shadows of the warehouse's interior, I couldn't help but marvel at the change in him. No longer the cold-blooded killer from Racing Days, nor the looming figure that had so often intruded on my dreams in the days since, I realized that Donnie was also not merely the pitiable, even comic figure that I'd met the week before. I couldn't be sure what he was into or how much of his trouble was of his own making, but I was sure that standing before me now was a real person, someone I'd been asked to look after and someone who truly needed my help.

"Maybe we can do something about that," I told him.

"Yeah," he said. "But maybe it'll roll over you, too."

## Chapter Ten

I had nearly an entire day to fill before my meeting with Donnie, and I was determined to spend the time wisely. The first thing I did was to drive over to St. Paul and the Grand Avenue Grill for one of their enormous Cajun breakfasts. Eggs, cheese, onions, mushrooms, green peppers, and spicy hollandaise sauce layered atop a bed of perfectly crispy hash browns, the crew at the Grand will make you either a half or a whole order. The half order's big enough to share. The whole order's the size of a manhole cover. I restrained myself. I got the larger version but skipped my usual side of andouille sausage. After all, I'd made dinner plans with Donnie.

Beloved though the Cajun breakfast was to me, ordinarily, I wouldn't have driven clear over to St. Paul just for a morning nosh. But I felt it best to arm myself with a little more information before meeting again with Donnie, and one of the things I decided might be useful to know was who actually held the deed to the house he shared with Tousignant and Bollok. An acquaintance of mine worked at a title company in St. Paul's Highland Park neighborhood, only a couple of miles south of the Grand. Of course, I could have just called my title company guy on the phone, but then I would have missed out on the breakfast. Besides, I find that people are more apt to do me favors when I make the request in person. I like to think it's my winning smile, but it might have something to do with the reputation I've garnered over my years as an investigator—large and potentially unstable. In any case, after a few minutes of cheerfully looming over the guy's workspace, his co-workers casting wary glances in my direction, I had the information I desired.

Surprisingly, it turned out that it was Donnie, or rather Donnie and the good folks at Wells Fargo, who owned the house in North Minneapolis. In fact, he'd owned it for some seven years. And his record, at least as far as the title company was concerned, was spotless. Granted, it was a modest home, but he hadn't fallen behind with the payments, and the property had no liens against it. That was all good for Donnie, but it didn't seem right to me. It's not that I begrudged him having attained the American dream of home ownership— something that, pointedly, remained out of my grasp— it's just that I hadn't known many ex-con junkies who had the kind of discipline required to set aside enough each month for even an affordable house payment.

Of course, Donnie might be relying on more than just his paycheck to keep the creditors away. I mean, his housemates were drug dealers and, from what I'd seen, successful ones. They'd certainly be making more than enough to pay the mortgage. But that morning outside the warehouse, Donnie had seemed almost desperately attached to his job. He'd been afraid to punch in late and had panicked at the thought that his employers might learn of his drug problem. That would be understandable if Donnie was a normal working stiff struggling to keep a roof over his head. But why would he worry so much about holding down some ill-paying, blue-collar gig when he could throw in with his more prosperous pals?

I left the title company and drove to my office, all the while wondering about the relationship between Donnie and his housemates. Donnie had told me that Tousignant was from Baltimore and that Tousignant and Vernon Murdoch had known each other there. It would be interesting, I thought, to find out when Tooz had decided to make the Gopher state his home.

My dad had an old friend named Davidson who still worked for the Apple Valley Police Department. Like Burnsville, Apple Valley was a growing suburb south of the Twin Cities, a place that had changed mightily since the days when Dad and Knuck and this Davidson had first put on their uniforms. But one thing that hadn't changed was the loyalty that these cops had for one another. And even though Dad had driven a patrol car in the next town over, Davidson was somebody that my dad had long ago told me that I could trust. I called down there, and although it took a little convincing, Davidson agreed to run Tousignant for me.

By early afternoon I'd learned that Tousignant, not surprisingly, had himself a rather colorful record. He'd graduated from penny-ante juvenile stuff in his native Arkansas to a far more distinguished career in Baltimore. There, he'd been arrested for simple assault, assault with a deadly weapon, armed robbery, possession with intent, and once for practicing dentistry without a license when he removed a bicuspid from what the transcript described as an "unwilling colleague," using a pair of slip joint pliers and a ball-peen hammer. But these arrests had not resulted in Tousignant doing any serious jail time, leaving him clear to continue plowing his own furrow through the local criminal landscape.

Alas, no path is without obstacles, and Tousignant's

was suddenly halted when, at the age of thirty-two, he was convicted of second-degree murder in the shooting death of a Balto drug dealer in what the prosecution painted as a robbery gone bad. Tousignant and a guy named Samuel "Stubby" Petoskey had been apprehended at the scene, but witnesses indicated that a third perpetrator had escaped prior to the arrival of the police. Despite various offers of clemency, both Tousignant and Petoskey refused to cut a deal in exchange for information as to the identity of this third individual. This, even though it was clear that the individual in question not only ran out on his colleagues but took with him their only vehicle and thus their most likely means of escape. That kind of loyalty is, to say the least, curious.

Tousignant and Petoskey were both sentenced to twenty-five years to life, but it turned out that a life of confinement didn't agree with Petoskey. He was stabbed to death in a prison yard altercation after serving only a few months of his sentence. Curiouser and curiouser.

Tousignant did only marginally better. Since "twenty-five to life" usually means neither twenty-five nor life, you'd have thought Tousignant would have been out after some eight to ten years of thoughtful and penitent time served. Instead, he did twenty-three years, all of it under maximum security. I didn't have transcripts from his parole hearings, but my guess was the extra time was the result of his inability to work and play well with his fellow inmates.

Tousignant's conviction occurred the same year Donnie and his family moved to Burnsville, and he'd only been released some eighteen months previously. I asked Davidson if there was any mention of a Janos

Bollok in connection with Tousignant. He said there was nothing in Tousignant's record, and he grumbled disagreeably when I asked him to run Bollok for me as well. I let it drop, cheered that I'd gleaned at least two potentially important bits of information—that Tousignant had been in stir at the time of Donnie's parents' murders and that Donnie appeared to have been doing well enough to hold down a job and afford his home for years before Willard Tousignant reentered his life.

After I'd filed away my notes, I glanced at my watch and realized that if I wanted to get a strategic advantage before meeting Donnie, it was past time to head for Yippy's. I got in my vehicle, and with a little luck—and by rolling through a couple of streetlights that weren't exactly yellow anymore—I managed to arrive at the restaurant some ten minutes before my appointment with Donnie.

It was both too late for lunch and too early for dinner, so other than the three Spanish-speaking employees behind the counter, I had the place to myself. I found a booth in the back corner with an excellent view of the front door and the parking lot beyond and eased my bulk into it with my back to the wall. Multi-tasking, I kept a watch out for Donnie and, at the same time, let my mind wander over both the details of my conversation with Davidson and Yippy's main menu options. I'd soon narrowed the more important matter of my dinner down to a decision between the two-thirds pound Double Bacon Cheeseburger and the more diminutive Grilled Sourdough Burger. A large order of curly fries was, of course, de rigueur. I was still making my final selection when a car entered the parking lot.

It was an El Camino, from the late 1970s by the look of it, and to my untutored eyes, in mint condition to boot. The chrome gleamed like a smile in a Pepsodent commercial, and the definitely custom, fuchsia-toned paint job was flawless enough to have been sprayed on within the last hour or two. It rolled to a spot just in front of the restaurant's glass doors and out stepped Willard Tousignant and Janos Bollok.

Despite a chill to the air, Tousignant wore no coat over his white pocket tee. As he entered, I scanned him for weapons. His jeans were boot-cut so, although I saw no evidence of it, he might have had an ankle holster under there. But the only potential weapon of Tousignant's that I could see was a black leather case threaded to his belt that apparently held a jackknife. Closed and covered by a snap, it didn't pose much of an immediate threat.

My bet was that the El Camino belonged to Bollok. That or at least he'd had sizeable input into the choice of paint since the vivid purple-red dress shirt he had on nearly matched the finish on the car. Over the shirt, he was wearing the same tweed sports coat that he'd worn when we first met. I surveyed the cut of the jacket. He could have virtually anything under there.

They took their time crossing the room. When they reached me, I placed my hands on the table where they could both clearly see them, then looked up to catch Tousignant's gaze. "What's it mean when somebody tells you to 'get a hat?'" I asked him.

Momentarily taken aback, his eyes went slightly wide, but he recovered quickly, flashing a half smile—the right side of his mouth opening to reveal a dandy bit of bridgework. "What's that you said?"

I shrugged. "I was in my car this morning. Driving right around here, as a matter of fact. Anyway, I was caught behind a bus, not really making much forward progress, and this guy in a sports car pulls up from behind me. As he goes past, I swear he yells, 'Get a hat!' Got any idea what that could mean?"

I turned from Tousignant to Bollok. Tousignant blinked a couple of times, but Bollok's face remained impassive. On one side, just south of his cheekbone, I could make out what was left of the contusion I'd given him when last we'd met. I couldn't hold back a smirk. Staring down at me, Bollok's eyes glittered with malice.

I turned back to see a slow smile spreading across Tousignant's face. "Well," he said, chuckling, "you are one to say the unexpected. I'll give you that."

"I'm a cipher," I agreed. "Does that mean you don't know about the hat thing?"

He kept his smile in place. "Didn't exactly come by to talk about hats, friend."

I shrugged again. "You want to sit?" I asked, pointing at the empty space across from me. "The fried chicken's not bad. I'm probably going with a burger, myself."

Tousignant chuckled some more. "I'll sit," he said, "seeing as how you're being so hospitable. But I'm thinking we won't be here long enough to share a meal."

Tousignant lowered himself slowly into the booth. "You might as well take a load off yourself, Janos," he said to his partner.

"I prefer to stand," Bollok said. He spoke slowly, his words so thickly accented they seemed viscous. I half expected to see a trail, like a snail track, left in their wake.

"Suit yourself, Bella," I said, beaming up at Bollok. "By the way, last time we got together I neglected to mention how much I loved you in *Spooks Run Wild*."

Tousignant issued an amused little grunt but raised a cautionary palm. "You might want to go easy there, friend. Old Janos is pretty sensitive about the way he talks."

"I'll keep that in mind," I told him. "It's a pity you're in such a hurry, Mr. Tousignant. It's also a pity that Donnie couldn't join us." I paused. "He *was* the one I invited."

Tousignant ran a hand over his bald pate. "That's what we came to talk to you about, friend. Donnie…ah, shit, you know, Donnie. He gets himself all…whatchacallit…flustered. Sometimes the easiest things just seem to be so hard for that boy. Take your visit this morning, for instance. Easiest thing in the world for old Donnie to tell you he's not interested in, uh…uh, renewing your relationship. But he gets himself so damn flustered. You know what I mean?"

I grinned but didn't reply.

"He gets so flustered," Tousignant continued, "that he needs me and Janos here to deliver a simple message."

Tousignant leaned forward. "Thanks, but no thanks," he said emphatically. "That's the message. Our boy Donnie would rather you didn't come around no more."

In my peripheral vision, I caught a glimpse of movement. One of the restaurant employees had stepped out from behind the counter and was peering at us. He saw me looking at him and quickly disappeared from sight.

"How do you like the Twin Cities, Mr. Tousignant?"

I asked.

"I like it fine."

I nodded. "You winter here yet? Gets pretty cold in the winter."

"So I hear."

"Then there's the snow." I sniffed loudly. "Not much like Baltimore."

Tousignant glanced briefly up at Bollok. "Gets cold in Balto, too," he said.

"You move here on account of Donnie?" I asked as casually as I knew how. "Or was there some other reason?"

Tousignant leaned back, shifting in his seat. "Sort of wore out my welcome in Baltimore. If you know what I mean."

"I think I know what you mean, all right. You see, I checked. You got yourself quite a legacy out that way. You should be proud. It's not everyone can do twenty-three years and come out so…" I paused. "So, well-adjusted."

Tousignant let go a laugh caustic enough to strip the finish off an armoire. "That's me, friend," he said, "well-adjusted."

Even Bollok allowed himself a flicker of a smile.

Tousignant's laughter cut off abruptly. "So, it sounds like you've been doing your homework."

"Thanks for noticing. Always trying to make Mom proud."

Tousignant ignored me. "But you know, I got to ask myself, why are you so all-fired interested in me?"

"That's a fair question, Mr. Tousignant. But rather than wait all evening for you to come up with an answer on your own, maybe I should just tell you. I'm trying to figure out why, after all that time in prison, your first move is to track down Donnie. It wouldn't have anything to do with the robbery that sent you to the joint in the first place, would it?"

Tousignant's eyes narrowed. "Just how does that concern you, friend? I paid my debt. If I want to look up the son of an old bud, that's my business, not yours."

"Ordinarily, I'd agree with you, Mr. Tousignant. But you see, Donnie and I have history. I can't just sit here and watch as you and this Lugosi wannabe waltz into town, take over Donnie's house, take over Donnie's life, and leave him strung out and jobless. I let that happen, what's that say about me? Suppose the story got around. Suppose folks at our old high school found out that I could have given Donnie a hand but did nothing." I shook my head. "There'd be a lot of wagging fingers come reunion time."

Tousignant leaned in and tapped the tabletop sharply with a calloused forefinger. "You think you know what you're dealing with, friend?"

I leaned in to join him. "I'm not saying I haven't got a question or two, but yeah, I got some idea what I'm dealing with. I know that a few years back—back when you were young and likely had a whole bunch more hair—you and two friends decided to rob a fellow Baltimore drug dealer. I know that things didn't go too well. There was a murder. And you and some guy named Stubby ended up sentenced to some serious jail time. I guess that brings up my first question. How does a guy get stuck with a moniker like Stubby?"

Tousignant snorted. "Well, Stubby was missing the top joint of one of his pinky fingers. But, just between you, me, and the lamppost, I remember hearing one of

Stub's lady friends once complain that old Stubby had himself one depressingly tiny pecker."

He waited a moment, then chortled so abruptly and with such force that a pea-sized globule of mucous shot from his nose. It splatted onto the table in front of us. "Guess it could have been that," he added, wiping up the snot with a finger. "You got any other questions, or are we about through?"

I shrugged. "Maybe just one more. I was wondering, was Vernon Murdoch the third guy in on that robbery back in Baltimore?

Tousignant's smile froze on his face. Bollok inched forward as if to block my exit.

"Murdoch being your accomplice would explain your devotion to Donnie," I continued. "Whoever it was took off, leaving you and Petoskey standing there with your dicks in your hands. In Petoskey's case, at least, a tiny, little one. Then Petoskey gets himself killed, and you end up squandering your best years doing time. There's bound to be hard feelings. Screwing with Donnie could be some kind of payback for his old man running out on you all those years ago." I paused. "Heck, it might even explain why he and Donnie's mom got killed in the first place."

We stared at each other, silence seeping in between us, Tousignant's eyes shining, his smile still fixed like the reaper's grin. "You accusing me of killing Vernon and Pam?" he asked at last, his voice brimming with forced incredulity. "Like you said, I was in Jessup when they met their sad end."

"No," I told him. "I'm not forgetting. But what about Vlad the Impaler here? He doing time with you?"

Bollok didn't even bother looking at me. Instead, he

reached up with both hands and carefully adjusted the collar of his vibrantly colored dress shirt. As before, despite the absence of a tie, he wore the shirt buttoned to the top as if he were trying to hide the growth that, like a bruised pluot, sprouted from his neck. "Why discuss this any further?" he asked his partner. "Let me kill this fellow and save ourselves the bother."

Tousignant laughed, short snickers that grated like a chisel against granite. "Why, Janos," he said, "It's no bother. You know how I love to jaw." He coughed up some more laughter, then added, "But I must say, our friend here's being a bit stingy. Seems he wants to choose all the topics himself."

"Something you want to discuss, Mr. Tousignant?" I asked.

"Well, now that you mention it, there is something," Tousignant replied, tilting his head back to give me a swell view of his untrimmed nose hair. "I'm a lucky guy, Dahms. I got…whatchacallit…resources. I ain't punching no time clock. I can take a late breakfast of a morning. I even have time to read the paper. That's what I was doing…What was it? A day or two ago? Anyway, I'm reading the paper, and I come across this item that kind of catches me off guard. According to this article, you and some retired Burnsville cop…cop name of Fullmer? Said you and this Fullmer shot somebody down the other day."

I pushed back a bit and let my right hand disappear from the top of the table. "Is that what it said?"

Tousignant's gaze followed my hand. "That it did. And, well, naturally, I asked Donnie about it. You and him being old friends and all. I'll tell you what, Donnie got all upset. Told me he'd had enough of the two of you.

You and this Fullmer."

"Me and Fullmer? Come on. I doubt Donnie's seen Knuck Fullmer since high school."

"That what you think?" Tousignant asked, arching his eyebrows. "No matter. In any case, the whole deal made Donnie real nervous. First, you poking around him after all them years, then him hearing about how you and Fullmer had teamed up." He lowered his voice conspiratorially. "Teamed up and shot somebody down."

Tousignant raised his hands, spreading them wide in a gesture of wonder. "You can hardly blame him. Especially after…after I guess what you'd call the *ugly shadow* of this Fullmer and your dad and what went down with Donnie's old man."

"What *ugly shadow* is that, Mr. Tousignant?" I asked as pleasantly as possible.

"I did some checking of my own. As you say, Vernon Murdoch was a friend of mine."

"Friend. Accomplice. You say potato—"

"A man's friend gets blown away like that," Tousignant interrupted, "he gets interested in knowing why. So, like I say, I did some checking. Turns out, after what happened to Vernon and Pam there was an investigation. Turns out some people got to wondering if the police weren't involved. Least ways maybe they…How shall I put this? Maybe they hastened old Vernon along to his maker. If you take my meaning."

I stared at him. "You got something to say, Mr. Tousignant, you go ahead and spell it out."

"According to what I heard," Tousignant said amiably, "the cops claim to have found Pam dead and Vernon dying on the floor. Both of them filled with buckshot. But then, the cops turn their backs, and suddenly Vernon's got a .38 slug—bam!—right there in his head. Convenient how they didn't see nothing. And pretty damn strange, if you ask me, how them cops claim they never saw Vernon with no gun at all just before he supposedly done himself in with one."

Tousignant made a little clicky noise with his tongue. "There's folks that say that story just don't add up. There's folks that say the cops weren't telling all they knew." He lowered his voice to a feathery rasp. "There's even folks that say maybe them cops had themselves a shotgun. Maybe Vernon and Pam getting killed like that ain't really no mystery at all."

I had to admit that Willard Tousignant was pretty good at pushing buttons. I struggled to maintain at least an outward calm. "That's quite a theory, Mr. Tousignant," I said. "These *folks* of yours say why the cops would have done any of this?"

"Maybe Vernon had something the cops wanted," he speculated. "Something they didn't mind killing to get. Maybe them cops were nothing more crooks."

"You know that my old man was one of those cops?"

"Oh yeah. I know that ."

"So, these *folks* are calling my dad a killer?"

Tousignant leaned toward me once again, his smile still crinkling his eyes, but menace beginning to crowd the amiability from his voice. "Fullmer? Your father? What'd you say before? Po-tay-to, po-tay-to? What's the difference? Personally, I never met no cop wasn't above just doing what he wanted, then making up a story afterwards."

As I get along in years, more and more I'm forced to look back and admit that I've done things of which

I'm not very proud. There have been frighteningly many instances where I failed to handle a situation with the delicacy and diplomacy that was required. But I can be proud of the way I handled myself at that moment with Tousignant. Proud that I didn't blow that sonofabitch away where he sat.

Instead, I forced a smile. "You've given me a lot to think about, Mr. Tousignant."

He chuckled. "Happy to oblige, friend. We all need something to while away the hours."

I laughed along with him briefly, then thought I'd take a shot. "You know a kid named Latrine Hawkins? Or Mason Slidel? Goes by the name 'Cleanhead?'"

Tousignant's smile withdrew into a grim line; the merry wrinkles around his eyes smoothed, and his gaze became as cold and piercing as an ice pick. "It's time for Janos and me to be going," he said crisply. "It's also time for you to get your nose out of my business."

"You telling me Hawkins and Slidel are your business?" I pressed.

Tousignant rose slowly to his feet, his eyes carefully tracking me as I slipped my hand beneath my jacket to within easy reach of my .38. This was Bollok's cue to undo the single button that secured the front of his sports coat. He reached around behind his back, the tail of his jacket flapping. But when Tousignant cast a sharp glance at Bollok, he immediately let his hands fall to his sides.

"You and me, Dahms," Tousignant said evenly, "we're done here. We meet again, things won't be so friendly."

"Ah, say it isn't so, Willard," I cooed.

Tousignant smirked in reply, then leaned down close, his mouth only inches from my ear. "You fuck with me," he whispered, "you fuck with my business; you fuck with my associates; you end up as dead as your old man."

"He died asking me to look after Donnie," I reminded him, letting anger enter my voice. "You honestly think I'd disgrace his memory, scared off by some cheap hood?"

Tousignant snorted. "Cheap or not, being on my bad side just ain't gonna be healthy for you, friend. You need to die for a memory, I can oblige." He reached down to tap the table again, causing me to flinch involuntarily. He noticed and smiled broadly.

"This ain't just some memory I'm trying to protect," he continued. "Memories fade. Memories get forgotten."

I thought about that for a moment. "You're wrong," I told him, surprising myself with the renewed calm in my voice. "It's people that fade. In the end, their memory is all you have."

Chapter Eleven

After my encounter with Tousignant and Bollok, I didn't feel much like talking to anybody. Since there's always somebody at the Bijou willing to ignore my occasional need for privacy, I decided to take in a movie instead of going straight home. Three movies, it turned out. The "Man with No Name" trilogy was playing at the Oak Street Cinema, a rep house in Stadium Village, just across campus from my home in Dinkytown.

By the time I got there, I'd missed most of *A Fistful of Dollars* but saw all of *For a Few Dollars More* and *The Good, the Bad, and the Ugly*. It made for a pretty late night, but watching Old Squinty deal so much more effectively with his foes than I had with mine felt somehow redemptive.

The next day, I awoke late to an uncharacteristically quiet Bijou. Edgerton was off to his copy shop job, and the other denizens were off doing whatever it was they did. I showered and dressed, then searched my cupboards for something to eat. It was only after several minutes of unsuccessful rummaging that I remembered the dogs.

Edgerton, I thought, was sure to have taken them out for their morning constitutional. After all, they'd spent the night in his room, and he'd been up well before me that morning. There was simply no reason to doubt that he'd seen to their needs before going to work. Except that Edgerton's sense of responsibility was a slippery thing. To the best of my knowledge, he'd never been late to work and had always paid his rent on time, even if he sometimes had to borrow it from me. Plus, he always labored mightily to meet the self-imposed deadlines he set for his many creative endeavors, whether they be penning a new comic book, fashioning a piece of medieval armor, or editing the latest film project that he composed on his cell phone. Satirical short subjects had become a new passion for him.

But it was a rare thing indeed for him to clear a table or wash a dish, vacuuming was unknown to him, and his trips to the laundromat were so infrequent as to be on a par with sightings of the comet Kohoutek. He was equally slipshod in his approach to canine management, frequently leaving the dogs alone in the house tasked with Herculean feats of bladder control. In the absence of more responsibility on Edgerton's part, I was oft called upon to take on the role of Basil and Nigel's paterfamilias and, as such, decided I'd better check on them before going in to the office.

The instant I opened the door to Edgerton's room, Nigel leaped from the shadows, flying paws first across the room and ramming into me so forcefully that I doubled over. Basil, who'd been lying quietly on the bed, barely raised his head.

I smiled at him ruefully.

When Edgerton had first brought Basil home less than a year previously, he'd been a squirming, buff ball of energy. Whenever he spotted anyone—me, Edgerton, the mailman, the occasional process server—he became a dog possessed, barking, whimpering, and wagging his rear so vigorously that I constantly feared he'd poke out one of his own eyes with the blunt end of his bobbed tail.

But Nigel's arrival put a stop to that. Although Edgerton had brought Nigel home to serve as a companion for Basil, it was soon clear that Nigel's adoption into the family was something with which Basil would never completely come to terms.

Instead of frolicking playfully with his new brother, as Edgerton had hoped, Basil had become increasingly lethargic when in the presence of the raven-haired interloper. It was now Nigel who dashed insanely through the house when the doorbell rang, Nigel who performed spectacular vertical jumps, his tongue darting as he tried to French kiss anyone entering the room, while Basil simply yawned diffidently. But there was a longing that lingered in Basil's eyes as he watched Nigel gambol about the house—a muted though still clearly distinguishable glimmer that indicated that had he not been blessed by a sibling, Basil would be up for some gamboling of his own.

I retrieved the dogs' leashes out from under a stack of photocopies that Edgerton had piled haphazardly on his desk—Edgerton took full advantage of his job at the copy shop, making free copies for himself of anything a customer dropped off that caught his fancy—and gave Basil an extra rub behind his ears before leading both dogs out back to take care of their business.

If living with Nigel had made Basil less lively, he made up for it by becoming ever quirkier. From the moment we got him, Basil had exhibited no shortage of eccentricities, the most noticeable of which was his unnatural fear of vinyl flooring. But now, in addition to my having to drag him through the kitchen—all four legs stiff, gliding like a first-time figure skater on the points of his outstretched nails—Basil had decided that it was necessary for him to "drop his load," so to speak, the instant he was through the back door.

It used to be that I would lead the dogs out the door, around the cars parked and rusting out back, and over to a patch of green near the far end of the house that Edgerton and I had designated as their "Elimination Zone." Nigel was only too happy to oblige, but Basil had recently taken to eliminating just as his rear legs hit the back steps. To counter this new tendency, I was now forced to take off at a trot, pulling the dogs along behind me, hoping to reach the "zone" before Basil was able to make the bulk of his deposit.

I often wondered what the neighbors thought, whether they ever glanced up from a crossword puzzle or perhaps were innocently gazing out a rear window only to see me emerge from the Bijou tugging frantically at the dogs, Basil in full hunch, turds popping out of his rear end like candy from a Pez dispenser. It probably explained why I never received invitations to neighborhood watch meetings.

Eventually, I got the dogs back in the house and locked safely away in Edgerton's room. My day stretching before me, I climbed into my Ford and first drove to nearby George's Bakery for a couple of cream cheese kolaches. From there, I headed to my office, where I brewed some coffee, ate my breakfast, checked my messages, and even returned a few phone calls before once again turning my attention to the Murdoch matter. It appeared murkier than ever.

One thing did seem clear. I was not going to easily get any information from Donnie. Even if he knew anything, he was too scared to share it, although it wasn't clear whether he was scared of me, scared of his housemates, or, if Tousignant was to be believed, scared of Knuck Fullmer. If I was going to continue to explore what happened with Donnie's parents, I would have to look elsewhere.

But before I could know where I needed to go, I'd first have to figure out exactly where I was. I took out a clean sheet of legal paper and made a list of everything I knew, or thought I knew, about Vernon and Pam Murdoch's murder and Willard Tousignant's possible involvement in it. After a few minutes, I had what I considered to be a pretty plausible working hypothesis. Vernon Murdoch, I speculated, had been the third perpetrator in the Baltimore robbery that sent Tousignant to prison. Tousignant had protected Vernon's identity because Vernon made off with some or all of the loot, and if Tousignant divulged this to the cops, it would have ended with both Vernon and the booty in the hands of the authorities. While in prison, Tousignant had gotten word of where Vernon was hiding and had an accomplice track him down, resulting in both Vernon and Pam's murders. If I was lucky, my hypothetical accomplice would turn out to be Janos Bollok, and once this was proven, both he and Tousignant would spend their sunset years in an exercise yard trying to pull their tough-guy routine on their younger, stronger, and meaner fellow inmates. It was an act that I suspected wouldn't run long.

Unfortunately, there were several things that I simply did not know, the first being if there was any actual loot missing after the robbery. Certainly, Tousignant and company wouldn't have planned to take down that particular drug dealer without hope of reward, and though the robbery had clearly been unsuccessful from the standpoint of Tousignant and Stubby Petoskey—they landed in jail, Petoskey never to emerge—that didn't mean that the reward part of the plan had also been unsuccessful.

One thing I've discovered over the years is that it is supremely difficult to get good information from a distance. You can get some good leads by reading contemporary newspaper accounts. If you're quite fortunate, you might track down a witness or two by phone, and if you're even luckier, they won't lie to you too much, but by and large, reliable information is best obtained in person. If I'd been working for someone willing to foot the bill, at this point in the investigation, I'd definitely have argued that my next move be a trip to Baltimore, complete with an expense account to cover airfare, a rental car, and reasonable accommodations, with a dinner allowance big enough for me to order my weight in crab cakes. But I was on my own dime on this one and an expensive East Coast excursion was not in my budget. Instead, I was going to have to rely on a less costly alternative.

With that in mind, I fired up my computer and began to search cyberspace for help. I eventually wended my way to the website of the Maryland Alliance of Licensed Professional Investigators. MALPI, for short. They had a nifty logo consisting of their initials forming a banner flying over a rendering of the scales of justice next to a huge eye peering through a magnifying glass. All of this was encircled by something in Latin printed in a script too small for dust mites to read. Below the logo was their mission statement which read, in part, that MALPI was formed "to further a mutual feeling of trust, goodwill, and camaraderie among investigators." Although they were likely referring to investigators willing to pay annual dues to the organization, I decided to ignore that in the hope that I'd stumbled on a fraternity of fellow gumshoes who'd fall all over themselves to help out a brother in distress.

I clicked on "Membership Directory," then "Baltimore" and was soon shown a lengthy directory of names, addresses, and phone numbers. As I knew no one in Baltimore, I simply scanned the list, hoping for inspiration to strike. I bypassed an Eric Brackman, a Stan Davenport, a Melba Hirschfeld, and a guy with the rather too obviously made-up moniker Rex Justice, before lighting on the name Harley Rocker. Bingo. Now there, I thought, is a good name for a P.I. Like the fictional detectives of my youth—men like Hammer, Cannon, and Mannix— a guy named Rocker was sure to have buckets of testosterone coursing through his veins. Who better to serve as my proxy? I jotted down his number and picked up the phone.

But at the last second something stopped me. I glanced over at my nice sheet of legal paper. I read, then reread my list of facts. My theory of the case. Completely missing was any mention of either Knuck Fullmer or my father. My dad, I reminded myself, was the reason I'd become involved in the first place. I pictured him on his deathbed, so troubled by whatever happened with the Murdochs that it consumed him during his final hours. And Knuck Fullmer? I pictured him too—not just the man I knew from my childhood, laughing with my Dad and smiling at his daughter, but also the one I'd seen so recently standing unmoved over a dying Latrine Hawkins. I'd been so focused on my desire to see Tousignant and Bollok do a perp walk on the ten o'clock news that I'd been ignoring facts, likely unpleasant facts, about both Dad and Knuck that were almost sure to come out if I pursued the matter. And while it was true that Dad had gotten me into this, he'd merely asked me to see if Donnie Murdoch was okay. He hadn't asked me to expose any family secrets. If I kept poking around, if I risked involving another P.I., any secrets he had would threaten to spill out.

But Dad had set me on a path, a path Knuck Fullmer forced me to keep walking by involving me in that business at the restaurant. If, as Augie Tarkof had hinted, there was a sinister connection between the murders of Pam and Vernon Murdoch and Knuck and my dad, I was going to have to deal with it. It was just another part of the responsibility of being my father's son.

I called Rocker. A woman answered—a woman with a voice that made me sit right up in my chair. Whiskey-smooth, sultry, and imbued with mystery, I was so taken by the voice that I was a couple of minutes into the conversation before it hit me—Harley Rocker was a broad. And disappointed though I was initially that my Balto connection would not come stoked with machismo, having launched into my story, I was most impressed with the care she took listening to me. She repeated back all the information I gave her and promised to get back to me within a couple of days with all she could glean about the robbery that had sent Tousignant to prison. She even sounded apologetic when I asked if she could offer me a professional discount.

With Rocker working from her end, I decided I'd better do something from mine. If she found evidence that a substantial take had gone missing along with the third robber in Tousignant's ill-fated heist, it would be up to me to try to figure out where it had ended up. My theory was that it had come to Minnesota with Vernon Murdoch, but the Murdochs hadn't lived like people who had sacks of cash hidden in their floorboards. Oh, they'd been secretive enough, keeping mainly to themselves, but they did it in a weathered, creaky old farmhouse that looked like the next good thunderstorm would render it into kindling. And folks in the neighborhood used to speculate that Pam Murdoch was so devoted to her vegetable garden because there wasn't really money in the family kitty to otherwise stock the larder.

If Vernon had escaped with enough loot to warrant his confederates coming after him, it certainly showed great self-control on his part not to spend some of it. Of course, he may have simply been too scared, keeping it somewhere safe until he was convinced that his former colleagues wouldn't come to claim it. Or he may have absconded with the booty only to lose it or be forced to hide it somewhere inaccessible. Perhaps he hadn't run out on Tousignant at all. Perhaps he'd been keeping the stash intact, waiting to split it up after Tooz's release. Whatever the case, I needed an "in." I needed to get in contact with someone who knew the Murdochs, had socialized with them, and could tell me if anything about them seemed suspicious.

The trouble is, to the best of my knowledge, no such person existed. The Murdochs were not friendly. I remembered my mom telling me that the local ladies had tried to invite Pam Murdoch over for coffee a couple of times when they'd first moved to Burnsville, but she had politely refused. A contingent had even brought over a welcome basket—brimming with fresh fruit, coffee cake, and neighborhood gossip—but although Pam met them at the door, she had pointedly not invited them in. And as for Vernon Murdoch, his stony demeanor and the gun rack in his truck tended to put off even the most community-minded of neighbors. I tried to remember if Donnie Murdoch had had any close friends in high school, someone who had maybe spent some time with him at home, but no one sprang to mind. Certainly no one had visited him during the brief time he lived with us.

Then I thought of Marisa Algren. If anyone had a candidate for me to speak to, it would be Burnsville High's most ardent class chronicler. The phone rang several times before she picked up. When she realized it was me, she let out a strangled gasp. "Lyle Dahms!" she squealed. "Just this minute I was cutting out an article about you. It's just…just freaky!"

I didn't know what she was talking about. "What kind of article is that, Marisa?"

"Why it's one from the Star-Tribune," she replied. "But there have been others. Several over the last couple of days. And not just in the Strib. From the Pioneer Press. The Sun. Oh, it's been a gold mine."

I still wasn't following. "What are all these papers doing writing about me?"

Marisa clucked disapprovingly. "How could you not know? You've been all over the papers for days. It's about the shooting, of course. Outside the restaurant the other day? The shooting? What else would I be talking about?"

"I guess I wasn't thinking, Marisa."

"How could you not? I know if I was mentioned in every paper, I'd—"

"Sorry," I interrupted, heaving a sob into my voice.

"I've just…I've been trying not dwell on it, is all. I haven't been reading the newspapers. I guess I didn't want to keep reliving it." I mustered up what I considered a convincingly poignant sigh before closing with "I'm sure *you* know what I mean."

"I understand completely," she replied, suddenly sounding quite motherly. "If must have been dreadful."

"Oh, it was," I assured her. "But I must ask, why are you clipping articles about me? I thought you only kept records on people from your own class."

"Well, they're not just about you," she said, a note of defensiveness now vying with the maternal solicitude in her voice. "They're also about Mr. Fullmer. And his Mindy was co-chair of our Spirit Squad."

"Ah, yes."

"And, as I explained when we spoke earlier, anything that concerns a classmate needs to be included in the archive."

"Of course, it does. In any case, I didn't call you about any of that. I'm calling again about Donnie Murdoch."

"Are you telling me that Donnie was mixed up in that shooting?" Marisa asked, her excitement returning as she mentally compiled a juicy new archive entry.

"I'm not, Marisa," I told her. "Again, this is an entirely different matter."

"So, you didn't get together with Mr. Fullmer over anything about Donnie?" Her disappointment was palpable.

"Sorry. Donnie had nothing to do with that."

"Even so," Marisa said, "you can't blame me for wondering. After all, what Donnie did after graduation remains an ugly stain on our class record. I'd just as soon forget him entirely. I'm sure the Fullmers would agree with me. I mean, they wouldn't want Donnie back in their lives, would they? It's a sad fact that not everyone we knew back at BHS is someone you want to remember." She sighed. "It's the whole melting pot thing, I suppose. High school is like this big pot we're all put into. Some folks just don't melt in like they should."

"I know what you mean, It's like finding a jalapeno bobbing around in your cream of wheat. But what's that you said about the Fullmers not wanting Donnie back in their lives?"

"Well, you know, with Mindy and Donnie and all that."

"What about Mindy and Donnie?"

This time Marisa didn't just cluck her disapproval. She crowed. "I can't believe you're asking me that. Aren't you supposed to be some kind of investigator?"

I ignored her. "What about Mindy and Donnie?" I repeated. "I know they were classmates of yours, but—"

"Well, I guess I shouldn't be so hard on you after all. Now that I think about it, I remember it was supposed to be some big secret. Of course, the whole school knew. Everyone important, anyway."

"Everyone knew what, Marisa?"

"Knew about Mindy and Donnie, of course. They were way into each other. I mean, Mindy once told me that she and Donnie were true soul mates. I kept waiting for it to end, you know, for her to take the blinders off and see what she was getting herself into. I mean, after all, remember that hovel the Murdochs used to live in? Who'd want to settle for that in their future? But they got even closer after…you know, after his parents died." She sighed again. "Then we graduated, and Donnie goes and shoots someone." She paused. "A lot of kids had trouble relating to life after they graduated. Even I had my struggles. Didn't shoot anybody though."

"Did Mindy say why she and Donnie kept their relationship a secret?'

"Mindy said something about how her father wouldn't like it. But I don't think that was the real reason. Heck, none of us liked it. So what if her dad wasn't thrilled? I mean, that's a father's job, right? Not liking his daughter's boyfriend."

Of course, Marisa was right, but Knuck had a couple of things that most other fathers lacked. He carried a gun and, as I'd found out recently, a willingness to use it.

"Maybe Mindy was afraid that if he knew, her father would do something about it," I suggested. "Something he'd regret."

"That's just silly, Lyle. Mindy's dad was a pussycat. I know you wouldn't think it at first. Him being a cop and carrying a gun and all. But do you remember the annual Spring Athletics fundraiser? The carnival? Mr. Fullmer volunteered at the carnival for years. Even after Mindy graduated. Used to dress up as a clown." She paused. "Yes sir, his Mr. Fluffy Pants was a Burnsville High tradition."

"I'm sure it's a cherished memory, Marisa. But all the same, you can't always predict what a guy will do based on the size of his shoes."

"I never thought of it that way," she replied. "By the way, about Mr. Fullmer and the boy that died? Was his name really Latrine?" She giggled. "'Cause that name is about the silliest thing I ever heard. I mean, who would ever—"

"Yeah," I agreed, cutting off her laughter. "Ain't dead people funny?"

Chapter Twelve

"Are you going to tell me or not?" I asked, barely able to keep an edge of desperation from registering in my voice.

Both Edgerton and our mutual friend Irving "the Milkman" Mulligan, a former professional wrestler whose bulk teetered uncertainly atop the bar stool, swiveled around to glance at Skip, who was standing behind the bar, his arms crossed, keeping his usual watch on the motley combination of earnest students, long-time losers, and certified nutbars that made up McCauley's clientele. Although he didn't bother to return their looks, I could have sworn that the side of Skip's face that wasn't paralyzed brightened infinitesimally.

Turning back around, Edgerton heaved a dramatic sigh. "What can I say, man? I could explain it to you, but here's the thing…I really can't vouch for its veracity and sending you out into the world armed with another piece of faulty information just wouldn't be right. There's no telling what kind of damage you could do." He grinned. "Don't ask me to be your enabler. We all know what a loose cannon you can be. Particularly when it comes to…" He paused to consider just the right phrase. "Particularly when it comes to specious rumormongering."

"*Specious rumormongering*?" I repeated. "Name just one time I—"

Irv chuckled lightly.

"On top of that," Edgerton continued, "my guess is that the genesis of this particular expression is not based on actual empirical data but rather only on anecdotal evidence. And you know what a slippery slope that is."

"I'll give you a slippery slope," I warned. "Now, can we get back to my question? What does it mean when someone tells you to 'get a hat'?"

Edgerton picked up his beer, examined it minutely, then slowly raised it to his lips before taking a long slug. "You know, Lyle," he said, "patience is something you could stand to work on."

"For the love of God!" I cried much louder than I'd intended. "Just tell me what it means!"

Both Edgerton and Skip immediately burst into laughter. Not your normal ha-ha laughter either, but a kind of paint-stripping, braying donkey laughter that turned every head in the place. The sight of preternaturally stoic Skip actually laughing out loud was unusual enough that it transfixed many of the regular patrons. Some sat bolt upright, gaping over at him with stunned, even panic-stricken expressions. But as the initial shock slowly melted away, most felt compelled to join in with nervous little twitters of their own.

Irv cast me a sympathetic glance. "Maybe you should just tell him, Stephen," he said, his tone weighted with concern.

Edgerton continued to laugh but, I thought, a trifle less vindictively than before. Finally, he reached out and placed a hand on one of Mulligan's massive shoulders. "Just giving old Lyle a hard time, Milkman," Edgerton assured him.

Mulligan smiled shyly, shuffled his feet, and ran a

hand through his thick thatch of reddish-blond hair. "I know, Stephen. And it's not like you guys shouldn't have your fun, but… You can hurt a guy's feelings if you ain't careful."

Edgerton, his eyes softening, patted Mulligan's shoulder. "Okay, Lyle," he said. "Here it is. Have you ever noticed that when you get stuck behind someone driving really slowly—or worse, driving really slowly with their left turn signal blinking continually for miles—that the driver is generally wearing a hat?"

I thought about that for a moment. "No," I told him. "I never have."

Edgerton shrugged. "Me neither. But lots of folks swear there's a correlation between hat wearing and a propensity to drive at speeds that might best be described as glacial. So, when that guy in the Norwegian sports car blazed past you, he was suggesting that you identify yourself as a slow-moving menace by donning appropriate headgear."

I blinked a couple of times. "Are Saabs Norwegian?"

"You know, I'm not sure," Edgerton admitted. "Norwegian. Swedish. Definitely one of those melanin-deficient, Nordic countries."

Having done his part to reconcile us, a gleeful Mulligan stood and threw an arm around each of us. We lurched forward from the force of his embrace, nearly upsetting our beers and his ginger ale. "Feel better now, Lyle?" he asked, flashing a smile as bright as all the headlights in Norway.

Irving "the Milkman" Mulligan was, without a doubt, the most kind-hearted guy I'd ever known. During the day, he worked as a custodian at a community center that offered career counseling, job training, and adult literacy programs. But he'd also spend most of his nights volunteering his scant free time to a whole panoply of causes. He manned a suicide prevention hotline, spooned out casserole at a local hot meal program, and stacked chairs at his regular Alcoholics Anonymous meeting. He even pitched in Saturday mornings as a babysitter at a nearby YMCA childcare facility. Simply put, he was a guy you could count on—charitable enough to help you change a tire but with mettle enough to help you face down a guy with a tire iron. And he did all this without complaint or expectation of reward, certainly making the Milkman stand out among my acquaintances. The other thing that made Mulligan stand out was his size. I mean, I'm a big guy—six foot one, two hundred seventy pounds—but next to Mulligan, I looked like an undernourished wood sprite. Mulligan was six foot six and had to be over three hundred pounds, none of them flabby or soft—something that, alas, could not be said of my extra pounds. Instead, Mulligan was as rock hard as he'd been a decade before when he'd made his living in the squared circle.

I'd been a fan of Milkman's in those days, little dreaming we'd ever actually become acquainted. In the ring, Milkman Mulligan had been a beloved underdog, his fans cheering as he leaped, body slammed, and pile-drove his way to near victory. Actual victory, however, belonged to others. Despite the energy he brought to his matches and the ardor of Twin Cities fans, Mulligan was never able to make a name for himself on the national stage. He stayed strictly bottom of the card for his entire career—cannon fodder sent in against the big guns. When Mulligan finally hung up his tights, he had little more to show for his efforts than an alcohol problem and persistent tinnitus from being repeatedly smacked in the head. Although, over time, he'd managed to beat the bottle, and the ringing in his ears eventually quieted to little more than a tinkling, I often wondered if the real legacy of all those blows was his rather simple view of the world. But then maybe it wasn't head trauma that caused him to so zealously offer his time to others or to risk his own well-being for something he believed in. Maybe it was just that he was a legitimately nice guy. Huge, sometimes dangerous, but really, really nice.

"I'm great, Milkman," I told him. "Thanks for asking."

Mulligan glanced nervously around and lowered his voice to a gravelly whisper. "I know you guys like to…whatchacallit, rib each other and all, but I thought, you know, with what happened with your dad and that business I read about you in the paper. You know, the shooting and all? I just kinda, you know, kinda thought you might like things a little, you know, a little more subdued, I guess you'd call it."

"I appreciate your concern, Irv."

Mulligan stared downward as he lightly tapped one of his substantial work boots against the bar. "All that work out for you?" he asked. "You know, the shooting and all?"

"Yeah," I told him. "Just fine."

"That guy you were with? Stephen told me he was a friend of your dad's?"

"My dad's old partner."

Mulligan's brow crowded. "Funny. Him involving you in something like that. So soon after your dad passing and all."

"Yeah," I agreed. "Funny."

Mulligan nodded some more, then hooked a thumb in the side of his overalls before turning to scan the room, then swiveling to face me, effectively blocking the rest of the room from view.

"Was me," he added, "I'd a left you outta that."

I grunted. "The man was trying to protect his daughter's place. What are you going to do?"

"Yeah?" Mulligan's frown deepened. "Stephen said there was something else."

"There might be," I admitted. "I'm looking into it."

Edgerton stuck his head out from in back of Mulligan like a chipmunk peering around a redwood. "You find out anything yet?" he asked.

"Nothing useful. Nothing that directly connects the Murdoch business with those chowderheads that tried to shake down Mindy Fullmer. However, I did find out that Donnie Murdoch used to be sweet on Mindy"

Edgerton hummed. "She sweet on him back?"

"Long time ago, yeah."

"How long ago?"

"Back in high school."

He hummed again. "Before Donnie's parents were killed?'

"Yeah."

"That give you anything to work with?"

"Not that I can see."

Edgerton rubbed his chin lightly, his fingertips barely mussing the hairs of his well-trimmed beard. He likely thought this made him look penetrating, but— exposed to repeated viewings—I found the pose more than a little insufferable. "Hold on," he said. "Didn't you know these guys in high school?"

"Yeah."

"And you didn't know they were going out?"

I shook my head. "It's not like I was their freaking social secretary."

"Yeah, but you went to school with them. Donnie even lived with you, for chrissakes. And you didn't know they were an item?" He chuckled. "I can see that your raptor-sharp powers of observation have been with you from the beginning."

"Bite me," I told him. "I didn't really know Donnie until after his parents were murdered and Mindy…You know how it is. Our parents were friends. We'd get forced together every now and then, but I don't remember ever having even one genuine conversation with her. We really didn't have much in common."

Edgerton tickled his beard some more. "Your dads were both cops. That's something."

"Sure, but that's where our similarities ended."

"Yeah?"

"Yeah," I insisted. "Mindy was older, so we really didn't have friends in common at school and besides…the dynamic was so different. You know, the Fullmer family dynamic was one thing; ours was quite another."

"How so?"

I squirmed. "Why are you so interested?"

Edgerton shrugged and took a sip of his beer. "You've mentioned Knuck and Mindy but never a mom. Is this Knuck married?"

"Yeah. Phyllis."

"She and your mom close?"

I motioned to Skip for another beer. "Not really. I don't think she and my mom ever got together without the boys or anything. And when they were together, they didn't seem to spend much time catching up. My mom would generally sit in the living room listening to Dad and Knuck talk. Phyllis Fullmer would mostly hover and refill drinks."

"Mindy close to her mom?" Edgerton asked.

"I guess. But not as close as she was to her dad." I smiled. "I'll tell you one thing. Knuck Fullmer positively doted on his daughter. Still does. You should have seen him at her restaurant. He even helped pick out the décor." I paused. "I've been in my office…What? Six years? My dad never set foot in there. Not one time."

Skip brought my beer over and set it in front of me. Edgerton drained his, then raised the glass and held it up briefly to his eye, peering through it like a telescope. "You think Mindy and Donnie going out and Knuck Fullmer taking such an active interest in his daughter's welfare might have given him reason to go after Donnie or his family? I mean, the last time we know of Mindy Fullmer getting hassled, her dad capped someone."

"Since when do you say 'capped'?"

Edgerton shrugged. "My dad sent me a set of *The Sopranos*. Season one. On DVD. You think it might be motive for your buddy Knuck to have taken out the Murdoch family?"

I sighed. "I suppose. You can always argue that a father will go to nearly any lengths to protect his daughter. But motive alone doesn't prove anything. Frankly, that guy I told you about—Willard Tousignant? I'm hoping to show he was involved."

"That clown-looking guy? Didn't you say there was a problem with his being the killer."

"Well, he *was* in prison at the time."

Edgerton grinned. "Prison. The big house. The hoosegow."

I groaned. "Nobody says 'hoosegow' anymore. Seriously, Tousignant could have ordered it done. He could have had his flunky Bollok take them out. And you're right. It could have been Knuck. But heck, it could even have been Donnie or Mindy that killed the elder Murdochs."

"Really?" Edgerton asked, perking up. "You think so?"

"No. Not really. The Murdoch killings were a very big deal at the time. The whole force was in on the investigation. I mean, it's not like the Burnsville PD is Scotland Yard, but I don't think a couple of high school kids could have been clever enough to knock off one kid's parents and then hide their tracks well enough to escape arrest. And even though Donnie ended up killing somebody else a short time later, that murder was different. That grew out of his losing his parents."

Edgerton nodded. "But, you agree, it could have been Knuck?"

"It's possible."

"Or your father, for that matter."

I swear I actually heard a clicking sound in my head, like an electronic ignition sparking a furnace. My cheeks warmed so suddenly that I was afraid they were glowing. I leaned in to draw his gaze, but Edgerton's eyes wouldn't meet mine. When I opened my mouth to challenge him, Mulligan interrupted. "Do I know any of these people?" he asked.

"No," I snapped, turning to face him. "And you don't want to either."

Mulligan shrank a little at the sharpness of my reply

but still managed to maintain a dejected little smile. I smiled back an apology and tried again to get Edgerton's attention. But he'd turned to Skip. Skip was still behind the bar but now was staring out into the dim room even more attentively than usual. Focused on the front door, his gaze had become steely; his head tilted back expectantly like a pointer eyeing a tell-tale rustle in a patch of brush. "Dahms," he said softly.

I stood up. Knuck Fullmer was standing just inside the door. A faux Tiffany lamp hanging down precariously close to his head swathed him in a pale yellow light. I caught my breath, holding onto it as a brace against the gulf that opened in my belly.

Knuck was disheveled—his shirt tail not quite tucked into his waistband, his tie decidedly askew. But it was the look on his face that was most shocking. His color was a splotchy red, and the hollows of his enflamed cheeks were streaked with tears. His eyes were wide as though getting used to the dim light of the bar, but they swirled with a darkness of their own. His mouth was slightly open, his lips slack as if the muscles in his face had somehow gone dead. He spotted me at the bar and approached with a halting gait—a condemned man slowly marching toward judgment.

"Good God, Knuck!" I exclaimed. "What's happened?"

At first, he seemed unable to speak. Instead, his mouth merely twitched as though spurred by an intermittent electric current. Finally, words began to form.

"It's Mindy," he sobbed. "They've got Mindy."

"Who's got—" I began.

"You got to help me, Lyle," Knuck implored, his

voice rising in a piteous wail. "Someone's kidnapped my little girl."

Chapter Thirteen

The barroom became so quiet I swore I could hear the blood draining from my face. When Knuck first arrived, Edgerton, Skip, and Mulligan had, as if by unspoken command, all drifted back out of the way to give him room. But hearing the news of Mindy's kidnapping, Edgerton and the Milkman inched back toward us. They moved tentatively, two skittish crabs crossing a beach bristling with seagulls. For his part, Skip slid further away down the bar, careful to keep his gaze fixed on the distraught Knuck.

"Who has Mindy?" I demanded.

Knuck simply gaped at me. I leaned forward. "Who kidnapped Mindy?" I repeated.

Knuck blinked but still said nothing.

He was in shock, I realized. I gave him a reassuring smile and motioned him toward an empty barstool. The Milkman, who'd been standing nearby, stumbled as he hurried out of the way. Knuck, however, appeared incapable of any action, even sitting down. "Knuck," I said, "tell me everything you know."

"They called," he said, at last, his voice so quiet I had to strain to hear. "They said they left a message at the restaurant, but they reached me at home. They, uh…they said that if I didn't give them a hundred thousand dollars, they'd…they'd kill her. They said they'd…they said they'd—"

"Who said?" I interrupted. "Do you have any idea who we are dealing with here?"

Knuck's jaw began to quiver, barely noticeably at first, but growing until he was trembling like a Parkinson's patient. "I could hear her in the background," he said. "I could hear them slapping her. I could hear her crying." He swallowed hard. "They said that if I didn't get them the money they'd start, uh…they'd start sending her back to me in the mail. First her ears, then her…her eyes. Her fingers. I could hear them beating her." He paused. "They kept on beating her. After making me listen for a while, they asked, 'When do you want us to stop?'"

"Who asked?" I pressed. "Was there just one voice? Two? What did they sound like? Did you recognize—"

"When do you want us to stop?" Knuck repeated. "That's what they asked me." His head dropped submissively.

I stared at him. Obviously, he was in no shape to take charge—that was up to me—but what was I supposed to do? I forced myself to slow down, to take even breaths. I knew I couldn't do a thing unless I had a clearer idea who'd taken Mindy. I remembered back to the incident at Mindy's restaurant the other day, to Latrine Hawkins and his partner, Mason Slidel— Cleanhead—the hood who got away. Was this payback for Knuck shooting down his partner?

Slidel was certainly a likely candidate, I told myself, but he just was a punk; he thought like a punk, acted like a punk. If he wanted revenge, he'd take it. It wouldn't be about money. It would be about punishment. The ransom demand, brutal though it was, showed a kind of subtlety for which I couldn't give Slidel credit. The kidnappers were punishing Mindy all right—and Knuck, too—but in addition, they expected to make a profit. It was a strategy that showed a kind of merciless shrewdness. No, I decided. Someone far cleverer than Slidel was behind this.

It had to be Tousignant. Willie Tooz hadn't exactly been on my short list of potential prom dates, but if he was the one threatening to send Mindy back to Knuck in a series of envelopes, I was now determined to make sashimi out of his tender regions. But I needed a plan—as well as a place to start. I could run up to the North Side, I thought, but what did I expect? Tousignant to be at home waiting for me? I thought back to the Yippy's, to the last time I'd seen him. Had I missed something? Something that should have tipped me off that he'd make a move like this, something that would help me now. He'd mentioned Knuck, I remembered, but not Mindy. And the only person Tousignant had directly threatened was me. A cold shiver ran up my spine. Was he doing this to get back at me? Was this my fault?

I glanced at the well-smudged phone bolted to the wall behind the bar. I knew what I had to do. "Skip," I said, "I gotta make a call."

Skip silently nodded his approval.

I was nearly to the phone when Knuck's head suddenly snapped up. "No cops!" he cried. "They said, 'no cops.'"

I spun back around. His face was still without expression, but his voice was steely with resolve. "Think, Knuck," I appealed to him, forcing myself to sound reasonable, "Of course, they said, 'no cops.' But that doesn't mean we listen to them. If Mindy's been kidnapped, we both know that her chances of *survival…*"

He flinched at the word, an arc of fear crackling briefly in the deep nothingness of his eyes. "We both know," I continued, "that the chances of getting Mindy back safe are much better if we call the cops. They've got the experience, the manpower, the resources."

"God damn it!" he exclaimed. "They said no cops!"

"I know, but—"

"Now you listen to me!" Knuck cut me off, his voice rising to a jagged shriek that rent the air. "This is my fucking daughter! Do you fucking understand that? Nobody does anything that might get her hurt. Nothing! You understand me?" His whole body shook with an incendiary mix of fear and rage. "Do you understand me?" he seethed. "Do you understand me, you fat fuck?"

The epithet, coming so suddenly, so unexpectedly, stung more than I like to admit. Although since I was a kid, I'd suspected that both Knuck and my dad had made jokes about my weight, but they'd always kept it private. They'd never done it in front of me. And never in front of my friends. I knew I shouldn't let it get to me. I knew that as distressed as he was, Knuck couldn't be held responsible for anything he said. Still, I had to take a moment to blink back my anger.

"You're overwrought," I said at last. "It's clouding your judgment. If this was anybody but Mindy, you'd be insisting on the cops. You'd know that this is too important a thing to go about half-assed." I paused, giving him a moment to see reason. "We have to get the professionals involved. It's the only way."

I was sure I'd reached him. His shaking diminished. He turned away from me; he even nodded thoughtfully. But when he turned back around, his face had contorted into a grotesque, hate-filled mask. Only an arm's length away from me, he wavered for an instant before angry decision flamed up in his eyes.

I braced myself for his attack. But instead of rushing me, he flung open his sports jacket and made a grab for the revolver in his shoulder holster. I got lucky. His anger made him clumsy. He had to pull at it two or three times before it cleared leather, leaving more than enough time for me to pull my own. I stared at him down the barrel of my gun. He froze, his .38 held off to the side but gripped so tightly his knuckles went white.

"Put the gun down, Knuck," I ordered. "You're not thinking straight."

A soft knock, like the rap of knuckles against the wooden bar, sounded from down where Skip had been standing. Knuck's gaze flickered in that direction for an instant but quickly returned to me. When it did, he brought his revolver level with my belly.

I should have shot him. If he'd been any other person at any other time, I would have shot him. But this was my dad's best friend. More than that—his partner. Hell, I had a hard time even keeping my gun trained steadily on him. I took a deep breath and, forcing calm into my voice, said, "We start shooting each other, neither one of us will be here to help Mindy,"

Again, Knuck glanced down to the end of the bar. This time I let my eyes follow. Skip was still there, only now in a shooter's stance—shoulders squared, feet apart, both hands wrapped around an enormous handgun. Big as my dad's Desert Eagle. I returned my attention to Knuck, to his clenched jaw and the unwavering revolver in his hand. I remember thinking I didn't know what to be most afraid of—Knuck shooting me in the guts or

Skip blowing Knuck's brains all over me. Fortunately, I didn't have to wonder long. After a tense moment, Knuck exhaled heavily before letting his gun fall to his side. "No cops," he repeated weakly.

I holstered my .38 and slowly approached Knuck. As I did, I cast a glance at Mulligan who was standing nearby with his shoulders thrown back and his arms spread curiously as though he were trying to catch a beach ball. I took a moment for me to realize that he was puffing himself up, making himself a larger target. If I could have seen around him, I was certain that I'd find Edgerton shielded behind him.

Knuck flinched only slightly when I placed my hand gently on his gun. Nodding, he unclasped his fingers and let me take the revolver. As I slipped Knuck's gun, barrel first, into my waistband behind me, Skip lowered his weapon, and Edgerton popped like a shaggy jack-in-the-box out from behind the giant Milkman.

"No cops," Knuck said again.

I shook my head. "Come on, Knuck. You know better than that."

He started to argue, but I held up a palm. "We'll talk to them when they get here. If things go right, the kidnappers will be wearing handcuffs before they even know the police were involved."

"The guy who called," Knuck replied, "he said they'd know. He said they had someone on the inside that would tell them."

"Of course he did," I chided. "He'd have told you they had spies staking out your Fruit-of-the-Looms if he thought it could get you to just hand over a wad of cash without bringing in the police. Whoever these assholes are, they want every advantage they can take. Don't give 'em any."

Knuck lowered his eyes and ran a palm across the lower half of his face. He seemed about to say something but stopped himself, then carefully tucked his shirttail back into his waistband. He raised his head, and, as if in a gesture of defiance, he adjusted his rumpled tie with a deft twist.

"I know what I'm doing, Lyle," he said calmly. "I came here for your help, not your advice. There's no way I let anybody dictate to me how this goes down. This is my family we're talking about here. My fucking family. You don't want to help me, stay out of it." He paused. "But if you're not going to help, promise me you'll keep your goddamned mouth shut. You hear? No going to the police."

"Jesus, Knuck!" I exclaimed. "You *were* a cop! You know this shit! You're the last person who should be calling the shots. You've turned into the fucking poster child for bad decision-making in a crisis. You pulled a gun on me, for chrissake!"

I expected a reply—a curse, an apology, anything—but Knuck was silent. This was not, however, the same mute stupor he'd suffered from when he first came in. This was different. This was like he didn't feel like he should bother to respond to me.

A bubble of rage rose within me. I took another deep breath, then swallowed hard. "I guess it's understandable after that call you described," I continued, showing more self-control than I'd have thought I possessed. "But we've got to get past that. We've got to do the right thing right now. What's your plan? To give them the money? You gotta be kidding me. A hundred grand? Who the fuck has a hundred grand?"

"I can get it," Knuck assured me. "There's at least that in the restaurant. There's my house. I can get it."

I shook my head. "Even so, why would you? It's not like you'll give them the money, and it'll all be over. You know it doesn't work like that. You give them what they ask for, they'll want more. They'll take all they can get, and you might still never see Mindy again. Not alive anyway. You know the drill. You play it that way, you give them what they want, there's no reason for them to give you anything in return."

"It doesn't always work that way," he insisted. "Lots of times guys like this they—"

"And lots of times they don't," I snapped.

Knuck gave his head a violent shake. "No. No. We get the money together. We make a drop or whatever they ask for. We see if we can trust them."

"Trust them?" I blurted in disbelief.

Without warning, Knuck reached out with both hands and grabbed me by the shoulders. Startled, I took a step back, pulling Knuck with me in an awkward tango. Another knock, this one louder than before, sounded from Skip's end of the bar. Both of our heads immediately turned. Skip had the Magnum resting on the bar in front of him. He hadn't raised it, but his message was clear. If there was trouble, he'd be the one taking care of it.

Knuck backed off. "Please, Lyle!" he pleaded. "You didn't hear them. You don't know. I tell ya. We fuck this up, they'll do it. I know they will. They'll cut her up. Can you imagine? Can you imagine what it will be like to get that first package? To get it and to know that there will be more. Can you imagine?"

I could. Unbidden, pictures flashed through my

mind. First, Mindy sobbing, then mute, her eye sockets empty, her features carved from her face, pawing at her captors with spade-like hands.

"I'm trying *not* to fuck this up," I assured him. "And I still think we have to—"

"We can call the cops in later," Knuck interrupted. "If we need them. But we gotta try it my way first. Shit, Lyle. It's my daughter. My money. We gotta play it my way. We don't, and things go wrong, I'm never gonna forgive myself. I'm never gonna forgive you. Please, Lyle. Please."

I stared at Knuck, cringing as he pleaded with me. I couldn't help but think of my dad on his deathbed, also pleading—pleading with me to make things right. I'd tried, I told myself, but somehow my doing what he'd wanted, my going to see Donnie, had spawned all this trouble. And now Mindy Fullmer had to pay. With that weighing on me, I wasn't certain I was in a better position than Knuck to decide the best course of action.

"What would you do?" I asked Skip.

Skip smiled his half-smile. "I'd do it his way," he said, motioning to Knuck.

I wasn't expecting that. "Really?"

Skip nodded. "'Course, I've never been real crazy about calling in the law."

I allowed myself a smile. "I knew that about you."

Turning back to Knuck, I said, "If we haven't got the cops, we're going to need help. It won't work just you and me. We're going to need more people on it."

"I'm in," Skip said simply.

I stared. "Why on earth—"

Skip shrugged. "'Cause I'm used to you, that's why. I let you go off with this guy without me and I end up having to break in a new regular." He paused. "That's just more work than I care for right now."

"I'll help too," Mulligan chirped in enthusiastically. "Some little girl's in trouble, you know I'll help out."

"She's not so little, Irv," I told him. "She's nearly forty."

"Oh." Mulligan's eyes went a little vacant. "Still, she's *this* guy's little girl, huh?" he said, eyeing Knuck eagerly. "Just tell me what you need me to do."

Knuck's expression clouded noticeably.

"Thanks, Milkman," I said.

Edgerton came forward. I thought I detected a slight hesitation in his step, but he pushed his hair back from his face with a confident wave of a bony arm and asked, "What can I do?"

Although the rail-thin and geekily intellectual Edgerton had worked every summer for many years at the Midwest Renaissance Festival and was actually a pretty fair hand with a broadsword, he wasn't exactly my first choice of confederates when fists and bullets were flying. The few times he'd been with me when violence broke out, I'd been so worried about him that I'd had trouble keeping my head in the game. It was a risk I didn't want to take unless I had to.

I cleared my throat. "When the time comes, it would be great if you could stay by the phone. You know, in case something goes wrong. In case we, uh…need anything."

"Is that all?" Edgerton asked, pursing his lips into either a frown or a pout. I wasn't sure which.

"We go with our strengths," I told him. "We keep you free for more, uh…" I paused to think of the right word. "For more strategic matters. The rest of us have more experience with the frontline stuff."

By now it was clearly a frown he was wearing, but although unhappy, he seemed to accept it. At least he didn't argue with me.

But Knuck seemed anything but satisfied. He raised both of his hands in front of him as though surrendering and backed off warily. "Now, hold on a minute, fellas," he said. "Lyle and me. We gotta have a word."

He tugged me a few feet distant, but not, I thought, entirely out of earshot. "Like I said, Lyle. My family, my way."

"What are you saying?"

"I know a couple of guys," Knuck said. "Guys I used to know on the force. If we need more manpower, I say we use them." Then he smiled at me. A smug, patronizing smile.

I suppose I should have been cheered by his recovery. After all, he'd gone from near catatonic, struggling father to anger-blinded madman to take-charge kind of guy all in a matter of a few short minutes. But I wasn't cheered. Something was definitely off. With Mindy in danger, you'd expect Knuck to be acting erratically, but the way his mood had been swinging—so quick, so drastic, so, I don't know, purposeful—it was as if someone was flipping a switch. As if he was on stage taking direction from a schizophrenic director.

Why, I asked myself, was he so dead set against calling in the police? He was, after all, an ex-cop himself. And why did he come to me if he had these "guys" he knew that could help him? It just didn't add up.

I stared at him, at the self-assured gleam that now shone in his eyes, the confidence he now radiated—the same cocky aplomb he'd exhibited just before he went out to put a bullet in Latrine Hawkins—and I became slowly, inexorably, more and more pissed.

"You want my help?" I asked.

"Yes, but—"

I turned to glance back at Skip and the Milkman. Irv was leaning forward, his eyes wide and expectant, like a kid peering over the counter at a soda fountain. Skip was using a fingernail to scrape a little dried-on something from the rim of a beer glass. "If you want my help, these guys are in," I told Knuck flatly. "That's non-negotiable."

Knuck drew me in closer to him. "Come on, Lyle. I mean the one guy's big enough, but I don't get the impression there's much going on upstairs." Knuck tapped his head with a forefinger. "And the smoke?" he asked, lowering his voice and giving me a little wink. "I was a cop long enough to know a hood when I see one."

I glanced over at Skip. He didn't move; his expression didn't change in the slightest. He heard, I thought. He had to have heard.

I placed a friendly hand on Knuck's shoulder. "They've both saved my ass in the past," I told him, my voice tightening. "Which is a helluva lot more than I can say for you. I trust them. Again, more than I can say for you. And, by the way, if you refer to Skip as a 'smoke' in front of me again, I'll lay you out. Understand?"

Knuck took half a step back and blinked rapidly several times, his mouth just slightly agape. "Okay," he said finally. "Shit, I figured…" He paused. "Okay."

I clapped him amicably on the shoulder and turned him back to the bar. Only one of us was smiling.

"Let me ask you again," I said when we'd rejoined the others. "Do you have any idea who these guys are?"

Knuck shook his head.

"Could it have been that kid Slidel? The one that goes by the name Cleanhead?"

Knuck shook his head again. "I suppose," he said, "but I don't think so. It didn't sound like him."

"Did the guy have an accent of any kind?"

"No," Knuck replied. "Not unless you mean American."

I nodded. "Do you know a guy named Willard Tousignant?"

Knuck blinked. "Who?" he asked. "Willard what?" He shook his head. "Nah, I don't know any Willard Nothing." He paused. "You think this Willard's got something to with this?"

"I don't really know. We'll get to that later. Did the caller give you any instructions?"

"He said he'd call back tomorrow. Said that would give me enough time to get the money together. Said he'd tell me how he wanted it to go down when he called."

I looked at my watch. "Does that give you enough time?"

Knuck nodded. "I think so. Shit, I've never had to get my hands on this much cash before. But I think so."

"You sure you want to do this?" I asked. "You really gonna give him the money?"

"I really am," Knuck assured me. "I can get it together. I'll do whatever it takes to get my Mindy back."

"You sure?"

Knuck let his head drop slightly. "Shit no, Lyle. I'm not sure. It's the only option they're giving me. All I know is that if we fuck this up—"

"I know," I said, "you'll never forgive yourself.

Okay. We try it your way. They'll probably have you make a drop somewhere. Somewhere public where they can keep an eye on you. Never mind, we'll be there too, keeping an eye on them."

"Hold on now!" Knuck said, his voice rising. "I told you I—"

"We gotta play the percentages," I insisted. "If we can spot them, follow them without tipping them off, it will greatly improve our chances of getting Mindy back safe."

"What if they spot you?" Knuck squalled.

"You'll have to trust us," I said, glancing over at Skip and the Milkman. "We've done this kind of thing before."

Knuck lowered his eyes to the carpet. "I do trust *you*, Lyle," he said quietly. "It's just…I don't know. It's just everything is happening so fast. Maybe it's these guys," he said, pointing at Skip and the Milkman. "I'd feel better if you'd let me bring in those guys I know."

I shook my head. "We covered that, Knuck. No way. It's these guys, or you can count me out."

His head jerked up, indignation pulsing in his eyes. "So, I got no say in this? It's my life, my daughter, and it's out of my hands! I gotta sit with my thumb up my ass and trust Mindy's life to someone who—I'm sorry to have to tell you this, Lyle—but someone whose own father used to refer to as a second-rate P.I? I gotta put her life in the hands of some big dimwit I've never met before, and this, this…" He waved a spastic finger at Skip. "…this smoke friend of yours?"

I hit him on the jaw. Right hand. Got good weight behind it, too. His head whipped around, a rope of saliva spiraling out into the room. Surprisingly, although

Knuck's knees immediately buckled, he managed to stay on his feet for a moment before he crumpled into a pile at the foot of the bar. The look on his face was one of pure astonishment. It struck me as incredibly comic. I had to work to keep from laughing.

"What the—" he cried.

"I warned you," I reminded him. "Now, unless you got more objections, I suggest we get to work saving your daughter."

Chapter Fourteen

Some years earlier, a newly-elected Republican governor of Minnesota—in a move that showed a clear nostalgia for such golden-age of television staples as *Bonanza* and *Gunsmoke*—spearheaded a bill through the legislature designed to turn Minneapolis into Dodge City. Together, they passed the "Minnesota Citizens' Personal Protection Act," a move that greatly widened the right of the citizenry to carry concealed weapons in the state.

The bill did something else, too. Prior to the new law, folks would generally assume that the mom pushing a cart down a crowded grocery store aisle or the guy yakking into his cell phone on the elevator next to them was not packing heat. Let's just say that the act disabused us of that quaint notion. No, a gun permit now allows the security-conscious to carry their guns, concealed or not, into any and all private establishments unless the owners expressly forbid it.

And property owners wishing to curtail the rights and liberties of the gun-toting public can't simply shake their heads and waggle their fingers to make firearms disappear from the buildings they own. Instead, they are enjoined to hang a sign lettered in black Arial typeface, at least one and a half inches high, on a bright contrasting background, more than one hundred square inches in size, four to six feet above the floor, and within four lateral feet of the entrance of said establishment. So it was that as Knuck and I entered the west entrance to Bloomington's Liberty Mall, the nation's largest shopping mall, the first thing that greeted us was a sign which read: *"The Liberty Mall Bans Guns in These Premises."*

Knuck and I exchanged glances and then wordlessly patted at the shoulder holsters we'd both concealed under our jackets.

I'll admit I felt a little bad about having slugged Knuck in the bar, his daughter having just been kidnapped and threatened with dismemberment and all. But Knuck had seemed to settle down quite a bit after I let him have it. At least he'd lost the more manic qualities he'd been exhibiting. He was outwardly calm as we waited to receive the call for Mindy's ransom payment. He was businesslike as he went off to speak to his accountant and to make the necessary withdrawal from the bank. He actually managed an off-handed charm as he contacted the press to tell them that the opening of Mindy's restaurant had been delayed, assuring them that it was nothing more serious than a little retooling needed in the kitchen and things would soon be back on track.

This delay, he explained to his wife Phyllis, was the reason he'd be so busy the next couple of days, and didn't it make sense for her to visit her sister in Rochester instead of sitting home alone while he and Mindy pulled all-nighters at the restaurant? He was every bit the concerned husband as he gassed up her two-door sedan, marked a highway map with a yellow highlighter, and sent her off with a mechanical peck on the cheek and no clue that her daughter was in any danger. And later, as he sat with me in the darkened restaurant, an old college backpack of Mindy's at his feet, bulging with currency, he showed no trace of either the paralyzing fear or the ruthless cockiness that I'd seen from him earlier. He still wasn't too happy with my insistence that we involve Skip and the Milkman, but he seemed genuinely glad to have my help and so didn't mention it more than a couple of times. When the phone finally rang, it was with a quietly resigned sigh that he told me where the kidnappers wanted him to make the drop.

I couldn't fault them for their choice. As in real estate, when arranging a ransom drop three things are important: location, location, and location. You need a place where you can be hidden but where your patsy— the worried loved one leaving the money—remains in your full sight. A crowded area is generally best. A crowd can help shield you as well as provide a distraction should one become necessary. Good lighting is a big plus, and perhaps most importantly, you need multiple avenues of escape lest your patsy not be so foolish as to come alone. The Liberty Mall had all of this in spades.

But since its opening, the very existence of the mall has disquieted me. Prior to 1982, the land in the Minneapolis suburb of Bloomington, on which the Liberty Mall now stands, had been home to storied Met Stadium, where I spent my earliest days watching such baseball luminaries as Harmon Killebrew, Tony Oliva, and Rod Carew play for the Minnesota Twins. Well, it might not be entirely correct to say that I watched them at the Met. My old man only managed to take Chuck and me out to the old ball game a couple of times when we were little kids.

But all summer long, he'd have the game on, his radio tuned to mighty WCCO AM and the voice of play-by-play man Herb Carneal. For us, baseball wasn't something that we saw but rather something that we heard. The game was the soundtrack of summer, a constant presence in the background, always there but mostly unobtrusive, its slow rhythms forming a gentle current that urged us through the sweaty afternoons and breathlessly muggy nights. Gentle, that is, until a crack of a bat sounded, and the noise of the crowd swelled like waves of pelting rain against a tin roof, Herb's voice rising majestically above the din. The game, so mundane yet so sacred, emanated from a place also equal parts sacred and mundane. Met Stadium may have been nothing but an oval of concrete rising from the sleepy plains in a sleepy suburb of a minor and climatically challenged U.S. city, but when Killebrew crushed a ball over the center field fence, or Carew snapped one into the gap to score a man from second, when the crowd rose as one, and normally staid Midwesterners shouted full-throated hallelujahs to the pagan god of baseball, Met Stadium revealed itself a cathedral from whence glory overflowed.

Then, in 1982, the Twins moved to the newly constructed Hubert H. Humphrey Metrodome at the edge of downtown Minneapolis, and overnight, the former cathedral became a shabby derelict, its wellspring of glory capped, the mighty deeds once staged there but ghostly memories. And so it remained for a decade until, with great fanfare, it was announced that on this formerly hallowed ground, developers built what they referred to as "the largest, fully enclosed retail and family entertainment complex in the United States."

Where the old Met had once celebrated the deeds of men, the Liberty Mall celebrates something that, although tawdry, turns out to be far more potent. The power of the almighty dollar. While my fellow Minnesotans flocked to the opening, I refused to set foot in the place on principle. But after years of steadfastly maintaining my integrity, Naomi—normally not someone I'd call a clothes horse—insisted that I accompany her to a shoe sale at Bergen's that she described as "the opportunity of a lifetime." I ended up trading my principles for a pair of "darling Cole Haan slingbacks" that I think she wore only once.

Housing some five hundred and twenty-five specialty stores, four national department stores, fifty restaurants, seven nightclubs, a fourteen-screen multiplex, and an aquarium, the Liberty Mall attracts some forty-two million guests each year, pretty much guaranteeing a crowd for Mindy's kidnappers to hide in. And the drop, Knuck had told me, would be taking place in the most crowded part of the mall. At its very center, three stories tall beneath a glass ceiling supported by a network of latticed girders and gray metal catwalks, is the largest indoor theme park in America.

We entered Bergen's on the second floor. Just inside the doors was a pair of elevators. Knuck nodded to me, then punched the "Down" button. We'd agreed that we would split up once we got inside. The kidnappers had, of course, insisted that Knuck bring the money alone. They had to. It's in the script. Right after insisting that the money be in small bills—nothing bigger than fifties—the caller is supposed to lower his voice threateningly and say, "Make sure you come alone." The guy paying the ransom is supposed to agree, all the while planning to have at least some kind of backup. Knuck may have nixed police involvement, but he never for a moment considered doing this solo. And I suspect the kidnappers never really expected him to. But there's no sense in rubbing their noses in it, so we agreed to go in separately.

Knuck vanished behind the closing elevator doors, and I stayed on the second floor, heading out of Bergen's and into the mall. I turned right down a wide concourse that, although lined with brightly lit shops, seemed strangely dark. I turned right again down a narrower and even darker concourse, proceeding until it widened to accommodate a cluster of kiosks, one proffering shiny Italian charm bracelets, another kitchen magnets that stood in front of a glass, torpedo-shaped elevator. The expanse beyond the elevator was open and filled with brilliant light. As I stepped forward to a railing, looming in front of me like the monumental statue of a pharaoh guarding his tomb, towered a massive effigy of that beloved cartoon character Sammy Squirrel. I had reached Camp Sammy.

One paw raised, this voluminous, two-story-tall squirrel jiggled. Letting my eyes run down the length and girth of the giant Sammy, I realized that it was inflatable. As the giant Sammy balloon shook its booty above, at its base was a large rectangular enclosure made of the same rubbery fabric. Through the clear walls of the enclosure, I could make out several toddlers bouncing happily inside. Outside milled a multitude of camp visitors, gawking, pointing, and reaching for their wallets.

I took a step back, retreating to an area closer to the elevator that was partly in shadow, and began to survey the park in earnest. Unfortunately, from my vantage point, I was able to make out surprisingly little of the expansive amusement park. I could see that in front of

Sammy lay an enormous pile of acorns—a spout at the apex spurting forth a fountain that ran merrily down the pile. Immediately to his left stood a giant, steel arm, also painted red and even taller than Sammy. Called the Mighty Axe, one end of the arm sported what looked like a double-edged blade while the other end grasped what resembled the wheel of an old paddleboat into which some two dozen lunatics had allowed themselves to be strapped. The wheel tumbled over and over while the whole contraption spun end-over-end. There was neither enough booze in the world nor a pair of Depends leak-proof enough to get me to climb on something like that.

High above the park snaked the tracks of a roller coaster. They were narrow, and the girders of the supporting trestle appeared as thin as gossamer. But along the tracks improbably raced a line of cars, clattering and filled with screams. The middle of the park was a noisy blur of brightly lit and colorful contraptions—racing, rising, falling, and spinning, each issuing forth a dissonant cacophony of bells and horns and prerecorded announcements warning thrill riders to "remain seated with their hands and feet inside until the vehicle comes to a complete stop." And people. There were lots and lots of people streaming into the park from all sides and then disappearing into the blur.

At the far end of this vortex, rising nearly to the ceiling, was an ersatz sawmill emblazoned with large letters that spelled out the words "Paul Bunyan's Log Chute." Under the peaked roof was painted an enormous mural depicting the fabled lumberjack, but unlike the blocky, hulking statue that my dad drove us all the way up to Bemidji to see when I was eight, this Paul Bunyan was blond and blow-dried, baring a distinct resemblance to the Brawny paper towel man. I had to wonder if the good people at Georgia-Pacific had greased the artist's palm.

While I was wondering, Knuck came into view.

He emerged near the acorn fountain, coming to stand amidst a group of swirling children who were all wearing the same color t-shirt and being shepherded by a pair of young women who seemed bent over with exhaustion. Knuck leaned back up, closer to the fountain, one strap of the backpack clutched tightly in his hand. I scanned the crowd, not really expecting to pick out anyone suspicious, instead hoping for a glimpse of either Skip or the Milkman, who I knew to be there somewhere, keeping watch. I shouldn't have bothered. Even though the Milkman was big enough that every time he got between me and the sun I expected to see its corona, I knew that Skip would manage to keep them both out of sight. Although I couldn't see them, it was comforting to know that they could contact me if they needed me. Or if I needed them. Feeling suddenly vulnerable, I reached into the pocket of my jacket and drew out my cell phone. Knowing that both Skip and Knuck could reach me made me feel a little less vincible. I checked to be sure that I'd actually turned it on, returned the phone to my pocket, and went back to watching the crowd.

I heard a distant squawk off to my right and turned to find a security guard walking slowly in my direction. Unlike a lot of places that opt for a more casual look, the Liberty Mall had gone all out making their security guards look official. This guy was decked out in dark uniform slacks with a white shirt, a badge, a cotton police hat with a shiny vinyl bill, and a Batman-style utility belt featuring a .38 caliber service revolver, as well as a flashlight, what looked like a cartridge of pepper spray, and several snap compartments that I'm assuming he used for spare ammo, chewing gun, and the like. It also sported a two-way radio (the source of the squawk that I'd heard) with a cord that coiled up to a transmitter he had clipped to his open collar. He looked to me like he was about twelve years old, which meant he was probably still on the near side of twenty. He was skinny, with a sharp, beak-like nose, and was distinctly chin-impaired. Garbed in his full security guard regalia, he had the geeky look of a software nerd at a Halloween dress-up party. But he evidently took his job pretty seriously. He stopped to do a threat assessment on a couple of Black guys who were window shopping at a nearby electronics store, nodding his head knowingly as he stared hard at their backs, fingering his flashlight. When they moved on, having never even noticed him, he proudly stuck out what little chin he had and strutted on by as though he'd just run off a biker gang.

A deep boom sounded off to the left side of the amusement park, and I immediately turned my full attention back to Knuck. There was another boom, and Knuck stiffened, craning his neck. I moved forward to the railing and saw a small marching band making its way toward the uber-Sammy balloon: four guys, one playing a bass drum, another a kit that combined snare drum and cymbal, and bringing up the rear a trumpet and trombone—all banging and snapping and tooting. Kids pointed. Sammy jiggled.

As they reached him, Knuck turned away from the band and let himself relax back against the fence that cordoned off the fountain. I scanned the crowd around him, surveying the children now dancing to the band and the beaming grandparents capturing the scene on their cell phone cameras. Then, for the first time since we'd set up, I thought about Mindy. I thought about how she'd come over to our house with her parents when I was growing up. I remembered that when we were really young, we'd played together, but pretty soon, she was twelve and above playing with little squirts like Chuck and me. I remembered the three of us watching TV silently in our basement while our parents "visited" in the living room above. I remembered Chuck teasing me about her one time shortly after she grew boobs. I remembered flushing his Bozo Super-Flex action figure down the toilet and catching hell from my dad when he had to call Roto-Rooter. And I remembered Knuck's description of the call from the kidnappers and their talk of carving her up. I shook my head to clear my thoughts, gulped in some air, and went back to watching the crowd.

A man in his thirties, possibly Hispanic judging from his brown skin and dark curly hair, was hovering about five feet to Knuck's left. He had his hands in the pockets of a letterman-style jacket, blue with white sleeves, his eyes following the marching band as they finally took their act further into the park. Another man, this one in his early twenties, but white with brown hair worn nearly at shoulder length, approached from the other side. He was wearing blue jeans, a denim jacket, and a pair of pointy cowboy boots. The two men exchanged glances before closing in on Knuck.

I took a deep breath and held it as I watched the mute scene from above. I'd agreed not to interfere. I was to let Knuck hand over the money, he hoped, in exchange for Mindy's whereabouts. It had taken some convincing, but I'd agreed to simply let them go. Unseen, however, Skip and the Milkman would follow the money. I'd keep Knuck covered, and when we knew who and where the kidnappers were and only when we knew Mindy was safe would we exact any retribution.

Everything went swimmingly at first. Knuck was nodding agreeably. The Hispanic man flashed a bright smile. The guy with the long hair even lowered his head and began shuffling his feet in an aw-shucks, embarrassed cowboy fashion. He raised his head, however, when Knuck reached out, the backpack in his left hand, extending it toward the Hispanic man. Smiling again, the Hispanic man took the backpack, then slowly drew a hand from his pocket. It was cupped as though concealing something. I leaned forward, but whatever it was, it was too small for me to make out. The Hispanic man reached toward Knuck, and they appeared to shake hands. As he withdrew, Knuck was careful not to look down at his now cupped hand. Then, as both of the men who'd approached Knuck slowly turned to leave, all hell broke loose.

A gunshot sounded from the third floor above me. There was a loud knock, and a fist-sized chunk burst from the acorn fountain where Knuck was standing. He jerked, raising his arms in an almost flapping motion, as he wheeled around to try to spot the shooter. A young Asian woman, who had been walking along the railing some three feet away from me, pointed as the throng below pushed back from the fountain, several people falling, others tumbling over their prostrate bodies.

Another shot rang out. I couldn't see where it struck in the tumult below. Wheels clacked on the roller coaster tracks above me, the screams of the riders nearly drowning out the piercing cries of the people making desperate retreat beneath me. I heard a loud squawk. The security guard had returned. Standing only feet from me, he scanned the scene frantically, fumbling at his radio transmitter.

"Shooter's up there!" I yelled, pointing up toward the third floor.

He stared slack-jawed at me.

"Up there!" I repeated.

A third shot rang out, and I turned around just in time to see Knuck, who remained near the water fountain, slump to the ground. A couple of feet away from him, standing alone in a clearing left by the retreating crowd, a dark-haired little girl, about four or five years old, was clinging tightly to the string of a helium-filled balloon. The balloon, shaped like Sammy Squirrel's friend Freddy Ferret, was nearly as big as her. There was another radio squawk, and I turned to find the security guard had unsnapped his holster. Panic, like a downed power line in the rain, sparked in his eyes, but something else shone there too—a wild zeal, as though in spite of his obvious fear, he'd realized that his time had finally come.

His gaze fixed on the scene below, he drew his revolver and began waving it erratically before him. "I think I see something!" he screeched into his radio before moving his feet apart and taking a shooter's stance.

I looked back down at the girl with the balloon. The words escaped me before I realized I'd opened my mouth. "What the fuck do you think you're doing?" I shouted.

He didn't seem to hear me. He didn't seem to be in his right mind. He just kept waving that gun, first to the left, then to the right, searching the mob of innocents for a viable target.

"Put that damn thing away!" I demanded.

I turned back to Knuck. He was still down but stirring, trying to get his legs under him. I allowed myself a smile, but it was immediately erased by the retort of the security guard's gun. I watched in horror as the little girl let go of her balloon.

The gunshot seemed impossibly loud, momentarily swallowing up all other sounds, but as it died, I distinctly heard the anguished plea of the little girl below as she wailed, "Mommy!"

Realizing she was unhurt, I spun around, pulled my own revolver from its holster, and used the gun butt to clock the security guard hard on the head. He crumbled like a stale coffee cake. More gasps sounded around me as I reached down to take the .38 from the hand of the downed security guard. I didn't have time to explain my actions. I had to get down to Knuck. I took off running.

Slipping the security guard's gun into the pocket of my jacket and returning my own gun to its holster, stupidly, I headed first toward the nearby elevator as if it would be wide open and waiting for me. Blocked, I skirted the crowd that churned in front of the elevator and raced back toward Bergen's, and the only way I knew to get down to Knuck. As though I'd stepped into a torrent, the river of shoppers also trying to make their way to the safety of the department store carried me forward. Rocked and buffeted, I made it inside Bergen's. I immediately realized that neither the elevator that Knuck had used nor the escalators, now jammed with a press of humanity, were remotely passable.

I remembered that there was a stairway in the

parking ramp, and I slowly shouldered my way toward it. Although quite wide, the stairwell, too, was clogged with frightened people fleeing for their cars. It was like trying to dog paddle out to sea through an incoming tsunami, but I somehow made it to the first floor. Breathing heavily and sweating so profusely that I half burrowed, half slid my way through the last of the mob, I finally broke free into the now deserted section of the amusement park. It was quiet—quiet enough that as I approached Knuck's position, I could hear the low hum of the motor that pumped air into the nearby Sammy balloon.

It had been a few minutes since anybody had taken another shot, so as I walked out into the open, I really had no reason to fear myself a target. Still, I felt an odd tickling sensation, as though someone was tracing something on the skin between my shoulder blades.

Knuck lay at the base of the fountain. I blanched when I reached him. Both his blue sports jacket and his white dress shirt were soaked with blood from a gunshot wound in his chest. His eyes were closed, and his head lolled on his shoulders. His breathing was the ragged gasp of an overworked bellows, but when I knelt down beside him, his eyes flashed open. "We gotta go after them!" he insisted, his legs twitching uselessly.

I thought it best to try to calm him. "Don't worry about them," I said, my voice as gentle as a mother lulling a newborn. "Remember, we got that covered. We've got people—"

"Fuckers shot me," he wheezed. "They took the money, and then the fuckers shot me."

"Don't worry about that," I repeated. "Just take it easy. We'll get you a doctor. The rest of us can handle—

"

"Shit!" he exclaimed. "They still got my Mindy. They still got…they've got—"

"Stay calm," I urged him. "Those assholes won't have her for long."

"I can't feel my hand," Knuck wailed suddenly. "Shit! I can't feel my hand."

His arms barely moved, but both of his fists were clenched in rage. "You're shot," I told him. "You're shot in the chest. It's not good, but you'll be okay. Your hands are fine."

Knuck's eyes widened. "My hand!" he cried. "You dumb fuck, it's in my fucking hand!"

"But there's nothing—" I stopped myself when I remembered. After he'd turned over the backpack, the Hispanic guy handed Knuck something. As carefully as I could, I lifted Knuck's right hand and pried open his fingers. Crumbled inside was a wad of paper. I unfolded it to reveal a three-by-five index card marked with a Minneapolis address. "Did the guy say this is where Mindy is?" I asked.

Knuck nodded.

"Did he say anything else?"

"You gotta go get her!" Knuck insisted, ignoring my question. "Don't worry about me. You gotta go get Mindy."

"Of course," I assured him. "But first, just let me—
"

"There he is!" a voice called out from somewhere above me. "That's him right there!"

I raised my head. The security guard that I had laid out was back on his feet. Flanked by two other young men in uniform, he was pointing an accusing finger directly at me.

Ignoring the accusation, I shouted up at them. "This man's hurt! Call an ambulance. He needs to get to a hos—"

"That's the guy!" the first guard shrieked. "Goddamn it! That's the guy that slugged me!" While the first guard continued to jab at the air, his two fellow guards stared at him incredulously, their palms hovering over their holsters.

I slipped the address into my jacket pocket and slowly got to my feet, careful to hold my hands high and away from my body. Then I forced a benign smile, hoping they'd take me for a peaceful innocent singled out by a madman. "Your pal's obviously lost it," I called up to them. "But this guy down here? He's been shot. He needs your help right away."

All three stared motionlessly at me for a moment until the guard on the left reached up and pressed the button on his radio transmitter. I heard the words "medical emergency" and the acronym "GSW." I turned back to Knuck. When I did, the guard that I'd belted squealed, "He's getting away!" Because I had his revolver in my pocket, I got cocky, deciding I really didn't have to pay him any attention.

Not until I heard the gunshot.

I spun around to find both of his confederates gaping in shock at the first guard, who, having grabbed one of their guns, had not only fired at us but was still aiming it unsteadily at Knuck and me, ready to pop off another round. As the echo of the shot died away, fearing he might have been hit again, my eyes darted toward Knuck. But almost immediately, from behind me, a harsh grinding sound rent the gathering stillness.

I spun around, suddenly aware of a lengthening shadow creeping over us. The huge Sammy balloon that had been towering above appeared to have bent over slightly as though making a little bow. For what seemed an eternity, I stood transfixed, the angry security guard still brandishing the handgun; the gargantuan figure of the inflatable Sammy, its pumping mechanism evidently struck by the guard's wayward bullet, had ground to an abrupt halt. With horror, I realized it was about to collapse on top of us.

I lunged forward, hunching down, hoping to scoop the wounded Knuck up and out of harm's way. I didn't make it.

Before I could budge him, we were blanketed by Sammy, the thick, rubberized canvas shrouding down around us. It was heavy, enveloping me in a darkness so complete that I immediately lost any sense of where Knuck was. Panic rising, I struggled beneath the suffocating fabric, feeling around desperately for the now-vanished Knuck but finding only that my antiperspirant had not been equal to the challenges of the afternoon.

At last, my foot connected with something solid, and after much fumbling, I managed to grab hold of both an arm and a leg. Heaving, I soon tugged Knuck out from under the flattened kiddie icon, the back of my head rubbed raw by the heavy fabric.

I thought he was dead. I could no longer make out his breathing, and he lay on the ground before me as unnervingly still as a CPR dummy. But after a moment, I heard a whisper. "Go find her," he said.

As though coming out of some kind of sonic tunnel, I suddenly became aware of the sound of heavy footsteps closing in on me. Adrenaline kicked in, and I scrambled to my feet. As I rushed deeper into the park, I heard someone shout a furious "Hey!"

Ignoring the shout, I hurried down a series of mazelike paths that ran between the various rides, most lined with greenery that ranged from small shrubs to large trees. When I no longer heard pursuers, I slowed my pace, staying close to the edges of things and trying to stay out of sight. But coming once more into the open, I looked up and saw figures lining the railing on both of the floors above me. Spectators watching me, many brandishing cell phone cameras, as I jogged past a silent carousel.

About halfway across the park, I began to hear voices—lots of voices—the sound of a crowd gathering. Now that the gunfire had ended, adventurous types were returning, hoping to catch a glimpse of the bad guys and get interviewed for the TV news.

I was walking now; several clumps of gathered men moved into sight. Not wanting to be caught by a mob bent on vigilante justice, I began to gesticulate wildly as I approached them. "I think I saw them!" I shouted, pointing back toward the downed Sammy. There were guards everywhere, man! I think they got 'em."

A couple of the guys looked pretty skeptical, but others beamed with excitement. "You can see for yourself," I prodded. "That is if you can get over there before they haul 'em away."

That was enough for most. As they moved forward, I was able to slip past.

An announcement blared that the mall was closing and implored shoppers to exit the building. Folks who hadn't already fled began to move toward the exits. I joined them, making my way back up to the second floor, grateful for the opportunity to let my heartbeat return to something approaching normal. Before exiting to the parking lot, I managed a glance back down to where I'd left Knuck. He was gone, taken away, I hoped, to the hospital and not the morgue. A great circle around the fallen Sammy was now strung with yellow crime scene tape. Patrolmen were conducting interviews. Both the cops and the tourists snapped their photographs. And high above, nestled against the sun-washed glass ceiling, that balloon, the Freddy Ferret balloon released by the frightened little girl, stood sentinel—orphaned, adrift, and alone.

Chapter Fifteen

A lot of people had seen me running away after Knuck was shot. God knows how many of them may have captured the moment on their cell phones. It would be only a matter of time before the police identified me and put out a bulletin on my car.

What I really needed was a different ride, and as I walked through the steadily emptying mall parking ramp, I eyed the few remaining vehicles covetously. I knew, in theory at least, how to boost a car, but I also knew that lacking the tools and experience, helping myself to someone else's vehicle would take an impossibly long time. And if the address the Hispanic guy had given Knuck really was where Mindy was being held, I had no time to waste. So, I returned to my car, plotted the address in my phone's GPS app, and turned over the engine. There were plenty of patrol cars around, but I got lucky. No one stopped me as I pulled out of the ramp.

The address was in the Phillips neighborhood of Minneapolis, just south of the West Bank campus of the University of Minnesota. I'd normally have taken surface streets, but I didn't want to risk a lot of stops at traffic lights. Instead, I took the freeway, heading north up 35W, then east on I-94, before finally getting off at the West Bank exit.

To the left, staid and sturdy, the campus overlooked

the Mississippi River. On the right, clustered around like sugar ants on a discarded lollipop, a semicircle of restaurants, bars, retailers, offices, and even a Holiday Inn fed off the disposable income of the University's staff, its students, and their anxious-to-please parents. One of these nearby enterprises was Balmer's Bar, which, before I centered on Dinkytown as the locus of my personal and professional existence, had been a favorite watering hole of mine. Balmer's had the two things I find most important in a bar—good beer and good bouncers—and there was no better place to get thrown out of on St. Patrick's Day.

Passing the corner of Cedar and Riverside, I gazed nostalgically at Balmer's, sheltered in the shadow of the enormous Cedar Square West apartment complex that towered above it. Urban renewal on a grand scale, it was the first federally funded "new town-in-town" development in the country. The architects had idealistically striven to create a city within a city—a high-density high-rise close to schools, shops, and cultural activities with a range of units designed to appeal to everyone from low-income wage earners and students on up to high rollers interested in a room with a helluva view. Their vision was never fully realized—egalitarian utopias being so much easier to create on paper than in brick, steel, and mortar. More recently, the complex had become home to many newly arrived Somali immigrants, providing inexpensive lodgings from which to pursue their promise of a better life.

Continuing south on Cedar Avenue, however, I entered a neighborhood where most people had watched their dreams evaporate long before. There were no more quaint shops or pubs. No cheap/chic ethnic restaurants.

No Holiday Inns. Instead, there was the Little Mountain housing project, another remnant of urban renewal, this one devoted to low-income members of the American Indian community—folks who knew something about loss and broken promises. Past Little Mountain, the houses became notable for listing porches, weathered siding, and brown, scrubby lawns. A single convenience store, whose business plan—judging from the signs hung in its barred windows—was centered on the sale of cigarettes, vape pens, and single cans of malt liquor, squatted shabbily on a corner. A couple of blocks east of the store, on Sixteenth Avenue, I found the house I was looking for.

It was a yellow two-story, which, like most of the houses in the area, was fronted by a spacious open porch. But nothing about the house looked inviting. The wooden steps leading up to the porch had long since rotted away, and an overturned plastic milk crate had been drafted to serve in their stead. The porch was bare save for a thirty-gallon trash can made of green plastic, heaped with refuse. Although large windows opened to the street, they were completely shrouded by what appeared to be blankets stapled to the casing on the inside. I drove past and turned at the corner. An alley ran the length of the block, allowing access to the back of the house, but I didn't turn in. People don't like strangers driving down their alleys; it draws attention. So instead, I stuck to the street, slowing to peer down the alley and spotting a small yard behind the house largely given over to parking. There appeared to be no fewer than three vehicles back there. That wasn't good. It meant that I could be facing a pretty crowded house when I came a calling.

I parked my own car another street over and dug in my jacket for my cell phone. Although I hadn't heard it ring, I dialed up my voicemail just to make sure that Skip hadn't called me since the shooting. He hadn't. Taking no chances on missing the call when it did come, I checked to make sure that the ringer was set at maximum volume and, for good measure, set the phone to vibrate as well before slipping it back into my pocket.

I told myself that it was a good sign that Skip and the Milkman had yet to check in with me. If they'd lost the guys Knuck had given the ransom to, they'd have called right away. Their continued silence likely indicated that they were still busy following the men with the money bag. But if I was to go busting into that house looking for Mindy, I'd need backup. Even so, I hesitated before dialing. Skip wasn't someone who was known for graciousness when interrupted. But then, I reasoned, he needed to know that Knuck had been slipped an address. He needed to know that it was possible that we already knew where Mindy was.

I punched in his number. After a single ring, a computer voice came on and allowed me to leave a message. Skip was working, I reminded myself. Too busy to pick up. He'd maybe even turned the ringer off because he didn't want it to be heard. It wasn't like he'd gone home or anything. He was still out there. It wasn't like I was alone.

So, I waited. I waited as the sun slowly dipped in the sky and the shadows around me lengthened. I waited as gray crept over the street, nearly matching the gloom that was seeping into my insides. Then suddenly, out of all that gray, I was confronted by a memory as vivid as the flesh inside a blood orange. I don't know whether I'd subconsciously blocked it or if it had simply been waylaid amidst all the other dubious recollections of my growing up, but all at once, I remembered back to the time right after Vernon and Pam Murdoch were murdered, back when the Burnsville PD felt compelled to investigate the rather improbable story that Knuck Fullmer and my old man had reported with regard to Vernon Murdoch's last moments. Both Dad and Knuck had been asked to take vacation while the investigation was being conducted, and one afternoon, I returned home from school to find the blinds drawn, the lights in the house dark, and my father at the kitchen table, ostensibly reading the newspaper. We weren't really talking to one another at the time, and he barely grunted when I came in to check the fridge for something to snack on. The pickings were slim, and I was about to leave empty-handed when the phone rang. When I crossed the room to answer it, my dad leaped from his chair, nearly knocking me to the ground as he pushed past. But instead of answering the phone, he grabbed it, base and all, and ripped it off the wall. I remember the ringer tinkled a couple more times after he dashed it to the floor.

This was hardly the first time I'd seen something set him off. I'd been witness to similar scenes throughout my childhood and young adulthood, and instead of being cowed, I got cocky. Smirking, I nodded at the remains of the phone. "Someone you'd rather not talk to?" I asked.

Dad shrugged. "It was probably Knuck."

"What makes you think so?"

He shrugged again. "I asked him to call me."

Puzzled, I shook my head. "That makes no sense at all."

Dad looked at me for a moment. A genuine

expression of solemnity shone in his eyes, dampening their normally steely blue gray to a soft mist. "Sometimes things don't make sense."

I hadn't thought of that incident in years, but sitting in the car, I couldn't get it out of my mind. He was right. Sometimes things don't make sense. For example, what happened at the Liberty Mall didn't make sense. Knuck had complied with the kidnappers' demands. He'd even handed over the money. So, why'd they shoot him? They could have grabbed the cash, used the anonymity of the crowd to mask their escape, then, if they still wanted him dead, send him seeking his daughter in a much less public place. A place where a successful ambush would be more certain and much less risky. A place, I realized, like the address they actually gave him.

My anxiety level rose like stink from a plate of French cheese. This time I didn't hesitate to dial up Skip's cell phone, but I got the recording again. I left a second message, and let's just say that this one was decidedly more animated than the first. It's not that I thought he'd actually abandoned me. We'd agreed that he and the Milkman would follow the money, and I'd never known either man to shirk a responsibility once accepted. But Knuck had been shot, his daughter was still being held, for all I knew, still being abused, and, goddamn it, I'd been left stewing long enough. Of course, I immediately regretted having left the message. Skip may have been a friend (although that is, perhaps, not exactly the correct word for our relationship), but he was a pro. He wouldn't relish the prospect of going into a potentially dangerous situation with someone who couldn't keep his cool. I took a deep breath, then another, forcing myself to calm down. Alas, it took only a few minutes before my newfound patience was circling the drain.

I wasn't stupid enough to go barging into that yellow house alone, but it occurred to me that there was nothing inherently wrong with my getting out and stretching my legs. Clouds had rolled in, and even though it was only late afternoon and not yet evening, I decided that it was dark enough to risk a little clandestine recon.

I made sure to leave the doors to the Ford unlocked in case I'd be in a hurry to hop back in when I returned. I pulled on a navy Twins cap and sauntered off toward the house. I didn't exactly have a plan. I hoped to at least get a peek inside—the more details, the better for my report when Skip finally called. And since the front windows had been completely covered, I decided to first try around back. It may not have been the best idea I ever had, but I felt certain that if I forced myself to wait in the car even a few minutes longer, like a toddler strapped for too long in a grocery cart, I'd soon be pitching a serious fit.

I had the sidewalk completely to myself. Although only a couple of miles from the pedestrian-heavy University campus, there wasn't another soul out for a stroll. That wasn't necessarily a good thing. A solitary figure on a deserted street tends to attract attention, but although lights burned in several of the nearby houses, indicating that people were home, I didn't see any faces at the windows or any tell-tale twitching of curtains. I reached the entrance to the alley, confident that the good people of Phillips were heedless to my presence among them. But as I started toward the back of the house, my confidence was abruptly shattered when an unfamiliar voice beckoned to me.

It was a man's voice, and although its suddenness startled me, it was surprisingly gentle, with a lilt as if the man was chanting rather than speaking. "Hey, fucker."

I turned slowly. It seemed to be coming from across the street, but I couldn't actually see who was speaking to me. I sensed no alarm, however, no urgency or anger in his voice. Instead, it had a sleepy quality, like that of a tired father wishing his newborn sweet dreams.

"Hey, fucker," he repeated. Then, after a pause, he added, "Come here, fucker. I'll kick your ass for you, fucker."

You get called enough names by enough people over a long enough period of time, and you get inured to it. Ordinarily, a guy starts calling me names, and I barely notice. But there was something about the drowsily pleasant tone, the cadence, the way the unseen man's words floated lazily to me, wafting across the overcast street, that seriously creeped me out. It was like being threatened by an incongruously malevolent Mister Rogers.

I scanned the surrounding houses. I thought I made out movement behind some bushes in a darkened doorway opposite me, but it could have been a bird, a squirrel, anything. I listened intently but heard only my own breathing, which now seemed impossibly loud. I braced for an attack, expecting that at any moment, this likely intoxicated provoker would come after me. Or at least rise from the doorway. But nothing happened. Not until I heard a grunt and spotted an arm arcing in a hook shot above the bushes. An instant later, a rain of broken glass scattered in the street between us, gleaming fragments bouncing toward me.

I froze, ducking a little lest my invisible assailant

launch another bottle. But none came. I waited, then waited some more. A couple of minutes passed, but I neither saw nor heard anything from him again. If not for the broken glass in the street, I'd have thought I imagined him.

I nearly started back for my car but didn't think I'd be able to face myself later if I let some drunk with a beer bottle and bad aim run me off. So, instead, I entered the alley and began making my way toward the rear of the house where Mindy was likely being held.

The yard was mostly gravel with clumps of broad-leaved grass sprouting in irregular patches like hair on the pate of a chemotherapy patient. As I'd noted earlier, three cars were parked side by side along the edge of the yard, their bows pointed toward the alley. As I skirted the cars, my tennis shoes scraped noisily against the gravel. Music played. It was coming from inside the house, a thudding bass and the snap of a snare drum penetrating the walls. There was singing. I couldn't make out the words, but they were rapid-fire and strident. I spotted a door, two doors, really, an outer flimsy metal screen door and a heavier, probably fiberglass inner door with a shiny deadbolt lock. A bare light bulb burned harsh and white above.

Keeping to the shadows, I worked my way along the house until I came to two large, double-hung windows that looked into the kitchen. The curtains were drawn, but they were a porous lace, and although I had to stand on tiptoe, it was relatively easy for me to peer inside. Unfortunately, there wasn't anybody in there. Just a sink full of dishes, a '50s-era dinette set—a light blue Formica tabletop set in an aluminum frame with matching chairs with no fewer than three large glass ashtrays on the tabletop, each heaped to overflowing with stumped out cigarette butts. Evidently, that tobacco settlement money hadn't reached these people. I reached up and pushed gently on one of the windows. It was locked. I squatted down beneath it and waited.

It wasn't long before I heard the sound of voices over the music. They were loud and getting louder. I risked a peak through the window. A young Black man had entered the kitchen. He was tall with hair so closely cropped that the stubble on his head appeared to have been sprayed on with an atomizer. Another young Black man, shorter and with more hair, came in behind him. They were arguing, pointing. Pointing at a third young man who brought up the rear. This last guy I recognized. It was Cleanhead, the hoodlum whose nose I'd broken back at Mindy's restaurant. His eyes were still blackened, his nose a bit pulpy. I allowed myself a smile.

Not wanting them to spot me, I hunched down, staying as close as I dared to the window in the hope of making out their conversation. It wasn't easy. I heard one of the Black guys mention "the girl," and the other insist that something was "fucked up." He was pretty sure of himself. Although the first guy went on to make several additional comments, none of which I was able to accurately make out, the second guy kept repeating that things were "fucked up."

Cleanhead apparently didn't have anything to say despite the fact that the conversation between the other guys was growing more and more animated. Unfortunately, between the closed window and the pounding music, I couldn't be certain what they were discussing. I thought I heard one of them say, "We need to get rid of her." At least, that could have been what he said. It might have been, "We need to get windier," but that made less sense. I raised myself to peer through the window again, but when I did, Cleanhead, who had his back to me, cocked his head attentively and began to turn around.

I ducked back down, pushing myself against the wall hard enough to meld molecules with it. I listened but could no longer hear the voices inside the house. Time slowed to a syrupy drip, each second spinning long like strands of molten sugar. If Cleanhead had spotted me, I thought, at any moment, he and his pals would come barreling out the back door. I could make for the alley and hopefully outrun both the lads inside the house and, if necessary, their neighbor, the evil Mister Rogers. Or I could round the corner of the house and head for the front. I liked the second option. It was more unexpected. If I didn't make too much noise, I might even get lucky and escape while they searched the alley for me. I decided to break for it as soon as I heard the back door open. But instead of the door opening, I heard only a soft thumping that seemed to emanate not from within the house but from far off. It took a moment before I realized that it was the sound of my own heart beating against the wall.

I pushed back, ready to take flight. I stayed that way for a long time. Long enough for me to feel ridiculous. Long enough for me to decide that Cleanhead hadn't actually spotted me. I rose back up on my toes and again looked through the window. All three men had taken seats at the kitchen table; the two Black guys were both smoking cigarettes, while Cleanhead had assumed what I now recognized as his normal position, sitting slumped in a chair, his eyes sleepy slits.

I crouched back down out of sight. I'd done all I could. I hadn't confirmed whether Mindy was in the house but, excepting the unlikely circumstance of her suddenly appearing in the kitchen to make everyone grilled cheese sandwiches, I'd have to enter the house to do that. And going in without backup would be foolish. It was clearly time to go.

Since the boys in the kitchen had a pretty clear view of the backyard, I decided to circle around to the front of the house. I'd taken maybe two steps when something came alive in my jacket pocket.

Whatever it was began wriggling frantically against the fabric that confined it. Simultaneously, music began to blare. This music clearly wasn't coming from inside the house. It was much too close. Much too loud. I stopped in my tracks, swatting wildly at the quivering invader in my jacket pocket and spinning about, trying to determine the source of the music. The all too familiar music.

It was the Minnesota Twins fight song. Shit! It was my cell phone. I'd forgotten to silence the ringer. The movement inside my pocket was no wayward rodent but rather my phone vibrating; the blaring tune that so definitively announced my presence outside the house was my ringtone.

The rear screen door banged against the door jamb, and footsteps thudded dully on the hard-packed ground behind me. I didn't turn around. Instead, I put my head down and barreled around the front corner of the house. I stopped, plastered myself against the wall, yanked my revolver from my shoulder holster, and waited. The door banged again and then again. Cleanhead was the first to round the corner. He'd got himself another nine millimeter to replace the one Knuck and I had taken away from him at Mindy's. I took a shot at him before he could turn it on me, but my bullet went wide of target, grazing his left side instead of striking him dead center. He yelped and, grabbing at his injured side, dropped his gun. Things were looking up, I thought. But then Cleanhead's two confederates raced around the corner, both firing blindly. One, like Cleanhead, had a nine-millimeter semiautomatic, the other a fully automatic machine pistol. I dropped to the ground as the world around me exploded in thousands of tiny shards.

Above me, the air became a cloud of gun smoke swarming with bullets. The sound was deafening. I felt a couple of tugs at my jacket, and then my left thigh seared with sudden pain as though someone had pressed it with a branding iron. I gritted my teeth and closed my eyes, waiting for more bullets to find me. Waiting to be pierced in the vitals, for my blood to pool warmly around me. Instead, the shooting stopped altogether.

I lay face down in the unexpected quiet, pawing at the dirt with both hands, realizing forlornly that I'd lost my revolver. Something nudged me. A foot. I opened my eyes as someone grabbed me roughly by the collar. Someone else waved the machine pistol in my face, the barrel close enough to give a butterfly kiss.

"You know this fat fuck?" the tall Black man with the machine pistol asked.

Cleanhead hobbled over, grimacing frightfully and clutching his injured side. I was pulled to my feet.

"Goddamn right, I know him," Cleanhead replied. Despite his bullet wound, he smiled thinly. Then he reared back, his gun in his hand. I'm not sure what happened after that. The ground opened up and swallowed me whole.

Chapter Sixteen

I was swimming. It was my family's first trip to the ocean. Our only trip there. My kid brother Chuck was bouncing happily in the water beside me. Around us, waves rolled in endlessly—blue-gray and cold as ice. A mist hovered offshore, swirling at the base of the sea stacks that towered out there—improbable columns of dark brown earth stretching skyward, topped with pines that were gnarled and stunted from the wind. Chuck was trying to time the waves perfectly, leaping into the air just as they reached him, just as they curled into rams' heads that broke hard for the shore. I waded further out into the foam-flecked swells, shuddering as the frigid water slopped against my bare belly. Mom and Dad had both stayed on the beach. Mom was lying on her back on a blanket; Dad sat upright in a canvas camp chair staring out at the surf.

A wave lifted me. Laughing, I waited for it to set me back down, but after several seconds, my cycling feet were still vainly seeking purchase in the soft sand below me. I was floating.

I turned toward Chuck, who was still bouncing but now many yards away. I watched curiously at first but then with increasing panic as Chuck became smaller and smaller. I tried to call out to him when a surge took me, and Chuck was gone. Everything was gone, enveloped in a dense gray that stopped my nose and stung my eyes.

I was underwater.

I kicked, hoping to propel myself to where the gray seemed lighter—to the surface—but things only grew darker. The taste of salt in my mouth was now so intense that it burnt my tongue; the mocking water surrounding me dared me to drink. To quench the fire. Arms flailing, a dreadful pressure began to mount in my chest. I went limp, hoping that buoyancy would carry me to the surface, but instead, I seemed to remain suspended, motionless, the gray seeping into me, gathering into my chest cavity, curling me into a fetal ball. I closed my eyes tight and prayed. It took a few moments, but at last, the pressure simply became too much for me to bear. I opened my mouth to scream.

Instead, I coughed. Over and over—paroxysmal coughs that followed one after another, violent enough to turn me inside out. Finally, I managed to suck in some air. I held my breath, convulsing until the need to cough subsided.

My throat was raw. A thick liquid—salty like the ocean—dribbled from my lips. I was bone-chilled and shivering uncontrollably, but I didn't seem to be in the water anymore. I couldn't see anything, unsure whether my eyes were open or closed. My head seemed impossibly heavy. Far too heavy to lift. The left side of my face was strangely thick, the eyelid drooping as though filled with liquid. I was so numb that I could only sense, rather than actually feel, how injured I was. The pain, I knew, would come later. But there was a stench. A pungent combination of tangy sweat and something…something earthy. Something I'd smelled before. Something from a murder scene. Blood, I realized.

I tried to move my arms but couldn't even feel them. Perhaps, I thought, I no longer had arms. Still blind, I concentrated on moving my eyelids, up or down, it didn't matter which. After much experimentation, I became convinced they were closed, but they seemed gluey and heavy as a plate from a barbell. When I finally managed to pry my eyes open, the world was a gauzy blur. I stared vainly for several moments before the shadows began to coalesce.

A pool of saliva mixed with blood stained the front of my shirt. There was a carpet under my feet, so I assumed I was inside. I seemed to be sitting. Sitting in an armchair. A very ugly armchair upholstered in threadbare terrycloth dyed a peculiar shade of nearly iridescent yellow. A length of twisted linen encircled my left thigh. Freckled with pale blue flowers, it appeared to have been torn from a bed sheet. A tourniquet, I realized. Like my shirt, it was also stained with blood. Below the tourniquet, my leg seemed frozen, bristling with needles as though I'd been frostbitten. When I tried to wiggle my toes, the entire leg seared with pain. I let out a loud groan.

Slowly and with increasing pain, I managed to raise my head. I wasn't at the ocean, I realized. I was inside the yellow house. The ocean had been a long time ago.

I tried to stand. I tried hard, but the relays that connected my brain to my legs appeared to have been severed. They registered no movement whatsoever. I let my head sink back down to my chest.

Within moments, I was back in the water. This time, my head had cleared the surface, and my eyes searched for the shore. But the blue gray of the water surrounding me began to darken as though something murky beneath the water's surface was rising from the depths to greet me. Panicked, I pulled my legs upward as a large wave broke around me, pushing me forward. The wave saved me. I could now see the shore only some fifty yards distant. Now, if only I could move. If only I could swim to shore.

I tried to move my arms again, but my muscles had turned to sludge. My arms floated uselessly, pathetically, at my side. Another wave lifted me, heaving me forward once again, luckily even closer to the shore.

Incredibly, my dad was sitting there on the sand. There was no sign of Chuck or my mom, just Dad. Then, as though an apparition, Knuck was beside him. Both were calmly looking out to sea toward me.

"I've got you, Dahms," a soft voice sounded quite close to me. "We're gonna get you out of here."

My dad's voice, I thought at first. But no, I realized, not him. Someone, though. Someone I knew. I forced my eyes open. Skip's face floated lazily before me.

"Help me get him out of here," Skip said, and I felt myself being picked up, first to my feet, then up into the cradle of someone's arms.

"You're safe," the Milkman told me. "We're gonna get you to a doctor."

I opened my mouth. There was something I needed to say. Something important. But I just couldn't hold on to what it was. My thoughts, like shards of melting ice, kept slipping from me—skittering away, leaving watery trails in their wake. Soon, even these were gone.

When I came to again, I appeared to be moving, being carried along, bouncing painfully. And there was humming. Loud humming. Like I'd been packed in a crate along with a beehive. I wanted to scream, but all I could do was squeeze my eyelids tight against the bees.

Then, the bees were gone. I was no longer in motion. I had the impression that I'd been sleeping but didn't know how long. A long time, I feared.

I hurt bad. Really bad. Everything ached. My eyelashes ached. My fingernails. I felt like a bruised piece of fruit rotting in the sun. Only it wasn't the sun. It was a bright light. And people were talking. First a man, then a woman. Then someone completely different came in, talking loudly, trying to sell me a Honda. He assured me that there were dozens to choose from. Not real, I realized. It was the television.

I opened my eyes. Again, everything was shifting and indistinct. I could tell that I was lying flat on a bed. There was a light over me, reflecting brilliantly off the stiff, white sheets. The sheets smelled clean. The air smelled clean, too. Impossibly clean, even antiseptic. Something creaked next to the bed, like someone shifting in a metal chair. I tried to turn my head to see who it was but stopped when my neck gave off a muffled crack. I let out a low moan.

I heard a slight gasp, and then Naomi's gentle voice came to me. "Lyle," she said. "Lyle, can you hear me?"

I tried to answer. I even heard my own voice, but I could only make out garbled sounds—like a hoarse pig grunting underwater. I reached toward Naomi, wanting to touch her, to be sure that she was really there, but stopped when I felt a sharp sting in my right arm. A needle. A needle attached to an IV. I stared at the narrow tubing flowing out of my arm. It seemed to be draining me, carrying me away. I was melting, blurring, taking the light with me, riding on it as though on water. Water circling down a drain.

More time passed. The light returned. Once again,

there were voices, but this time, I recognized them as coming from the television. But that meant someone might be there, watching. I listened. After a moment, I heard the creaking sound again. I tried to turn toward the sound, but my neck was now frozen in place. "Naomi," I called. There was more chair creaking. I was able to open my eyes. Things were still a bit smeary but much clearer than before. With slow effort, I forced my head to turn to the side, toward the chair where I'd seen Naomi waiting for me.

I felt a lurch in my guts when instead of my sweetie, Augie Tarkof's face swam into view. "Just in time," he smiled. "They're talking about you again."

Augie nodded toward the wall opposite the bed. I turned my head. It seemed easier now. On the television screen was a grainy longshot of Camp Sammy—rides twirling, kids squealing. There came a couple of popping noises, and suddenly, the squeals turned to screams. The crowd fell back, and the giant Sammy balloon began to crumple. The camera moved in tight as the fabric of the great fallen Sammy rippled, and a man emerged, dragging something with him. The camera moved in even tighter. There was no mistaking it. It was clearly me.

"They've been running it incessantly," Tarkof told me. "Like they can't get enough of it. Like it's that footage of the Hindenburg disaster or that bridge that blew down in Washington back in the '40s." He laughed. "And it ain't just the TV. It's the newspapers, too. You're everywhere. Got one right here if you want to see it."

I nodded.

Tarkof reached over to the bedside table and picked

up a newspaper. Beaming, he held it up to reveal a front-page photo of me, a close-up evidently taken from a frame of the same video the TV news crew was using. Above the picture, a headline read, "Sammy Assassin Sought."

"Shit," I muttered.

"Yep," Tarkof told me, "you're quite the media darling, Dahms. Your mug's been plastered all over town for days. So, I guess it's not so surprising that I get a call this morning from the charge nurse saying that the guy that killed America's favorite squirrel is in a bed down here after having had the absolute shit kicked out of him. Who did this to you, Dahms? Was it Sammy's gang? Freddy Ferret? Wanda Weasel? Was it revenge for what you did to Sammy?" He smirked. "Looks like that Patty Platypus isn't someone you want to mess with."

"Water," I said.

"What?"

I smacked my lips, so thick and swollen they barely moved. "Water," I repeated.

Tarkof looked around briefly before spotting a plastic cup beside a pitcher of water on a tray by the bed. He filled the cup and moved it slowly to within a few inches of my face.

"Straw," I said.

Tarkof screwed up his face in puzzlement. "Demanding, ain't you?" he asked as he hunted up a straw from the same tray.

He moved the straw close enough for me to reach it. I took a grateful sip. "How's Fullmer?" I asked.

Tarkof became suddenly interested in my IV, prodding the half-filled bladder of saline with a stubby finger. "Your dad's old partner?" he asked. "I was wondering how long it would take you to ask about him. To tell the truth, he's not doing very well. Took a slug in the chest, you know. They managed to dig it out of him, but…" Tarkof spread his hands apart helplessly before him. "Doctor says he'll probably make it. That is unless he gets an infection or something." Tarkof tapped the IV lightly with his fingernail before turning back to me. "Hospitals are the worst place for sick people. You know that?"

I nodded.

"Now I seen the tapes," he continued. "And we talked to about a zillion witnesses. We know it wasn't you that shot him. What we'd like to know is, who did?"

"Don't know," I managed. "Above and behind me. Didn't see nobody."

Tarkof leaned in toward me. "Okay, but you got some idea. You didn't go in there with no idea of what you were getting into."

I began to slip back into fatigue. My eyes closed. "You sure?" I asked.

I felt Tarkof's hand on my shoulder. I winced, wondering if any part of me wasn't bruised. Tarkof let go. "You need to stay with me, Dahms," I heard him say, although he now seemed quite far away. "We need to…"

\*\*\*\*

I didn't hear anything else for what turned out to be a long time. When I awoke, the room was dead quiet. No television chatter, no beeping machines, nothing. I wondered if I were still in the hospital.

I opened my eyes. Edgerton was in the chair beside my bed. He had a pair of half-moon reading glasses perched low on his nose and a thin, hardbound book open on his lap.

"How we doing?" I asked.

Edgerton closed the book. "I'm doing fine," he told me. "Thanks for asking." He smiled thinly. "Against all odds, you're doing pretty good too. You got a couple of cracked ribs, a nasty cut on your thigh, but they stitched that up, and your nose…Well, for a while, your nose looked like it pulled stakes and tried to move across your face. But they pretty well fixed that. How do you feel?"

"Spiffy," I mumbled.

Edgerton shrugged. "Not that any of this makes any difference to you," he said. "After all, you decide to get yourself beat to a pulp just because you can't wait around for your backup, it's really nobody's business but yours."

"You're pissed," I said. Actually, my mouth was so dry it sounded more like *"Chore piffed."*

Edgerton understood anyway. "I suppose I'd be pissed if I thought about it. I mean, if you die, I'd have to break in a new best friend. Still, no big deal. I've got the Milkman on the bench, and he's not the kind to ever pull anything this selfish."

I tried to smile, but bruised and as puffy as a blowfish, my mouth barely twitched. "Best friend?" I slurred.

Edgerton ignored me. "The cops have been by," he said. "They promised to come back. Your mom's been by, too. She's a bit of a mess. Too many Dahms men in the hospital over too short a time. But Irv took her home and has been looking in on her. You should call her as soon as possible."

I nodded slowly. "Any word on Fullmer?"

"From what they tell me, he's doing pretty well. He's going to be here a while, but they say he's improving slowly."

"Mindy?" I asked thickly.

Edgerton put his lips together grimly. "No."

I pointed at a plastic cup of water with a straw on the tray poised above my bed. Edgerton picked up the cup and moved the straw to my pursed lips. "She wasn't in the house?" I asked at last.

"Not according to Skip and the Milkman," Edgerton told me. "You were all alone when they got there. You shoulda heard Irv berating himself for not getting there earlier. The guy can't help but blame himself anytime anything bad happens to a friend. You should talk to him, too."

I nodded. "How long?" I asked.

His eyes narrowed with confusion. "Since the incident?" he asked. "It's been three days."

"How'd they find me?"

Edgerton smiled benevolently, his face beginning to blur. "I'll tell you another time."

"And the money?" I asked as the whole room began to swim from view.

"Gone," I heard Edgerton say.

"Hmm," I moaned. "I thought sure Skip would get ahold of it."

"He may have been sidetracked."

I grunted. "Tell him he's fired."

"He's the one who brought you in." Edgerton didn't say it, but the last word in that sentence was "alive." Skip brought you in *alive*.

I tried to smile. "In that case, tell him I'll keep him on. But he's damn sure on probation."

## Chapter Seventeen

It turned out not to be much of a story after all. Skip and the Milkman had been watching carefully when the two guys grabbed Knuck's money. With Sammy collapsing spectacularly behind them, the bad guys headed out of the mall, and Skip went for his BMW while the Milkman trailed after them. Over an open cell phone connection, Irv was able to let Skip know which level of the parking ramp they were on and soon he and Skip were pulling out on the road behind a white four-door sedan driven by their quarries.

Everything was going smoothly. Skip and the Milkman followed the sedan up MN-77 and onto Cedar Avenue by the 5-8 Club at the south end of Lake Nokomis. They turned right onto East Fifty-Eighth Street, with Skip keeping his distance and his eyes squared on them. But along about Twenty-Second Avenue, a mom driving with her three kids in one of those big honking soccer mom vans pulled out in front of Skip at the precise moment a UPS truck began to pull away from the curb. Both vehicles entered the exact same space at the exact same time with the usual result— shrieking brakes, horns, and crumbled fenders. Skip was just far enough back to avoid them as they collided, but by the time he'd maneuvered around them, he'd lost the bad guys.

Skip then tried to reach me on my cell phone. No

luck. After a few more futile attempts, someone called *him* using my phone. That someone told Skip where to come find what was left of me. The voice was muffled; no way to tell who the caller was.

When they got close, Skip and the Milkman drove through streets filled with squad cars, lights flashing, spotlights sweeping. Whoever called in the report of shots fired must have been directionally challenged because the cops concentrated most of their activity about a block and a half north of where I actually was. Skip was able to park right in front of the yellow house and, to hear him tell it, he and the Milkman just ambled up to the front door like they owned the place. They didn't even have to break in. The door was unlocked, and the house was empty. No one there but me.

The Milkman must have thought I was dead. He looked down at me, his cheeks glowing red and tears starting to form in his big, blue eyes. He was turning away when Skip tugged at his sleeve. I let out a soft moan, followed by what Skip described as the mother of all farts. "Big enough to be recorded by seismologists at the U of M," he said.

Why'd they call Skip? Why didn't they just kill me? Why, with the likelihood of cops swarming the house any minute, had someone taken the time to haul my ass into the house and even wrap a tourniquet on my leg? None of us could figure that at all.

Over the next couple of days, the cops kept stopping by my hospital room. Augie alternating with a younger, better-looking detective named Mickey Lydecker. Neither told me I was under arrest. Neither said I wasn't.

Skip, Edgerton, and the Milkman also seemed to alternate, so one of them was nearly always with me. To their credit, they each watched a lot of bad TV as I drifted in and out of consciousness.

To the best of my knowledge, Naomi did not visit again.

After five days in the hospital, I started to feel like maybe I would live. Over my strenuous protests, a tag team of nurses managed to force me to get out of bed and take my first steps since what everyone was still calling "the incident." By that time, I'd pretty much become a hospital bed habitué, and I was less than enthusiastic about having to abandon my new "supine" lifestyle.

But it turned out that I was powerless against the odd combination of bland smiles and steely insistence that characterized my nurses. Over the next couple of days, the nurse team increased both the number of times they came for me and the distance they forced me to walk. I eventually had to admit that the walking might be good for me as my strength slowly returned.

I also slowly started to think like an investigator again. I even remembered to call Harley Rocker in Baltimore to see if she had learned anything more about the robbery that had sent Tooz to prison.

She'd been trying to reach me. When she hadn't been able to, she'd done an internet search, so she knew all about my little visit to the Liberty Mall. But, businesslike, she kept the conversation to the facts of the long-ago robbery. She told me that the Baltimore PD had no record of a known accomplice of Williard Tousignant named Vernon Murdoch. Rocker went on, however, to interview a street hustler named Itchy Patinkin, who said he used to do business with both Tooz and his partner, Stubby Petowski. Itchy confirmed that "old Vern" was definitely part of the circle. After the robbery and

Tousignant's imprisonment, Itchy reportedly stopped seeing "old Vern" around the neighborhood.

Rocker also reported that the drug dealer killed in the robbery that Tooz did time for was part of a crew working with the Colombian cartel. By all accounts, they were well-connected and very successful. The cops had found neither money nor drugs in the house after the killing—just Tousignant, Petowski, and the corpse. If Murdoch had been involved and if he'd taken off with the goods, he might have been holding on to a small fortune. A lot of "ifs," but I had little else to go on.

Another thing Ms. Rocker did was examine the records that the prison maintained on the folks who visited Tooz during his twenty-three-year stretch. At first, there were quite a number. No fewer than four different women made nearly weekly independent visits until one Valentine's Day when they all logged in at basically the same time. None of them came to visit after that.

Janos Bollok, a frequent visitor throughout, was listed as having picked up Tooz the day he was finally released. And there was one very curious entry to the visitors' log. Not long after Vernon and Pam Murdoch were killed, Tooz was visited by two out-of-town police officers—John Fullmer and Raymond Dahms.

I suppose it shouldn't have surprised me that Knuck and my dad decided to do their own investigation of the Murdoch murders. After all, they were on suspension and likely thought that shedding more light on the circumstances would speed their return to duty. And my old man was always like a dog with a bone when it came to what he thought needed to be done. But Knuck had been definite when I asked him the day Mindy went missing. He said he didn't know Willard Tousignant.

Of course, he was distraught, not thinking clearly, and that visit to Baltimore had been a long time ago. Still…

I tried to remember everything that Knuck had told me. From the beginning.

The way he'd presented it, the meeting with Latrine and Cleanhead was about protecting Mindy and her restaurant. Actually, *their* restaurant. Knuck had said he'd invested in it, and, according to him, other than the amateurish attempts at sabotage, everything was all set for a successful opening and a successful father/daughter partnership. Then, before the first customers get to place an order, for no good reason, Knuck shoots a guy in front of the place, and a couple of days later, Mindy is kidnapped, and somebody shakes Knuck down for a hundred grand. He comes up with it, too.

I'd assumed that he'd invested most of his retirement savings in the restaurant, and if my dad was any example, a suburban cop's retirement nest egg would be more wren than ostrich-sized. If his money was tied up in the restaurant, how had Knuck come up with the ransom?

When I asked him, he'd said Mindy had investors. He'd been pretty specific, too. He said they were the guys behind Morey's in downtown Minneapolis.

I'd eaten at Morey's a couple of times. Mostly for the kitsch factor. When it had first opened, the place was a full-on tribute to funnyman Morey Amsterdam, with photographs from the Van Dyke show on every wall, and Morey's one and only hit as a songwriter, *Rum and Coca-Cola,* in heavy rotation on the background music. They'd since cooled on the concept, keeping the name but eliminating most of the Amsterdam paraphernalia. There was, however, still a small photo of Morey and his cello behind the hostess station.

I didn't know who owned the place now, but I did know a guy named Corey who worked there. I'd gotten to know him during his time as a line cook at McCauley's. He was a good-natured, enthusiastic kid who loved Pink Floyd. Whenever it was his turn to choose the music in McCauley's kitchen, Corey would play *Dark Side of the Moon*. If you looked over the counter and saw Corey working the grill, chances are you'd hear the strains of either *Money* or *Time* tripping into the dining room. After a few months, I thought I'd do us all a favor, and I offered to buy the CD from Corey. He immediately offered to make a copy for me and didn't seem to understand when I insisted that I wanted only the original. No copies allowed.

Corey eventually decided to make cooking his career, leaving McCauley's to get a culinary degree at Minneapolis Community & Technical College. I'd since heard that, armed with that degree, he'd found a gig at Morey's.

I called the restaurant and left a message for Corey, who they said would be starting work a little later that afternoon. When he called back, I asked him if he knew anything about Morey's owners investing in a new restaurant called Mindy's. He didn't but allowing to my recent celebrity status of having gunned down Sammy Squirrel and all, he was eager to look into it for me. It wasn't too long before he called back again, telling me that the deal between Mindy and Morey's had fallen through some time ago. Long before Knuck had asked me to back him up at the meeting with Latrine and

Cleanhead.

I was still turning that over in my head when Knuck came to visit me. Skip was sitting sentinel at my bedside. The door was open, and we both watched as Knuck moved slowly down the corridor toward us. Skip shifted slightly as Knuck approached but otherwise kept his eyes on the book he was reading. Knuck inched his way forward, one hand grasping the rolling metal pole that held his IV. A nurse hovered a step behind him.

He looked like hell.

Hunched over, he appeared to have shrunken a couple of inches, and his previously rail-thin build now seemed positively skeletal. His eyes were hollow, the skin of his face stretched tight across his high cheekbones, and he winced with each step, his grimace accentuating his skull-like appearance.

Watching him come, I was struck by something. I wasn't angry at him. Maybe I should have taken this as a sign of personal growth. Maybe it was just how helpless he looked, but after all he'd gotten me into, after all the lies he been telling me, after all the pain I'd been through, I wasn't angry at him. I guess I realized that my dad's old partner was simply a guy who did what he thought needed to be done. Not so unlike my old man. Through everything Knuck had put me through, from gunning down Latrine Hawkins to pulling his gun on me at McCauley's to risking his life out there in the open at the Liberty Mall, Knuck Fullmer was just a guy who did what he thought was necessary. No matter the cost. No matter who got in the way.

When Knuck reached the door, Skip turned to me and cocked his head in question.

"I gotta talk to him," I said.

Skip shrugged, rose to his feet, and aimed a huge if lopsidedly disarming smile at Knuck's nurse. Taking her by the arm, Skip began to escort her out into the hallway. "They'll be okay without us for a couple of minutes," he assured her. She looked dubious but followed him out the door.

They didn't get far. Instead, my nurse—a short, sturdy blonde with a bright white overbite and forearms like a Teamster—picked that moment to further speed my recovery. She breezed into the room, half saying, half singing, "Time for another stroll, Mr. Dahms."

"I got company," I complained, pointing at Knuck.

"Oh, good," she smiled. "It's high time that Mr. Fullmer was out of bed as well. We can all do this together."

"But I just took a walk a couple of hours ago," I reminded her.

"Then you ought to be better at it this time," she said, her tone becoming a trifle brittle.

"Can't it wait just a—"

Knuck may have looked like the walking dead, but he'd been a cop for a long time, and one thing an old cop lives for is busting balls. "Whatsa matter, Lyle," Knuck interrupted, his eyes brightening infinitesimally, "Too weak to go for a walk with an old man?"

My nurse patted my bed covers. "The sooner we get you up, the sooner you'll get to lie back down."

I sighed, sat up, and swung my legs over the edge of the bed. Too fast, it turned out. My vision blurred, and I had to press my palm against my forehead to keep my head from swimming away.

Knuck chuckled as the nurse helped me to my feet. "Christ, Lyle," he said. "I'm the one that got shot."

"I got shot, too," I protested, pointing to the bandage on my left thigh that was visible beneath the all-too-short hemline of my hospital gown.

"Shit," Knuck sneered. "I've cut myself shaving worse than that."

I raised an eyebrow. "Why are you shaving your legs, Knuck?"

Moments later, our nurses led us both out into the hallway, Skip following a discreet distance behind. Clutching our IV stands and making vain attempts to keep the backs of our gowns closed, side-by-side Knuck and I began taking halting steps down the hall. After an eternity, we made it to the end of one hallway and were about to head down another when I turned to my nurse, who held my arm just above the elbow with a vise grip. "I think I can solo for a while."

When she let go of my arm, Skip, who was following behind, took a long stride forward and turned to cut off both the nurses. "Let's let them go on a bit by themselves," he suggested. "They fall, we'll be right behind to pick them up."

My nurse started to protest but Skip asked, "Honestly, how far away from us can they get?"

I'm not sure they shared his optimism, but Skip can be pretty persuasive. I've seen him sit belligerent drunks down with little more than a glance. The nurse studied Skip's expression—smiling yet cast with an immutable insistence—and paused long enough to allow Knuck and me a measure of distance.

"Have you heard anything from—" Knuck began.

I shook my head. "Nothing. From Mindy or anybody else. You?"

He shook his head. "The cops have her apartment

staked out, but there's been no sign of her. No phone calls. Nothing. We can't just sit here. We gotta do something. We gotta—"

"We?" I asked.

Knuck stared. "You quitting on me, Lyle? Is that what this is?"

"You ever been to the coast, Knuck?"

"What the fuck's that got to do with anything?"

"I've been dreaming about the ocean is all," I said. "My folks brought Chuck and me to the ocean once. I think it was my sophomore year in high school. The Washington coast. Don't know why Dad picked Washington. Water was cold as a freaking Slushy, even in the summertime. Still, it was the first time I ever saw an ocean. Pretty impressive."

"What the hell you talking about, Lyle? I know you got hit in the head, but—"

"You and the family didn't make that trip with us, did you? I mean, our families spent enough time together. I sometimes can't remember what all we did. We went there during that time you and Dad were on suspension following the Murdoch murders."

"No, we didn't go with you that time," Knuck said. "You sure you're all right? I mean, this isn't a good time to reminisce about old times. My daughter's missing and—"

"You're probably more of an East Coast guy," I said.

He blinked a couple of times but didn't respond.

"You've been to the East Coast, right Knuck?"

"Of course, I've been to the—"

"You went to Balto with my dad once, didn't you? Back when you guys were looking into that Murdoch business?"

Knuck stopped walking. "What are you getting at, Lyle?"

I shrugged and took a toddling step forward. Knuck followed closely behind.

"The thing is, you haven't been straight with me from the beginning. You treated me like a goddamned mushroom since the day you marched into my office— keeping me in the dark and feeding me shit. I've been shot. I got beat to within an inch of my life. I've been fingered as the killer of America's favorite squirrel. And for what? I haven't the faintest idea."

"I did all that to help Mindy," Knuck insisted. "You know that."

We'd reached the end of the hallway. I glanced back at Skip and the nurses, then at a grouping of four chairs off to our right.

"Knuck and I are going to grab a seat for a minute," I said. "Rest up. We'll let you know when we're ready to walk back."

"I have other patients, Mr. Dahms," my nurse said. "I don't have the time to—"

"I can stay with them," Skip offered.

My nurse started to protest, but after staring at us for several seconds, she finally threw up her hands. "Let me know if you need help getting them back in their rooms," she said before motioning for the other nurse to follow her. They were long gone before Knuck and I were able to lower ourselves into the chairs. Finally settled, I waited for him to continue.

"I haven't been a very good dad," he said at last. "When she was little, Mindy wanted to spend every minute she could with me. It's funny what you remember. I mostly remember her hugs. She'd just come right up to me all the time and give me these great big hugs with those teeny, little arms."

He smiled. "I didn't have much time for her back then, and when I finally began to make the time, she wasn't all that interested anymore. Then, after years of barely tolerating me, she came to me with the restaurant idea. Asked could I put some money into it. Be an investor. I thought it was our chance to start over. But it went to hell." He paused. "Things always go to hell."

"Tell me about it, Knuck," I said. "The truth this time."

He paused. "The truth's a slippery thing, Lyle. You know that. It's hard to know where to begin."

"Let me help," I offered. "Why'd you shoot Latrine Hawkins?"

"It's like I told the cops. They made a play for me. I had to do it."

I smiled. "Bullshit, Knuck. They were unarmed. Latrine wasn't carrying and we had Slidel's gun. You went after them. You decided to take them out. You going to tell me why?"

"Some other time," he said. "Right now, we gotta—"

"I told you before. There's no *we*. Not anymore. Not unless you stop feeding me crap."

"I'm telling you the truth, Lyle. I didn't have no reason to go after them two. What would possibly possess me to step into that pile of shit?"

"Mindy," I said. "You were angry. You felt betrayed. You realized that Mindy had been lying to you. You weren't going to punish her, but you damn sure were going to punish someone. So, you went after

Hawkins and Slidel.

"Ah, Lyle! That's crazy talk. That's what that is."

"I know about your investors, Knuck. I know they pulled out. My guess is that you and Mindy were looking at some major cash flow issues. You'd put money in the restaurant, but not enough. And not as much as you could have. We know that because you came up with the ransom money. Did she ask you, Knuck? Did she ask you to put up more cash? And did you say no?"

Knuck turned to stare at the IV pole at the side of his chair. At the slow, monotonous drip of the saline solution. At how the plastic tubing ran from the bag into his arm.

"How'd you know they were working for Mindy, Knuck?" I pressed. "And when did you know it?"

Knuck fingered the band of tape that encircled his forearm, holding the IV needle in place. "Only way it made sense," he said at last. "It wasn't just one thing. It was everything. I kept thinking about it when we were talking to those two. Listening to their bullshit story. Wondering why they'd shake down an ex-cop. Wondering why they weren't afraid. Mindy and I…"

Knuck paused. "Mindy and I'd hit a rough patch. We had everything in that restaurant. And it wasn't enough. It *was* enough, but then, all of a sudden, our partners pull their investment. Concentrating on other opportunities, they said. If we were gonna open, we had to have more money. She came to me. She begged me. But I'd done all I was gonna do. She's a grown woman, and I'm a…I'm an old man. I just couldn't go into the poor house for her. Not for her business anyway. I couldn't do that either to her mother or to me. But she was determined. She was gonna open even if she had to bleed me dry. And you know what, I really can't fault her for that. I taught her that. I taught her not to back down. To always look for another way. To be resourceful. Bringing in those two to shake me down for more money. That was her other way."

Knuck flashed a brief smile at the thought. He was proud, I realized. Proud that his daughter had turned out so much like him. "You should know that I didn't mean to shoot that kid. I just wanted to find out for sure if she'd hired them. I *needed* to find out for sure."

"Did you?"

Knuck shook his head. "I asked. They wouldn't talk. Things happened."

"You think Mindy set you up at the mall?" I asked. "You think she staged her own disappearance? You think the ransom money went to her?"

It took him a while to answer and when he did, his voice was surprisingly calm. "I don't know, Lyle. It's possible."

"You know what that means, right?"

Knuck nodded. "They shot me. I gave them the money, and they still shot me. I can understand that Mindy thought she needed the money. I can understand her finding a way to get it out of me. What I don't understand is why she'd think she needed me dead."

"The money?" I asked. "The money you gave them. Where'd it come from?"

Knuck sighed. "Had to mortgage everything I had. Sold the boat. Cashed in some bonds. Even borrowed from some people ain't the kind you want to owe. Every fucking dime I ever saved and probably every dime I was ever gonna save. That's where it came from. Phyllis and me? We're never gonna get back where we were. But you know what, Lyle? It would have been worth it. It would have been worth losing everything just to have Mindy back and safe."

I shook my head. "You sure, Knuck? You sure that money wasn't from someplace else?"

Knuck face scrunched with puzzlement. "What you mean 'someplace else'?"

I shrugged. "You sure that money isn't from a long time back? Back when Vernon and Pam Murdoch were killed?"

Knuck stared me. "This ain't the first time you asked me about the Murdochs lately, Lyle. Something on your mind?"

I nodded. "Yeah. I'm wondering if something happened that day. The day you and my dad found them."

Knuck sighed. "Not this bullshit again. I'm tellin' ya, Lyle. People been asking us about that for fucking years. Your dad and me. We were investigated. We were cleared. What the fuck more do you all want from me?"

"Just the truth, Knuck. I'd like the truth."

Knuck was silent for some time. Then he looked me squarely in the eyes, his expression calm and sincere. "You shouldn't be asking about that, Lyle. It can't lead to no good. You know that if I was involved in that shit back then, your dad would have to have been involved, too. You know that?"

"I know."

Knuck turned his head, placed both his hands on the arms of his chair, and slowly pushed himself to his feet. I watched in silence as he began to make his way in an uneasy gait down the hall toward his room.

He was several feet away when he turned. "You

know, Lyle," he said. "Parents will do almost anything to protect their kids. Maybe sometimes you kids could do what you can to protect us back."

Chapter Eighteen

A couple of days later, they let me out of the hospital. To my surprise, no criminal charges had been filed. Tarkof said that after reviewing all the available videotape, it was clear that I hadn't shot anybody. Not even Sammy Squirrel. I did coldcock that security guard, but a review of those same tapes showed his actions had been reckless and endangered those he'd been hired to protect. As a result, he'd been relieved of his duties. Unfortunately, none of that videotape showed who *had* done the shooting. Tarkof and company had no idea who'd gunned down Knuck.

Although the medical people decided to let me go home, Augie informed me that I wasn't going to get off scot-free. The folks who manage America's biggest shopping mall made it clear that I would not be welcome there ever again. Just like that, I'd lost my chance to shop in a store devoted exclusively to flip flops or to buy a foam hat shaped like a wedge of Cheddar cheese.

Tarkof asked if he needed to worry about me interfering with their investigation of Mindy Fullmer's disappearance. I told him that I hoped I'd never again have anything to do with any of the Fullmers as long as I lived.

I spent the next couple of days laying around the Bijou resting, playing with the dogs, and listening to Edgerton play guitar in the next room. As with so many of his interests, his attention to music waxed and waned. There were weeks when he would be fanatically devoted, spending every available hour playing along to records as he cranked out near-deafening renditions of songs like Motorhead's "Ace of Spades" and Iggy Pop's "I Want to Be Your Dog."

At other times, his attention would be focused elsewhere, and his Stratocaster and suitcase-sized Marshall amp were consigned to a darkened corner. That week, however, he was fully plugged in, working out a bluesy version of the Space Jam that Mr. Spock and the cosmic hippies had rocked out to in the *Star Trek* episode "The Way to Eden."

Yay, brother.

Finally, when the walls began to close in around me, I decided I needed to get out of there. Remarkably, I still had my car. I'd left it parked on the street when I went to visit the yellow house where I thought I'd find Mindy and where, of course, I'd almost died. I'd have expected that, during my recovery, having left it so long on the street in that neighborhood, someone would have either boosted it or stripped it for parts. But when Skip went to look for it days later, he found it untouched, a testament, I think, more to the decrepitude of the vehicle than to the reputability of the neighborhood. So, I had transportation. Now, where to go?

Oddly, my first thought was to head south to Burnsville to visit my mother.

Mom and I had talked on the phone every day since I was released from the hospital, mostly short conversations about how I was feeling, whether I'd heard anything from Naomi, and what was that music she kept hearing in the background. That should have been enough for me, and even as I eased behind the wheel of my Ford, I kept asking myself why I was going down to my childhood home.

Traffic was light on 35W, making the commute a brisk twenty-five minutes. Definitely not sufficient time for me to figure out what had possessed me to make the trip. I was pulling into the driveway when I realized that I hadn't even called Mom to tell her I was coming or to make sure that she'd even be home. But the garage door was open, and I spied her car, actually my dad's enormous Buick, parked inside.

I parked behind it and, owing to my still tender condition, took rather longer than normal to get out of my car and to toddle up to the front door. On my way, I'd noticed that the place looked even spiffier than it had when I'd been down earlier with Naomi for tuna casserole and to dash whatever hopes Mom had of adding a daughter to the family any time soon. The lawn was once again freshly mown, and I wondered if Mom was handling that herself or if she'd hired a service or a neighborhood kid to do it.

Outside the front door was a new planter, a faux terra cotta plastic, at least twenty inches in diameter, with multicolored pansies ringing a spiky green plant that someone once told me was called a dracaena. And on the stoop in front of the door, a newly purchased all-weather mat, lime green with the legend "Welcome Friends," now greeted visitors. Definitely not something my dad would have chosen. I was about to ring the doorbell and experience some of that welcome for myself when something made me turn around.

I hadn't noticed it when I'd arrived, or maybe I'd seen it and somehow had mentally just refused to let it register, but down by the curb, pounded into that freshly mown lawn, was a post and a sign with a familiar red background and white letters that spelled out "Burnsville Realty."

My mother had put the house up for sale.

When I turned back to the door, it suddenly swung open.

Mom was startled. She evidently hadn't heard my car turn into the driveway. She was taking off somewhere, opened the door, and there I stood. There was a sharp intake of air, and she glanced around quickly and furtively before settling her eyes squarely on mine. She smiled. "Why, Lyle. You didn't call. I wasn't expecting you. What a fabulous surprise."

I smiled back. "Hi, Mom. Yeah, I know. Sorry I didn't call. I just—"

"Oh, tut," she said, ushering me inside. "Never you mind. I'm so happy to see you. I don't suppose you've had time for lunch. We'll have to do something about that."

"Mom, I—"

Her eyes widened. "You know what!" she exclaimed, taking me by the arm through the living room, down the hall, and into the kitchen. "I tried something new last night. Salisbury steak! Don't know what I was thinking. Something just got into me. It's like meatloaf, really, and you know how your dad loved his meatloaf. Well, it's just like that, only you fry it up into patties and serve it with brown gravy. I used a packaged sauce. Really easy. But you know, I'm just not used to cooking for only one. I used two pounds of hamburger, just as if I was cooking for your dad. I've got enough leftovers for thrashers. Enough for you, too, I hope. Just

249

be a second for me to warm it up. Oh, and I have some of those potato buds. They're pretty good if you use real butter. Sit down while I fix you a plate."

She motioned briskly toward a chair at the kitchen table.

Like the front porch, the kitchen appeared showroom-ready. Any sign of dinge from the lacy white curtains that had long framed the windows had been bleached away, and the stovetop shone with a preternatural glow.

I sat down at the kitchen table, unable to quiet a groan as I eased into the chair. Mom noticed and winced along with me before she began to bustle about, plating two manhole-cover-sized saucers of ground meat and covering them with a chunky brown substance before putting them in the microwave. She then reached down into the drawer beneath the oven for a saucepan for her potato buds.

"I didn't mean to put you out, Mom."

"Oh, tut," she repeated. "Like you could ever put me out."

I smiled. We both probably knew the truth. I'd finally come up with the reason for my visit. I wanted to put her out. I was feeling lonely, and I wanted to find out if I showed up and see whether she'd make a fuss. Like a stubby little top, she glided back from the stove and then spun around to reach into the refrigerator to snatch up a stick of butter, humming, beaming.

I thought about the for-sale sign in the yard. Turns out there was another reason for my visit. I just didn't know it when I left the Bijou. "Mom," I said. "I think maybe the reason I came down today was to tell you I'm sorry."

She'd poured the water into the saucepan, knifed a couple of good-sized knobs of butter into it to melt, and began measuring the potato buds into a plastic measuring cup.

"Whatever could you apologize to me for?" she asked. "If anybody should apologize, it's me. You've been at death's door, and I've barely been at your side. Oh, I called, but it's not the same. I've been…I don't know, selfish, I guess you'd say. Anyway, you're here now, and I'm so happy, Lyle. So happy."

"I'm happy too, Mom," I told her. "But really, it's finally hit me that losing Dad was the hardest thing you ever had to do, and I…I was off messing around with this Fullmer thing. I should have been with you. I should have been here, where I belong. Helping you get things ready." I glanced around the kitchen with a smile. "The place looks great, by the way."

The water was boiling. I could hear it bubbling away in the pan. Mom was silent as she poured the potato buds into the water, gently stirring them before placing a lid on top as she turned down the heat. "You saw the sign," she said.

I laughed. "You better hope I saw the sign. The place is for sale. It's best if people driving up can see the sign."

She sighed. "Are you disappointed, Lyle? You can tell me if you are."

I've never been the most demonstrative guy. That really wasn't a thing growing up in that house. But I didn't hesitate. I pushed to my feet and wrapped her up in my arms. "I think it's great," I told her. "I really do."

She extricated herself long enough to push the "Reheat" button on the microwave. The light went on, the motor hummed, and Mom stepped back to pat me on the arm and return her attention to the pot on the stove.

In minutes, my lunch was done and steaming on the table in front of me. The meat was as dry as sawdust, and the gravy was gritty and tasted like rock salt mixed with creosote, but that wasn't the point. The point was that my mom loved me. She finally took a seat across the table from me, smiling a tight little smile, her eyes alive and merry.

"So," I began. "You're selling the house. Where are you thinking of moving?"

Mom's smile broadened. "You remember I told you about Carla Haberman? Our old next-door neighbor? She's got a lovely place over in Edina. It's a condo. One bedroom with one and a half baths. It's got a balcony overlooking a courtyard, and the place has an indoor pool for, like, exercising. I hear they do water aerobics. You ever think I'd be doing water aerobics? But Carla says it's easy and fun, and it's just a bunch of old ladies like me, and afterwards sometimes they get coffee. Anyway, they have a unit for sale just like Carla's and…" She paused, and her smile vanished. She sighed, took a deep breath, and looked me square in the eyes. "I already put some money down on it, Lyle. It's kind of a done deal."

I reached across the table and took her hand. "I'm really glad for you, Mom. I think this is really the thing for you right now. I'm so happy you…uh, you're making such forward-looking decisions. Really, Mom. It's fantastic."

Her smile returned, now brighter than even the freshly bleached curtains. "I was worried, you know," she said. "I thought you might be upset about my moving. The last time you were down here, you seemed—"

I interrupted her. "It just took me a few days to get used the idea. Now I think it's just…swell. I think it's just swell."

She removed her hand from mine, stood, and went to the counter to fill a coffee cup. I went back to the Salisbury steak. When she sat back down, I asked, "Any problems with financing? I mean, selling the house. Buying a new one. Can you swing it all financially?"

"Your dad left me in really great shape, Lyle. Insurance took care of most of the medical bills. I'll make something off the sale of the house, and I've got both social security and his pension. I'll be just fine."

"Great, Mom," I said. "That's great. Dad never seemed to worry much about money. I mean, it's not like we were ever extravagant, but we had everything we needed, didn't we? I mean, we even went on that vacation that one time. To Washington? Do you remember that? First time I ever saw the ocean. That was quite a time, wasn't it?"

"It sure was," she agreed. "You know, I always thought maybe we could live out there. It's so green with all the trees and the moss. They have a rainforest, an actual rainforest, and there's the ocean so big and gray. That's the name of the county we visited. I remember. Grays Harbor County. Your dad had a friend that moved out there and worked for the Grays Harbor County Sheriff's Office. That's partly why we picked the place, so your dad could talk with them about maybe joining them. It would have meant a lot of change, but I liked it. In the end, you know, your dad decided to come home." She glanced down at the table, shaking her head slightly at the memory.

As I recall," I ventured, "we made that trip only a few weeks before Donnie came to live with us."

Mom raised her head, wariness clouding her expression. "That's right. It was right around that time."

I was silent for several seconds. "We took that vacation when Dad was on suspension, didn't we?"

Mom sipped at her coffee. "Yes."

"You know, I remember being surprised. That we took that trip, I mean. You know, Dad on suspension. He must have been worried about losing his job. About losing his salary. But we went on that trip. A pretty big luxury. Only trip like that I remember us taking as a family."

"We used to visit Grandma and Grandpa in Wisconsin most summers," Mom reminded me.

"I remember, but we flew to Washington. Stayed in a hotel. For the Wisconsin trips, we drove and stayed at their house for free. Not exactly the same."

Mom smiled. "True. I was glad we were able to take that trip to the coast. Yes, it cost more, but the memories…"

I nodded. "Didn't Dad take another trip right around that time? With Knuck?"

Mom crinkled her brow. "He did. He and Knuck flew to the East Coast just before our trip to Washington. But that was business." She paused. "Is something bothering you, Lyle?"

I shook my head. "Nah. It's nothing, Mom. I've just been replaying those days over in my head lately. It's just all this stuff with Donnie and Knuck and Mindy. It's got me thinking."

"Thinking about what?" Mom asked, caution entering her voice.

"About Donnie's parents' murders, I guess."

"You mean about how they thought maybe your father and Johnny Fullmer might not have handled everything the right way? You thinking about that?"

"Yeah," I admitted.

Mom shook her head side to side, but slightly and quickly, more of a shudder than an indication of disagreement. "They were investigated. Nothing came of it. There was some talk, but nothing came of it."

"Some folks think that maybe Vernon Murdoch had something stashed in the house. Some think it was cash. Cash that was never found."

Mom stood and went to the window. She pushed back the curtains and stared into the yard. After a moment, she asked, "Did you see the new planter? The one on the stoop. The realtor suggested it. Makes the house seem homier, she said."

I stood and joined her at the window. "This cash," I continued, "There's some who think that maybe it was on account of the cash that Mindy Fullmer was kidnapped. That maybe the guys who took her wanted their money back."

Mom spun around to face me. "That doesn't make any sense, Lyle. How could kidnapping Mindy get them back Vernon Murdoch's money? That would mean they thought that…" She turned and looked back out the window. After several seconds, she said, "That would mean they thought Johnny Fullmer had the money. That he took it that day…That day that Donnie's parents were killed. And if they think that, they'd think that your father—"

"That Dad was involved." I finished the thought for her. "That he helped Knuck take the money or at least covered up for him."

Mom remained silent, staring out the window. The clock on the kitchen wall clicked loudly. It was a classic Kit-Cat clock—black with a white bow tie, huge white eyes rolling, and a long tail sweeping back and forth, swishing away the seconds. Quieter but still distinct was the tick, tick, tick of the stove as the electric heating element, now off, cooled under the pan of potato buds.

"Lyle," Mom said at last. "I can't listen to any more of this. You can't honestly believe that your father would be involved in anything like that. You can't honestly think that he'd—"

"I don't, Mom," I told her. "I don't think that Dad would steal from a dying man, no matter how tempting it might have been. But I'm not sure that Knuck wouldn't. And I…I'm not sure that Dad would turn him in if he did."

Mom kept staring out the window. I listened to the clock. "He wouldn't have," she said. "He couldn't have turned Knuck in. He couldn't have done that any more than he could have moved us to the coast. He had to stick it out here. He had to stick it out with Knuck. He couldn't have it look like he'd turned his back on his partner. Your father didn't always approve of everything Knuck Fullmer did. He was upset with him plenty of times. But he always had his back. Always."

"And did Knuck Fullmer always have Dad's back?"

"I thought so," she said.

We sat back down at the table, Mom fingering the handle of her coffee cup. "Any word about Mindy?"

"None."

"Are you going to keep looking for her?"

"I don't want to," I told her. "I want to be through

with this. I never want anything to do with the Fullmers again. As far as I'm concerned, Knuck Fullmer brought all of this on himself. On himself and on Mindy. And it's not my responsibility to get him out of it."

"You want to be through with this? That's what you said. But that's not the same as being through with it. Are you through with it?"

It took a while to answer. "Probably not," I admitted.

Mom stood and went into the living room. I sat at the kitchen table and even had a couple more bites of Salisbury steak before pushing it aside. When she returned, she was carrying the case. She set it on the table in front of me. "Take it."

I reached out and rested my palm flat on the lid.

"Take it," she repeated. "He'd want you to have it."

I lifted the lid to expose Dad's great big Magnum shining blue beneath the glare of the overhead kitchen lights. "Mark XIX Desert Eagle," I said. "It's a beaut. One helluva piece of firepower."

I looked up at Mom. There were tears in her eyes. "Maybe it can help keep you safe," she said. "Look at you. Look at you here, all bruised. You were nearly killed. And still. I know you, Lyle. You won't quit. Damn your father. And damn you too, if you want the truth of it. I wish I could stop you. I could never stop either of you. Not really. Your father? Once he had his mind set on a thing, I could never get him to quit. No matter the cost. It's like they say, like father like son."

I stayed there for about another half hour. After a while, we began to talk about other things. She'd started going to a nearby Catholic church. Dad never had any time for church, but Mom had always felt a longing. It was fine, she said. They seemed like good people. They were starting a four-part study of the Book of Ruth. Stranger in a strange land. Not unlike herself, sitting alone in the pew, missing her husband.

I gave her another hug as I went out the door. She stood in the doorway a long time as I wobbled down the porch stairs and slid gingerly behind the wheel of my car, placing the case with the handgun on the passenger's seat.

It was a sunny afternoon; the streets were quiet. A couple of kids were riding bikes, and a slight breeze was ruffling the leaves of a line of alders. I noticed the tail only a few blocks from where I intended to pick up the freeway. It was Janos Bollok's El Camino, its flawless fuchsia finish gleaming about two blocks behind me. I turned onto County Road 5, which I knew would take me past Plain View Elementary School. It was summer, and the place should be empty. It had a large parking lot, and if I pulled into the middle of it, I'd be able to see them coming from every direction.

When I came to a stop sign, I watched in the rearview mirror as the El Camino pulled over to the curb behind a parked two-door sedan in an attempt to keep from being spotted. I remained at the stop sign a bit longer than I normally would. It gave me time to slide a loaded magazine into my dad's massive handgun.

Chapter Nineteen

I was lucky. There were no other cars in the parking lot. Plain View Elementary is a long, single-story building that takes up an entire block with a spacious parking lot on the north end. It's in a residential neighborhood with plenty of split-entries facing the building from the surrounding streets. But it's also lined with trees, some small and recently planted, others tall and flush with foliage, which would provide some cover from prying eyes. On the one hand, if these guys made a move on me, it might be good to have witnesses. On the other, I'd been at this long enough to know that witnesses tend to report seeing what they and the lawyers want them to have seen. Often, even with a clear view, the truth is as hard to spot as a beetle hiding in a dish of black jellybeans.

I parked my car at a diagonal in the middle of the lot, a few car lengths from the entrance off County Road 5. I slid out of the car and watched as the El Camino pulled slowly toward me. Bollok, who'd been driving, got out first and stood behind the open driver's side door. Tousignant followed suit a moment later.

The sunlight shone brightly off Wille Tooz's bald pate, his fuzzy hair fluffing out erratically, forming a kind of saucer around his head. He wore jeans, a white t-shirt, and a pair of what had to be size fourteen cowboy boots. Everything about him sang "Rodeo Clown."

Bollok was wearing the same thing I'd always seen him in—a gray tweed jacket over an azure dress shirt buttoned to the nape of his neck, that scrofulous, purple growth glaring over the collar.

Exiting the car, Willie Tooz broke into a big grin, slammed his car door loudly, and ambled forward. For his part, Bollok stood rock-still behind his open car door. An intermittent stream of cars passed by on the adjacent streets. None seemed to be too interested in us.

When Tousignant was within a few strides of me, he paused and laughed his raspy laugh. "Well, I gotta hand it to you, friend. You must be tough as alligator hide to be up and around so soon after that beating you took. I read all about it in the paper. They said you plumb got the shit kicked out of you. Didn't know for sure that you'd make it. But here you are."

The gun, in my right hand, was in plain sight down at my side. If Tousignant was intimidated by it, he didn't make it obvious.

"You telling me all you know about that was from the paper?" I asked. "You weren't any closer than that?"

Tousignant cackled once more. "Nope. It's like that Will Rogers fella. All I know is what I read in the funny papers."

"It's *papers*," I corrected him. "Not funny papers. Newspapers."

"Well, hot damn, son. It's good to be in the company of a scholar." He pointed at his partner with a crooked thumb. "Janos here probably never even heard of Will Rogers. Be good for the two of you to spend more time together. Might be you could teach him a thing or two."

I glanced at Bollok. He didn't look like he was anxious to spend more time with me. "I'm kinda busy right now," I said. "Have his people call my people."

Tousignant smiled. "That's pretty good. 'Have his people call your people.' But the fact is we're a might busy ourselves. We're spending all our time wrapped up in what you might call a quest. We're questing something that belongs to us." He narrowed his gaze. "We're questing for our money."

I thought about that for a moment, then patted my leg gently with the barrel of the Magnum. "You know, Mr. Tousignant, I'll admit I'm a bit confused. I mean, after all, Knuck turned over the money to your goons at the mall. You shot him anyway, but…hey, he turned it over. You expect me to believe you misplaced it since then. You don't strike me as the absent-mined type."

"Well, I guess maybe it's you that's got the absent mind, friend. Them 'goons' as you like to call 'em weren't mine at all."

I stared at him. "You telling me you're innocent, Mr. Tousignant? You saying this whole kidnapping and ransom isn't your work? Afraid I'm not buying that. We both know that you'd do anything, literally anything, to get your money back. It's an ego thing with you. Am I right?"

Tousignant started toward me. As he did, I raised my gun, gripping it with both hands and leveling the barrel at his chest. Out of the corner of my eye, I saw Bollok reach into his coat pocket. Tousignant stopped in his tracks and raised both hands before him in a gesture of surrender. "It's not my ego, I'm concerned about it, friend," he said. "It's my money. And it don't matter if you believe it or not. I don't have it. But here is something you can believe. I'm gonna to get it. I'm gonna to get it if I have to bleed every one of you. You, that Fullmer, and any other member of your family or friends that I think can help me get it."

"That's pretty loose talk for a guy with this much gun pointed at him," I observed.

"Ah, hell, friend. We both know you ain't gonna shoot me. You do, and Janos over there will drop you before I hit the ground. He's a wicked shot. He hit that Fullmer at, hell, that had to be forty yards. Maybe more. A lot further than what he's looking at here."

I glanced over at Bollok again. Like me, he had both hands wrapped around a handgun. I had to console myself by noting that it was a much smaller gun than mine. It would kill me just as dead if we took to shooting, but mine was definitely bigger.

I lowered my gun ever so slightly. "Okay, now I'm even more confused. You say the thing at the mall wasn't your play. Are you saying you didn't snatch Mindy Fullmer either?"

Tousignant nodded.

"And those guys Knuck handed the money to weren't your guys?"

Tousignant nodded again.

"But you admit that Bollok was there? That he shot Knuck?

"That he was."

"You there, too?"

"Absolutely. It just don't go to letting Janos here out on his own when there might be gunplay. The man just don't care who he shoots. Needs me to point out the right targets for him."

"And you pointed out Knuck? Bollok shot Knuck on your say-so?"

Tousignant shook his head ruefully. "Well, not

exactly that one time. It's more of a general rule. That time at the mall? That was a special circumstance. Janos saw the play going down and sort of just reacted on his own. If I had my druthers, I'd have preferred he'd a left it alone. Would have given us a better shot at following the money. As it was, with all them folks running and shouting and the security guards and the cops on their way, we had to hightail it pronto. Left us with fewer options. Options like following you down here. Now, forgive me for wanting to move our little tete-a-tete along with more...whatcha call it, alacrity, but I need you to tell me where I can find my money."

"Wait a minute," I said. "If you didn't set up the ransom drop, why were you there? The only people who knew about it were the kidnappers, Knuck, and me. We didn't even tell the cops. How did you know about it?"

Tousignant gave me an apologetic shrug. "We got a call. It's as simple as that. Somebody called and told us that Fullmer had our money, and we should head to that damn mall to get it. Even told us where he'd be waiting. If we'd a got there a couple of minutes earlier, this thing would have been put to bed. But, hey, finding a parking spot was hell, and once we got inside that huge fucking place, it took for-fucking-ever to find that ballooned-up squirrel. We got within sight just as Fullmer was about to hand over that backpack to them so-called goons. We saw that going down, and...Well, Janos acted a bit impulsively."

I thought about that. "Okay. Suppose I believe you? Suppose I believe somebody tipped you off, and that's why you were there? Suppose I believe you weren't behind the kidnapping? Who would have called you? The real kidnappers? Shit, Tousignant. You expect me to believe that the guys who set up the drop thought 'what the hell, let's invite a couple more guns to the party?' Makes no sense."

"Life ain't usually in the making sense business, friend."

I had to admit that he was right about that. I mean, there I was standing in an elementary school parking lot, beat to hell, both hands wrapped around the biggest gun I'd ever handled, facing off with a malevolent clown and an armed Count Chocula. Times like these make a man re-examine his life choices.

"Besides," Tousignant continued. "I really don't care what you believe. God's truth, friend. All I care about is my money." Tooz took a step forward, stopped, and eyed me appraisingly. "Times up, friend. Tell me where to find my money or Janos'll drop you where you stand."

I sighted my gun barrel in the middle of Tousignant's chest and, uncharacteristically, found myself without a snappy rejoinder. This bothered me more than it should have. A guy's gonna die, he should be able come up with memorable epitaph. It makes easing into the afterlife a bit more tolerable. But, drawing a blank, there was nothing I could do but shoot the bastard and take what was coming to me.

I was tightening my finger on the trigger when I heard the first whoop. It was loud and off to my right and was followed almost immediately by another loud whoop coming from my left. The whoops merged into a continuous *whoop-whoop-whoop* as lights flashed across the pavement and an amplified voice enjoined us, "Drop your weapons!"

I held mine steady as Tousignant broke into a wide

grin and slowly raised his hands.

I turned toward Bollok and found his gun was still pointed directly at me. To his right, a Burnsville patrol unit had swung into the parking lot, and two uniformed police officers stood behind its open doors, their guns drawn. I heard the scrunch of more tires across the parking lot beyond where Tooz was standing. The cops had come in from both sides. Bollok cast a glance from side to side and, without expression, let his gun slip until he was holding it by only one finger looped through the trigger guard. He raised it above his head. As he did, I slowly set the Magnum on the ground and nudged it forward with one foot. I watched it spin lazily away before lacing the fingers of both my hands behind my neck.

Chapter Twenty

My biggest problem turned out to be my choice of parking lots. I soon found out that there is a federal law called the Gun-Free School Zones Act that "prohibits any person from knowingly possessing a firearm that has moved in or otherwise affects interstate or foreign commerce at a place the individual knows, or has reasonable cause to believe, is a school zone."

And although I really wasn't sure what to make of that business about "otherwise affects interstate or foreign commerce," the officer in charge, a Sergeant named Harrison, assured me that it applied to my case because at some time or other all guns have "moved" in interstate commerce. Harrison was in his early thirties, short but sturdily built like those concrete "Dragon's teeth" they used to put in farmers' fields during WWII to slow down approaching tanks. He typed slowly at his keyboard using only his forefingers and pounded down so hard that the clack, clack of his typing, even in the noisy room, jarred like a toddler repeatedly squeezing off a cap gun.

The penalty for violating the Gun-Free School Zones Act, Harrison had told me, was a fine of five thousand dollars, imprisonment for not more than five years, or both. His eyes took on a quiet luster when he emphasized "*or both*."

While Harrison worked, I was kept standing in front

of a counter, both hands cuffed behind me. I'd been there for quite a while, and frankly, I really needed to go to the bathroom. When I mentioned this to Harrison, he said something about "holding my water" and went back to his loud and extraordinarily slow typing. I had long since launched into the "pee dance" when I decided to see if I could get some courtesy by telling Harrison that my dad had been a long-standing member of Burnsville's finest.

"That so," Harrison intoned solemnly. The luster gone, his eyes were as hard and cold as black marble, and his gaze held mine for nearly a full minute before he went back to his typing.

But another officer, who had been passing behind Harrison, stopped when he heard me mention my dad. He was a tall African American, trimmer than you'd expect for a cop his age, which I figured to be in the late fifties. He had a deeply lined face, a strong jaw, and a full head of hair that was still mostly black but had grayed at the temples into two stark, almost white patches that crept up toward the top of his skull, framing his expansive forehead. When he looked at me, recognition flashed in his eyes.

He stood behind Harrison, watching the typing for some time before lightly tapping him on the shoulder and motioning Harrison away from the counter. They stood briefly in a corner, talking quietly and casting occasional glances my way. Finally, Harrison returned to his typing, and the other officer wandered out of sight.

Several minutes later, he returned holding a sheet of paper covered with dense writing. He set it on the counter in front of Harrison, tapping it with a finger. Harrison read it slowly, glanced only once back up at the older officer, and then went back to clacking at his computer.

"If you want, Essoe," Harrison said, "you can take him to the can. He's been asking, and this is gonna take me awhile."

Essoe nodded and came around the corner. He continued behind me, and I heard a faint click as he unlocked the handcuffs. I rubbed my wrists as he motioned me down the hall to the men's room. I was deeply grateful.

When I finished, I took pains to dry my hands thoroughly, and when I emerged to find Officer Essoe waiting in the hallway, I offered him my hand. He glanced first at my outstretched hand, then looked me deeply in the eyes before taking it. His was a solid handshake—firm, single pump.

"You're Lyle Dahms," he said. "Gabriel Essoe. Saw you on the news the other day." He paused. "I knew your dad when he was on the job."

"Glad to know you, Officer Essoe. I appreciate your kindness. Would you, um…Would you mind telling me what that paper was you gave the sergeant?"

Essoe smiled. "You have a carry permit," he said. "I checked. The thing about that *no-guns-in-school-zones* law is that it doesn't apply if the gun owner is licensed by the state where the school is located. You have a valid Minnesota carry permit. It doesn't apply to you."

"I appreciate your clarification on that, Officer Essoe. Your colleague, Sergeant Harrison, didn't seem to know that."

"Oh, he knew it," Essoe said. "He just put it out of mind for a bit, is all. I'd have done it myself. Put you in a cell for a while until the DA's office found time to review the case. He'd spring you, but it could be a day or two. Longer maybe."

"What made you intervene?"

Essoe looked at the ground. "Your old man was on the job when I first started. Things were a bit different then. Some of the old-timers weren't too keen on having a brother on the force. Not out here in the suburbs anyway." He raised his head to look me in the eyes. "Your old man was different." Essoe smiled. "Don't get me wrong. He was a complete asshole, but...he didn't give a shit what color a guy was. All he saw was blue. He'd bust your balls just like he would everyone else." Essoe shook his head. "A couple of the other guys...They were slow to come around. A couple never did. Even that partner of his, what's his name, Pussy Whipped Fullmer? Whatever his nickname was. That son of a bitch was fucking incorrigible. The shit he used to say. The names he called me when he knew damn well I could hear him. But your old man? He wouldn't stand for it. Back then, if I wanted to make it, I had to put up with it. But Ray Dahms. Hell no. He'd rock that fucking Fullmer back every time. Usually with just a look."

"I remember that look," I told him.

"I imagine you do." He paused. "Those two guys you squared off with? What's going on there?"

I shook my head. "I'm not sure. Not yet anyway. They're mixed up in Mindy Fullmer's kidnapping. I just don't know exactly how."

"You planning to find out?"

I nodded. "If I can. Wouldn't be all bad if Tousignant and Bollok were held up a while. Might give me a head start. They can be kind of...kind of distracting."

"Oh, I think they'll be held up a spell," Essoe told

me. "That one guy. Janos Bollok. That gun he had wasn't registered, and he's got a felony on his record, so no way he's getting a carry permit. Even if he had one, it wouldn't be from Minnesota, and the law says that a licensed gun owner can only possess a firearm on school property if the owner is licensed in the state where the school is located. He's fucked."

"How about the other guy? Tousignant? I don't recall seeing him with a gun."

Essoe spread his hands wide before him. "Hey, the gun they had isn't registered. Pretty hard to tell which one of them it belonged to. Better hold 'em both until that can be sorted out."

"Until the DA has a chance to review the case?" I asked, smiling broadly. "Could take a day or two, I hear."

"Maybe longer," Essoe reminded me.

Essoe took me back to the counter where Harrison was still clacking away at his keyboard. Essoe hadn't put the handcuffs back on me. Harrison noticed but didn't say anything.

When he finally finished up the paperwork, Harrison had another uniformed officer place me in a holding room, but after about another two hours, I was released. I called my mom, and she agreed to pick me up. When she got to the station, she asked Harrison if he'd given me back my gun.

Harrison started to argue, but Mom cut him off. "It's a family heirloom," she told him. "It belonged to my husband. He was a cop here when you were still in diapers. I'd like it back."

Harrison stared at her and looked about to tell her off when Essoe reappeared. "Seems like the right thing to do, Sarge," he said. There was nothing the least bit menacing or insubordinate in the way he said it, but I got a distinct feeling that there was something there. Not a threat, exactly. Just a sense of gravity that Harrison could not overlook. He stood and soon came back with the Mark XIX. Mom signed for it, and we left.

In the parking lot, I asked Mom if she knew Essoe.

"The Black man?" she asked. "No. I don't think so."

I thought about that. I thought about what Essoe had said about my father. About him being an equal opportunity asshole. Essoe clearly meant it as a complement. But I thought back to all the times Dad had had fellow officers come to the house. All the picnics. All the times they got together to watch football. I couldn't remember a single Black man ever coming to the house. Knuck Fullmer was always there, but never Gabriel Essoe.

Mom drove me over to the impound lot where the cops had taken my car. I paid the charge and waited as they drove the car around to the front of the building. Mom waited with me. When I climbed behind the steering wheel, Mom reached through the open window and placed Dad's gun, still in an evidence bag, in my lap.

"Be careful, honey," she said. "Stay safe."

"I will, Mom."

It had been a long day, and the sun was heading for the horizon, shadows creeping steadily across the parking lot. My first thought was to drive back to the Bijou to rest up and consider my options. But I'd been resting long enough, and despite the fact that I was still weak and very, very sore, I thought I'd better get to work. There was no telling how long Tooz and Bollok would stay behind bars.

That, of course, begged the question. What was it

that I was supposed to do? Who was I looking for, and where should I go to look? The easy answer was that I was looking for Mindy. Maybe she'd been kidnapped. Maybe, as Knuck had suggested at the hospital, she had staged her own kidnapping in order to get her hands on more of her dad's money. Mindy was the key. But where should I look for her? I had no idea.

The thing is, when you got nothing, it's all you got, and you better do something with it. I had nothing. This thing had started when my dad sent me out to make peace with Donnie Murdoch. To help him if I could. From what I could tell, I'd done exactly the opposite. Of course, I reminded myself, it wasn't my fault that Tooz and Bollok had shown up from Baltimore to hassle Donnie. They were already in his house when I got there. That was all I had, I realized. Donnie's address. I should go find him. Maybe he'd be home. Maybe he could tell me something he'd learned from living with Tooz and Bollok that would help me find Mindy. In any case, it was something. Even if it was nothing.

Chapter Twenty-one

I pointed my car to the North Side. I caught the tail end of rush hour traffic, but eventually, I was parked in front of Donnie's house. I entered the front porch and tried to peer through the brown paper that covered the windows. I couldn't be sure, but it did not appear that any lights were on in the house.

There were actually fewer cigarette butts in the big ashtray on the porch table than there was the first time I had visited. Standing at the door, I glanced down at the gaping crack where the porch floor separated from the outside wall. It appeared slightly wider than on my previous visit, but that was likely my imagination. I rang the doorbell several times, but when no one answered, I knocked loudly. Still no answer. I examined the front door. As I'd noted before, Donnie and friends were security conscious. There were actually two doors. The first was a steel mesh security door that fronted a solid wood door behind it. Both were secured with deadbolts.

There was a time when I might have tried kicking in the doors. The wood framing around a door is a heck of a lot more forgiving than a deadbolt, and often, you can simply boot the door and splinter the frame. But that makes a lot of noise, and when the homeowner gets back, there's no hiding that someone's made unauthorized entry. There was a time when I might have circled around the house looking for a discreetly placed window.

With those older, multi-paned windows you could always knock out one pane and reach in to work the hasp. But all of that was before Amazon. For only seventeen dollars and ninety-nine cents, plus shipping and handling, I'd been able to buy a full twenty-four-piece set of lock picks. It even came in a lovely leatherette case. Don't know how to work a set of lock picks? No problem. Just turn to YouTube. There, dozens of helpful do-it-yourselfers are happy to post video after video of those new lock picks in action, proving how easy it is for the absent-minded homeowner to gain entry to his house after inadvertently locking himself out. Or something like that. The upshot is that after quite a bit of practice I'd pretty much got the hang of it.

I'd really only ever used two of the twenty-four pieces. The first was a stainless-steel pick with a curved end. I slid this into the key slot of the first of Donnie's deadbolts, pushed up, and pulled it toward me several times, listening for the click of the pins. Then I inserted a small tension wrench into the lower part of the key slot and, placing the pick into the lock as well directly above the tension wrench, I wiggled the pick back out toward me while simultaneously turning the wrench to the left. The deadbolt turned easily. It took two tries to get the second deadbolt to slide open, but the whole operation took less than three minutes. I love the internet.

Once inside, I stood at the base of the stairs and listened. Nothing. Not the tick of a clock or even the hum of a light fixture. The house was dark and silent. After a few moments, I began to look around, heading first into the main floor living room. It was a mess.

There were dirty dishes everywhere—on the coffee table, the side tables that flanked the tattered brown sofa, even on the floor in front of the flat-screen TV, all flecked with ashes and covered with crushed cigarette butts. There was no art on the walls, no framed family photos, nothing personal except the litter of a disorganized life.

Beyond the living room, through a nice, naturally finished wooden arch, was a dining room. The table was a garage sale metal table with a Formica top and three matching metal chairs. There were no dirty dishes on the dining table. Instead, it was a riot of old newspapers and magazines, mostly porn, piled around a giant-sized box of vanilla wafer cookies. A built-in china cabinet took up most of the back wall of the dining room. It was gorgeous or would have been with just a little work. Dark, richly grained wood with glass-paned doors, each with a gothic arch and intersecting metal muntins that fronted…Well, nothing. The cabinet was completely empty.

Around the corner from the dining room was the kitchen. Light streamed in through its many windows illuminating more dirty dishes, crushed cigarette butts, and an electric stove so caked in grease that if it caught fire, it would burn for days.

From my previous visit, I suspected that Tooz's meth works were in the detached garage out back, but before confirming this, I headed up the stairs to check out the second level of the house. A rather narrow hallway ran perpendicular to the staircase. The first door to the left was a small bathroom. There were three small bedrooms, one directly ahead, the others at either end of the hallway. Each was a microcosm of its occupant.

The bedroom at the top of the stairs was the messiest, with clothes tossed in piles atop a visibly dirty floor, more dirty dishes on the dresser and nightstand, more cigarette butts, and a bed covered in a sheet and threadbare bedspread that could charitably be described as dingy. The bedroom down the hall to the left, on the other side of the bathroom, was nearly bare. Only a sheet and a light blanket covered a small bed. Again, there was no art on the walls, no framed photographs. There was a dresser that contained a few t-shirts, some boxers, black socks, and several brightly colored handkerchiefs. In the closet hung an azure dress shirt, a pair of black slacks, and nothing else.

The last bedroom was another matter. It was clearly Donnie's. On his dresser were several framed photographs—him as a young boy standing between his beaming parents, his high school graduation photo, and other shots of family. At the foot of the bed was a small, flat-screen television, a sturdy stand, and a DVD player tucked below. Several DVDs were displayed in an adjacent wire rack. To my surprise, most were classics. John Wayne westerns, the original Star Wars trilogy, and several vintage comedies, including the Marx Brothers, W.C. Fields, Laurel and Hardy, and even a set of silents starring the oft-forgotten Harry Langdon. It was an enviable collection and would not have looked out of place in my own room.

I hadn't known that Donnie was interested in classic movie comedies. Growing up, the great movie comedians had been a bit of an obsession with me. Mornings before school were filled with Our Gang comedies on WCCO TV, Sundays were for Laurel and Hardy, Saturday nights for the likes of the Marx Brothers, Fields, and only occasionally Chaplin. In junior high, I got my first projector, a silent Super 8 and, armed with a catalog from Blackhawk Films of

Davenport, Iowa, I started my own collection—Chaplin in *Dough and Dynamite* and *One AM*, Laurel and Hardy in *The Second Hundred Years*, and Elmo Lincoln's original Tarzan. Although I hadn't screened any of those titles in many, many years, the projector and all those reels still occupied a corner of my closet at the Bijou.

Maybe if I'd known Donnie was a film buff, things would have been different. Maybe instead of being suspicious of him, we could have been closer. But I hadn't known. I hadn't bothered to find out anything about him.

There was a nightstand beside a neatly made, full-size bed. Hanging from a small lamp was a black and gold tassel commemorating Donnie's graduation from dear old Burnsville High. Marisa Algren would have been proud. Next to the alarm clock was a photograph of him and a woman. It was a recent picture. Donnie looked exactly as he did when last I saw him. Only in this photograph, he was smiling—his eyes unclouded by either worry or drugs. Instead, they shone with joy. Even love.

The woman in the photograph with him was Mindy Fullmer.

I remembered what Marisa Algren had told me about Donnie and Mindy dating in high school. From the photograph, it looked like their romance had rekindled.

I thought about that as I made my way back downstairs and into the kitchen. I found a side door that opened out onto a set of concrete steps that were covered with glued-on artificial turf the color of a lime-green freeze pop. It was torn in several places, revealing an earlier attempt to coat the concrete in a thick layer of glossy, banana-yellow paint. At the base of the steps, a concrete patio spread toward the backdoor of a single-car garage. I tried the door to the garage and found it locked. This time I didn't even need the lock picks. There was no deadbolt and enough space between the doorframe and the doorknob to easily slide in a credit card and push back the bolt.

I was surprised at what I found inside. The place was immaculate. Its only contents were a few tools hanging from pegs along the walls and an electric lawn mower with what had to be a hundred feet of orange extension cord coiled on top. The floor was swept clean, there was no real odor to speak of, and there was, most assuredly, no sign of a methamphetamine operation. Tooz and Bollok had either moved their drug operation or dismantled it and moved on to another source of income.

I pushed the lock button on the garage door and closed it behind me. I was doing the same to the door to the kitchen when I heard a board creak. It came from the front porch. I hadn't locked the front doors behind me when I came in, which would likely tip off whoever had entered that someone was inside. I pulled my dad's gun out of the inside pocket of my jacket, held my breath, and listened. I heard the front door swing open and footsteps crossing the living room toward the kitchen where I was waiting.

I held the gun in a shooter's stance, my eyes and the gun barrel trained on the open passway into the kitchen.

"Tooz?" Donnie's voice sounded in the living room. "You home?"

I stepped into the living room, still pointing the barrel of the gun before me. Donnie's eyes widened as he spotted me. He took a deep breath and started to say something. I cut him off before he could speak. "Donnie, we have to talk."

He slowly raised his hands. "You gonna shoot me, Lyle?" he asked. His voice was level and soft, without a note of fear, accusation, or even wonder. It was simply a question.

"Probably not," I admitted.

"Then maybe you could put down the gun."

"We'll see. First, I gotta make sure we understand each other."

He nodded.

"You see, Donnie. I'm tired. I'm tired of being a patsy. I'm tired of getting beat up and threatened. I'm tired of being thrown in jail, and most of all, I'm tired of being lied to. I need to get some clarity. And you, Donnie, you're going to give it to me."

"I'm tired too," Donnie said softly. "But there's not much I can give you. Not much I can give anyone." He paused. "Pretty near everything I ever had's been taken away."

I glanced around the living room, at the dirty dishes piled everywhere, the cigarette butts. I thought about Donnie, a virtual prisoner in his own home since his dad's former partners moved in. I wondered what I'd do if I were him. I wondered how I'd deal with the helplessness. I suddenly became even more conscious of the gun in my hand. I lowered it to my side.

"They won't be back, Donnie," I told him. "Not for a while anyway. Tooz and Bollok are in jail down in Burnsville. I was there myself for a bit. We had…There was an incident. I've been assured that they will not be released for a day or two. It gives us a little time."

"Time for what?"

"Time for that clarity I spoke of."

"I don't know what I can say that would—"

"How's Mindy?" I interrupted. "Her dad's pretty worried about her. It's not right you guys keeping him in the dark."

"How would I know where—"

"Donnie," I snapped. "Remember, I'm sick of being lied to. Just tell me how Mindy is, goddammit."

"She's…She's…She's—"

"The truth!" I thundered, instinctively raising the gun, the barrel shivering with anger.

Donnie was silent for several seconds. There was a sadness in his eyes. "She's safe," he admitted at last.

"You're going to take me to her," I told him.

Donnie shook his head slowly. "I can't do that, Lyle. I gotta keep her safe. She's relying on me. She's—"

"She's got nearly a hundred grand of her old man's money, and she's lying low until she can safely surface and spend it." I said, finishing the sentence for him. "What's the plan, Donnie? New identities? You guys gonna blow town, set up somewhere else, and live happily ever after? Maybe spend your declining years dishing out Midwest/Asian fusion cuisine in some backwater somewhere? Not gonna happen, Donnie. She turned on her dad; she'll turn on you, too."

"She'd never do that. She loves me. We got a right at a life."

"Okay, but what you got right now is a big target on your back. Both of you. This Tooz isn't going to stop until he gets his money. He's told me so. He doesn't care who gets hurt. He's in jail now, but they don't have enough to hold him long. He's going to come looking for Mindy, and he's going to find you." I shook my head. "No. Running isn't the answer. You need to turn yourselves in. The cops can help you with this. If you're honest, they'll find a way. *We'll* find a way. But you gotta come in, you gotta tell the truth, and you have to return the money."

Donnie lowered his head. "There isn't any money, Lyle."

"Bullshit!"

"I'm telling the truth," Donnie insisted.

"Donnie," I said as calmly as I could, "I was there. I was there when Knuck put the cash in the backpack. I was there when he turned it over to the so-called kidnappers. I was there when Knuck got shot, and the bad guys got away with the loot. Both he and I are convinced Mindy set this whole thing up. That, at least, it started out as her attempt to get more money out of her dad for the restaurant. We're way past that now. People have been hurt. Shit, people all over the country saw America's favorite cartoon squirrel gut shot on the evening news. That kind of thing sticks in the national consciousness. There ain't no way you two are getting away with this. Either you turn yourselves in or wait for Tooz to find you. And if you come in, you gotta bring the money with you.

"I'm telling you, there isn't any money."

I shook my head. "Whatever, Donnie. That's not even my primary concern. We're going to take a ride. You're going to bring me to see Mindy. We're going to talk it out. We're going to find a solution. We're going to end this thing."

"Lyle, I just can't do that. I can't—"

"You can't what, Donnie? What are you afraid of? Can't you see I'm offering you a way out? You can't think I'd actually hurt either of you. After the shit storm

I've endured for you two, is that what you think? That I'm some kind of threat?"

Donnie raised his head. "Well, you are holding a gun."

I sighed. "Yes, I am. Whatever you and Mindy have done, whatever danger you have placed yourselves in, you brought me in with you. Earlier today, I was looking down the barrel of Bollok's gun. Earlier today, I was sure I'd seen my last sunset. Look out the window, Donnie. The sun's going down. And there aren't going to be many more sunsets for any of us—not for me, not for you, not for Mindy—unless we find a way out of this mess. Now, are you going to take me to her? Are you going to let me help you? Or are we all just going to face what's coming on our own?"

Donnie stared at me. At first, I thought I detected defiance, but as he continued to stare, it seemed a cloud came over him. Slowly, he sagged with an all-encompassing weariness. "I really don't know what to do, Lyle."

I lowered my gun. "Me neither," I admitted. "Let's find out together."

I followed Donnie upstairs to his room. He shoved a few items of clothing and some toiletries from the bathroom into a couple of plastic grocery bags and led me to the front door. "I only came home to grab a few things," he told me. "I've been staying here so that Tooz wouldn't suspect me of anything. I took some time off work so I could spend days with Mindy. The nights have been hard. Tooz has been real angry."

"Has he been taking it out on you?" I asked.

"No more than usual."

"And Mindy?"

"I've got her stashed at a motel up north of town. In Columbia Heights."

"I'll drive us there," I told him.

"And then?" he asked.

"We'll see what develops."

Chapter Twenty-two

The motel was only about six miles north, but with traffic, it took us some twenty-five minutes to get there. And it wasn't really in Columbia Heights. It was actually in the town of Hilltop, the self-proclaimed "Little City with a Big Heart" which at the last census boasted nine hundred and fifty-one souls.

Hilltop is noteworthy as one of only two cities in the United States that boasts a majority of residents living in manufactured housing. The other is Landfall, Minnesota, about twenty-five miles distant. Originally a swath of unincorporated dairy and horse country, in the 1940s, two separate entrepreneurs opened large trailer parks there. Having invested their livelihoods in providing inexpensive—if thin-walled and storm-vulnerable— housing options, the trailer park owners became fearful that their more well-to-do neighbors, who considered the expanse of tightly-clustered mobile homes an aesthetic embarrassment, might take action to have them removed.

To forestall this possibility, they circulated a petition to formally incorporate the land on which the trailer parks stood as its own municipality. Since nearly everyone in the designated area lived in a trailer, the petition passed easily. In time, Hilltop prospered, attracting the construction of a strip mall that included a supermarket, a drugstore, a liquor store, and a bowling alley. The finishing touch was the thirty-eight-room

Starbrite Motel that rose just off Highway 65. Alas, public perception of the city took a big hit when, in 1995, the Minneapolis Star Tribune named Hilltop the "Crime Capitol" of Minnesota after it logged one hundred thirty-one serious crimes in a single year. This worked out to one crime for every six residents. Like the city itself, the once-lauded Starbrite Motel also suffered in the public mind due to repeated health code violations and the fact that, over time, it began to draw a more disreputable and volatile crowd. But although it garners more 911 calls than any other address in the city, the Starbrite's towering red sign with its glowing neon star serves as a beacon, beckoning both the iniquitous and the unwary to partake of its dubious hospitality.

We arrived to find the parking lot half empty. Donnie directed me to the end unit on the lower of the two levels. We parked in a spot in front of the door to the last unit, my car headlights harshly illuminating its slate gray surface.

When we reached the door, Donnie knocked twice. No answer. He knocked again. Two knocks, not too loud, but certainly loud enough to be heard inside. Again, there was no answer.

"You have a key?" I asked.

Donnie nodded.

"Use it," I prompted.

The door opened into a shabby room. Centered against one wall was a queen-sized bed covered in a well-worn bedspread with a floral print. The bed was flanked on each side by small tables, and along the wall opposite the bed squatted a low dresser that supported a large, old-style tube television set. The single window was covered with a thick, green-striped curtain, pulled closed except for the gaps at the top where, in several places, the curtain had torn away from the rings. High up on the wall next to the window was an air conditioner—filthy, its white surface had yellowed and now served mainly as a habitat for insects snuggling comfortably in the thick dust that blocked the intake screen.

"Mindy," Donnie called. "You home? We have company, honey. Lyle's here."

The door to the adjacent bathroom was closed, and although there was no sound, if Mindy was there at all, she would have to be inside. We stood there, Donnie and me, staring at the closed door for nearly a full minute before it swung open.

Mindy was wearing a knee-length, cable-knit sweater, light brown, over black leggings. Her spikey hair with its platinum tips appeared damp from a recent washing. She stared at me, shaking her head dolefully. "Jesus Christ, Dahms," she said at last. "Haven't you caused us enough trouble? Can't you just leave us alone?"

"That's an interesting point of view, Mindy," I countered. "I caused *you* trouble? Doesn't really jibe with the facts, does it?"

She smirked. "What do you know about facts? You've been blundering about blind since my dad had the bad sense to bring you into it. The two of you! You couldn't have fucked things up worse if you'd been trying."

"What are you grousing about?" I asked. "You needed money. Your dad wouldn't give it to you, so you hired a couple of lowlifes to threaten your business, and when that didn't work, you staged your own kidnapping and got your dad to pay. What's the matter? A hundred grand not enough for you? Tell you what, I think I got a couple of fives on me. Happy to hand 'em over if it will make you feel better."

"I told you, Lyle," Donnie insisted. "There is no money. We don't have the money."

"And I told you that I saw the money, and I saw your partners take it from Knuck at the mall."

"Yes, but—"

"Forget it, Donnie," Mindy interrupted. "He's got his mind made up. Like all of them. He knows what happened, and no way could he ever be wrong." She crossed the room and sat down on the bed. "You and Dad can believe what you want. It doesn't matter anymore."

"I'm afraid it does matter," I told her. "If you don't cough up the money, you'll never be safe. Not with Tousignant and Bollok after you. You see, they figure that money is theirs. Don't matter if it is or not. They figure it is, and they're going to come after it."

Donnie slowly crossed the room and sat on the bed next to Mindy. He reached out for her hand, but she pulled it away. "You gotta understand, Lyle," he said. "About the money. First, there was no money. Then there was. But we don't have it anymore."

"I don't have time for riddles, Donnie."

"You don't have time for the truth either," Mindy said. "And that's just fine. But I gotta know, just why the fuck are you here, Lyle?"

"The fact is that I came here to see if you were all right. I don't really know why I should care. Not after the crap I've been through on account of you and your dad. But that's why I came. To see for myself that you are alive and to try to convince you to do the right thing and go on living."

"The right thing!" Mindy exclaimed. "The right fucking thing! Just what is *the right thing* according to you?"

"I don't know. Let's start by telling your father that you're alive. He took a bullet for you. You owe him that much. Don't you?"

Mindy glared.

"He bankrupted himself to keep you alive, even though he thought you might be behind it. He mortgaged everything to come up with your supposed ransom. Maybe giving him the money back would be the right thing."

"You just don't get it, do you, Lyle," Mindy said. "You don't get any of it. We don't have the money. We had it, but we lost it. And we lost it because of you."

"Me?"

"Yeah, you. If it were up to me, I'd have let them kill you. But instead, Donnie here made them a deal. The money for your life." She paused. "Lousy fucking deal if you ask me."

"Whoa," I said. "Slow down, Mindy. What are you telling me?"

Donnie stood and walked toward me. "It's like I said. First, there wasn't any money. Then there was, but we had to give it away."

"Give it to who, Donnie? Who did you have to give it to?"

"To that Cleanhead. To him and his pals. They were going to kill you, Lyle. First, they beat the hell out of you, and then they were going to finish you off. When I tried to stop them, they were going to kill me too. But when I offered them the money, they thought it was real funny. They said after the beating they gave you, you were never gonna be right anyway. They took the money and left all three of us in that house."

"But I thought—"

"I found your cell phone and dialed the last number you'd called," Donnie said. "You'd called it more than once. I figured it was someone you were counting on to help you. Maybe even Mindy's dad. It wasn't. It was this real intense guy." Donnie gave his head a shake at the memory.

"Skip," I said.

"Whoever. I nearly hung up on him. But I didn't. I told them where to find you. Then Mindy and I took off. I wrapped a piece of sheet around your leg, and we took off. I stashed Mindy here and went home so Tooz and Bollok wouldn't know that I was involved. I went home so Mindy would be safe. I've been living with them, waiting for the right time to get her away from here."

I stared at him, my mouth actually hanging open. It couldn't be true, I thought. Why would Donnie do such a thing? Why would Mindy let him? Or Cleanhead?

"Donnie, I—" I began.

"There's your truth, Lyle," Mindy spat at me from the bed. "You're alive because Donnie here saved your ass. And it cost me everything. Happy now? I know I am. Shit. Ain't everything just grand?"

You know how when you stand up too fast, you sometimes have that blurry feeling, like things are fading out, and you're going with them? As if everything corporeal surrounding you was somehow losing its substance and becoming misty with you particlizing along with it. I stood there looking at Donnie and Mindy and felt myself becoming misty. It took several seconds before I recrystallized and rejoined them.

"Thanks, Donnie," I said at last. "I mean it sincerely. Thank you."

Donnie shrugged.

"Why?" I asked. "Why save me? Why not just let them kill me?"

"Believe me," Mindy said, "I've asked him that question over and over."

Donnie lowered his head, staring at his shuffling feet. "I couldn't let them kill you, Lyle. Not after what your family tried to do for me back when…back when…" He was unable to finish the sentence.

"Really, Donnie," I told him. "Thanks. That's…unexpected."

I let the silence gather around us for a couple of seconds, but time was not on our side. I turned to Mindy. "But there are still plenty of questions."

"Oh, what a surprise," Mindy sneered. "The fearless detective has questions."

"Yeah," I said. "I do. We could start with why I should feel guilty because the assholes you enlisted to rip off your dad ended up ripping you off instead. But maybe we'll circle back to that one. Instead, let's start with your dad. According to Knuck, he was heavily invested in your restaurant. He thought it was bringing you two back together. What made you turn on him?"

"I never turned on him," she screeched. "He was my partner. We were in everything together. *He* turned on me."

"You mean when he refused to sink any more money into your restaurant? Is that when he turned on you?"

"I just needed him to see reason," Mindy whimpered. "We were so close. We were nearly open. A little more investment. A little more trust and we'd have been fine."

I smiled. "A little more *trust*?"

"I would have paid it back," Mindy protested. "I'd have earned it back. Every dime. The restaurant was a great concept. We'd have made it. Made it and then some."

"Hold it," I said. "I heard something like ninety percent of all restaurants fail in the first year."

"That is a complete myth," Mindy informed me. "The fact is that only fifty-nine percent fail, and that's like in the first three years."

"Well, I gotta tell ya, I'm probably not going to invest my hard-earned scratch in any venture that has a sixty percent chance of going belly-up within three years."

"It's fifty-nine percent," she repeated. "And he's my father. He's supposed to look out for me. He's supposed to believe in me. He owes me that."

"And what about you, Mindy? What do you owe your dad? You wiped out his life savings, and for what?"

"I took a chance. That's all any of us can do."

I sighed. "Another thing's been bothering me. Tooz and Bollok. Why were they at the mall? Tooz said someone called and told them to be there. That the ransom was being paid. Who would have called them? I didn't call them. Neither did Knuck. No way Cleanhead and his crew invited another couple of gunmen to the party. Who called them?

Mindy stood and stiffly crossed the room to a side table where her purse was lying. She dug through it until she produced a crumpled pack of cigarettes. She fumbled as she drew one from the pack. She seemed to regain control as she touched the end with the flame of a lighter.

"Shit," I exclaimed.

Mindy turned, triumph shining in her eyes. "What is it you think you know? You want to share it with us?"

"Why?" I asked her.

"Why what?"

I turned to Donnie. "Did you know?" His expression was blank, drained. He shook his head.

Turning back to Mindy, I said, "You called them. Christ! You called in the guys that shot your dad."

Mindy took several deep drags on her cigarette. "You don't know anything, Lyle. And you can't prove anything."

"I don't need to *prove* anything. I don't want to *prove* anything. But I do need to know, why the hell would you call those two in just when you were about to get everything you wanted?"

"Nobody ever gets everything they want."

"That's not an answer, Mindy."

She stared at me for a while. Then she turned to Donnie and stared at him a while longer. Finally, she walked to the open bathroom door and tossed her cigarette into the bathroom sink.

"It was Cleanhead," she said, not really looking at either Donnie or me. "I overheard him talking with the other guys. I brought them in and offered a reasonable split, but he planned to take it all. After all the planning. All the work. He wanted it all. Donnie couldn't help me. He'd be useless against them. I needed someone...I don't know, someone who wouldn't be scared. I needed a wild card. A monkey wrench. I thought Tooz would follow the money. I thought maybe I could reason with him. It wasn't a good plan. I wasn't thinking straight. But once I made the call, there was nothing I could do about it."

"So, your dad loses all his money," I said. "Then he takes a bullet because you had some idiotic notion of playing all sides against the middle and hoping like hell that you'd come out with the biggest prize. Shit, Mindy. Don't you care about your dad at all? Is he like everyone else? Just a means to an end?"

She was silent a moment. "It's complicated," she said.

"The fuck it is. He's your dad. You could have looked out for him."

Mindy bowed her head. Donnie crossed the room to her, touching her shoulder. She shivered at his touch.

"And what about you, Donnie?" I asked.

"What do you want to know?"

"Tooz and Bollok came out here from Baltimore looking for something. Your father was dead. My guess is that Bollok was the guy with the shotgun all those years ago. Not that we'll ever prove it. But there's the question of the money. Everyone figured your dad made off with a lot of money. Or drugs. Or both. Something valuable enough that Tooz would cool his heels in the joint for twenty-three years waiting to get his hands on. Something valuable enough to kill your dad for. That's the story told among the old timers in Baltimore. I know. I checked. And that's gotta be what brought Tooz and Bollok to town. They want their money. They think you have it. Don't they?"

Donnie shook his head. "No. Tooz knows I don't have it. He knows that if I had it, I would have given it to him. He knows another thing, too, although he doesn't want to admit it. There never was any money."

"Explain that to me."

"I've been living with this a long time, Lyle. It's like a tune that's always playing in the background. Sometimes, it's so soft I can barely hear it. Sometimes it's all I can hear."

He swallowed. "My dad didn't run out on Tooz because he'd stolen any money. He ran off because he was scared. When Tooz and them tried to rob those Colombians, my dad heard the shooting and bolted like a rabbit. When Tooz was arrested, Dad figured he'd blow town and set up someplace else. He made his way to Minnesota, found work, married, and had a son. But the fear never left him. It became part of who he was. It infected my mother, too. They were both scared. Scared all the time, but they wouldn't talk about it. And it turned out they had every reason to be scared."

"Was it Bollok?" I asked. "Do you know if it was him? Did he kill your parents?"

Donnie shrugged. "I'm with you, Lyle. I figure it was Bollok with the shotgun. I mean, who else? And if it was, he's the one that killed my mom."

"And your dad," I said.

Donnie shook his head. "No. Dad was hurt. Really hurt. Probably dying. But he wasn't dead. I got there too late to do anything about that. They'd already been shot. Mom was dead. The shooter was gone."

Puzzled, I said, "That's not how the police report reads. There's no mention in the report that you were there at all."

"The report is a lie," Donnie said. "I was there. And I'm the one who killed my father."

Chapter Twenty-three

Passing car tires crunched softly in the parking lot outside the motel room. A jagged beam of light swept the room through the gaps in the curtains. Donnie and Mindy stood close together, not looking at one another. Not touching. I listened as the car moved slowly on.

"I couldn't believe he survived the shooting," Donnie continued. "He was all opened up. His breaths were gurgles. He was talking, but I couldn't understand him. I knelt on the floor beside him. I couldn't make it out at first, but finally, I understood. Dad had a .38 he kept upstairs in a drawer of his bedside table. He asked me to get it for him. I told him that whoever had shot him had gone. That we needed to get him an ambulance. He got more agitated. He insisted I get the gun. I needed to calm him down. I went upstairs and got the gun.

"Your dad and Mr. Fullmer pulled up in their squad car as I was coming down the stairs. I watched them through the windows. I heard their radio squawk. I saw them get out of the car and run over to where my mom was lying. I saw Mr. Fullmer put his fingers against my mom's neck. I saw him shake his head.

"They come in, guns drawn, yelling. I think maybe they'll shoot me too. I freeze. I just stand there on the stairs. They call and call, but I can't answer. I hear them walking through the rooms below me. I see your dad at the bottom of the stairs. I don't move. I don't speak.

Finally, he spots me. He trains his gun on me. He shouts something, but I can't make out what it is. It's just more yelling. I close my eyes and wait. Wait to hear the shot that will kill me.

"All at once, he's got an arm around me. I'm still holding the gun. I watch as he puts a hand around mine. He's got big hands. His hand swallows mine up. He asks me for the gun. I don't remember letting go, but I remember us walking together down the stairs. When we reached the bottom, the gun was in *his* hand.

"I tell him everything I know. I tell him how I came home and found Mom dead and Dad dying. I tell him I needed to be with Dad. That it was important.

"Your dad makes me go sit in the living room. Mr. Fullmer is going from room to room. He passes us and goes upstairs, checking those rooms too. Then he goes into the basement. I ask your dad again if I can be in the kitchen with my father. It takes a while, but he finally lets me go.

"In the kitchen, I kneel next to my dad. Your dad stands over us, watching. I lean in close. My dad's voice is barely a whisper. He's asking about the gun. I look up at your dad. He's still holding it. My dad says it's over. He just wants it all to be over. I didn't know what he was talking about at first. Then he says for me to get the gun and help him make it all be over. He begs me to shoot him. He's in terrible pain. He's begging. I never heard him beg before, but he's begging. Then Mr. Fullmer comes out of the basement. He takes your dad by the arm, and they move toward the back door. Mr. Fullmer is pointing. My mom's out there. Just as they reach the door, your dad puts the .38 on the counter. Your dad and Mr. Fullmer step outside. They're just on the other side of the door. They could turn around any second. I have to move fast. I spring to my feet. I grab the gun. I kneel back down next to my dad and press the barrel against his head. I can't be sure, but I think I hear him right. I think I hear him say, 'Thank you.'

"I don't remember much after that. I remember the noise. I remember the gun going off. I don't remember much else."

Mindy turned and crossed the room to her purse. She pulled out another cigarette, lit it, and stood smoking, her eyes as cloudy and gray as the smoke from her cigarette.

Donnie looked up at me and smiled wanly. "They didn't tell anybody." Donnie continued. "They said I was in shock. They said I only did what my old man wanted. They said there was no way they'd let me do time for it. They wrote it up the way they wrote it up. They took shit for it, but they stood by me anyway. Your dad even took me in. Both your dad and Mr. Fullmer stood by me. They stood by me right up until I let them down. I bought a gun of my own. Little thing. I had it with me when I went to the fair. You remember? Racing Days. I shot that guy with it. Still not even sure why. Just seemed like I had to, I guess. I paid for that. Paid for a long time. I don't let myself touch guns anymore."

Mindy blew a cloud of cigarette smoke out into the room around us. Donnie shrugged and quietly crossed the room to her. When he drew close, she reached out and took his hand.

"I couldn't believe it when I ran into Mindy again after all those years," Donnie continued. "She was the best thing that happened to me in high school. I thought I'd lost her forever after I…after I was arrested. But she sees past that, and I guess I'm starting to see past it, too.

I'll do anything it takes to make things right with her. With her and me."

Donnie's grasp around Mindy's hand tightened noticeably. Both of their gazes, steady and cold, turned to me.

I knew it was my turn to say something. It was my party, after all. I'd insisted on the meeting. I'd insisted that I hear the truth. I guess I thought that if everyone came clean, I would know what to do. I didn't know a damn thing.

"You got a cell phone, Donnie?" I asked at last.

"Sure."

I pulled out my wallet and fished out a business card, stretching out my arm to hand it to him. "Text me the number," I told him. I waited. A moment later, the cell phone in my pocket chirped.

"Like I told you earlier," I said, "Tooz and Bollok should be tied up for a couple of days. You might want to lie low for a few more. Can you get time off work, Donnie?"

"Maybe. Probably."

"You got any money saved up?

He nodded.

"Enough?" I prodded.

He nodded again. "Enough for a little while."

I sighed. "Okay," I said, turning to leave. "I'll be in touch."

Donnie stiffened. "What are you going to do?"

I shook my head. "I really don't know," I admitted. "Something."

"You going to tell anybody?" Donnie asked.

"Tell anybody what?"

I left before he could reply.

The drive home took a lot less time than the drive up to the motel. Driving home always seems to take less time. I fiddled with the radio, but I couldn't seem to focus on the music. Instead, I thought about Donnie and Mindy. I didn't believe in their future. There was too much of the past in their way. I didn't even think I owed them anything. But now I knew their secrets. Now, they were my secrets, too.

I thought about my dad. Donnie's secret had been his as well. He'd hid it away. He'd let it eat at him. He died trying to be rid of it. He died passing it on to me.

I arrived home more tired than I remember being before.

## Chapter Twenty-four

Despite my fatigue, I had a difficult time falling asleep. Finally, I got up and took one of the remaining pain pills they'd given me when I was released from the hospital. I slept long but fitfully. There was a buzzing inside my head. I didn't hear it. I felt it. Like an electric current. A silent vibration that colored my dreams.

It was early afternoon before I got out of bed. I trundled down the hall to the bathroom, showered, and afterward, stood staring at the man in the mirror. I wasn't thrilled by what I saw. I returned to my room, dressed, and then made my way out into the living room. There, I found Edgerton sitting on the couch watching television. Basil and Nigel were curled up on the couch beside him. As I entered, Basil raised his head and eyed me indifferently. Nigel leaped from his perch, raced across the room, and tried to climb up my leg. Edgerton didn't even flinch.

He was watching an old episode of *The Twilight Zone*. I'd seen the episode before. We both had. Many times. Burgess Meredith plays Henry Bemis, a small, bookish man who is nearly blind without his glasses and whose only real love is the printed word. But he is frustrated by a cruelly nagging wife and an angry boss who both work to keep him from his reading—his only true escape from a small, inconsequential life. When he enters the bank vault, as is his habit, to steal a few minutes in solitude with a book, a hydrogen bomb explodes outside, destroying the world he knew. Hopeless, bereft, and utterly alone, Bemis contemplates suicide until his eyes alight upon a miracle—the ruins of a public library, its books intact and waiting for him. Enough books to last a lifetime. Enough books to retrieve his lost soul. Bemis gleefully organizes the books, creating enormous stacks and plotting out how he will fill the time he has left. But as he reaches for the first book, Bemis stumbles, and his glasses fall to the ground, where they shatter. The last we hear from him is his cry, "It's not fair. It's not fair!"

I stood behind Edgerton, watching, waiting until the episode concluded. In the quiet after it ended, I thought about what was fair, what was possible, and how the best-laid plans of mice and men, Henry Bemis and, yes, even Lyle Dahms, more often than not, lay crushed and shattered just when we thought we were about to succeed.

Donnie reunited with Mindy only to have that dream undermined by the arrival of Tooz and Bollok. Knuck's dream of re-establishing a relationship with Mindy dashed against the hard reality of financing. I'd sought to fulfill my father's dying wish. All I'd done was make things worse. And I had no idea how to make them better.

Edgerton turned to find me standing there. "I didn't hear you come in last night," he said. "It's good you were feeling well enough to get out. Where'd you go? How were things out in the world?"

I shrugged. "Interesting. I squared off against a couple of armed guys in an elementary school parking lot. I got arrested. I found Mindy Fullmer. Oh, and my mom is selling my boyhood home."

Edgerton stared, then nodded at last. "You eat?"

"Not today."

"In that case, I suppose you'll want to take me out for a bite."

"Oh yeah," I deadpanned. "That's the top of my list."

"I'll get my coat," he said. "McCauley's?"

"Sure."

Skip was behind the bar when we entered. He barely raised his eyes at us before turning his back to fiddle with a rack of beer glasses positioned below the taps. For Skip, this was tantamount to a hearty welcome. Edgerton and I grabbed a couple of menus and took seats in a booth in the corner of the room. The bar was nearly empty. The jukebox was playing the 1967 Bee Gees hit *New York Mining Disaster 1941*.

Skip came by, and I ordered a full breakfast—two over-medium eggs, sausage, hash browns, and sourdough toast. Edgerton went with the "Mexican pizza," a flour tortilla baked in the pizza oven topped with seasoned ground beef, tomatoes, onions, black olives, and cheese. He ordered two extra squeeze packets of sour cream. Quite the gourmet.

My phone rang before the food arrived. It was Gabriel Essoe, the Burnsville cop I'd met the day before. It was a courtesy call, he told me. He wanted me to know that Willard Tousignant and Janos Bollok had made bail.

"I thought you said they'd be in for at least a couple of days."

"I was wrong," he told me before hanging up.

Maybe it was the after-effects of the beating I'd received, and maybe it was that I just wasn't very good at my job, but I really didn't know what to do with the news.

Edgerton squinted. "You going to tell me what's going on?"

I did. I told him about how Tooz and Bollok had been waiting for me as I left my mom's house. I told him about the Gun Free Zones Act and how it didn't really seem to matter much. I told him about Mindy and the lost money and how she and Donnie probably saved my life. I told him about Donnie killing his own father and how Tooz and Bollok were still looking for a payday, and how they were determined to get one no matter who they had to threaten. And I told him that I was completely at a loss as to what to do about any of it.

"And now they're out?" Edgerton asked. "Tooz and Bollok?"

"Yep."

"They going to come looking for you?"

"I suppose. If Donnie stays out of sight like I told him to, there really isn't anyone else they can go after."

"What about Knuck?"

"I don't think so. He already called in every marker he had to get the ransom together. He couldn't come up with more money if his life depended on it."

"Which it might," Edgerton observed.

I nodded.

"Where else might they go?"

"I think you nailed it, Stephen. I don't think there's anyone else for them to come after. I think they'll come after me."

"That comforting," he said, grinning. "Particularly since we live in the same house."

I shrugged. "Hey, you could always stay somewhere

else. Maybe Skip would take you in for a few days. Or the Milkman."

"Or maybe *you* could stay somewhere else. You know, get a motel room or stay with your mom or—" Edgerton paused. "Okay, you probably don't want to stay with your mom. No reason to put a target on her back."

I thought about that. I thought about how Tooz and Bollok had braced me the day before as I was leaving my mom's house. I suddenly had an overwhelming desire to talk to her. I pulled out my cell phone. Edgerton's eyes crinkled with concern.

There was no answer at Mom's. Skip brought our food order to the table. He and Edgerton exchanged a significant glance. I tried the number again. Still no answer. "I gotta go," I announced.

"Wait a minute!" Edgerton exclaimed, getting to his feet. "Think this through. If there is something going on at your mom's house, you're going to need backup."

I stood and pushed past him. "No time," I said. "Besides, it's probably my imagination. I'll run down there. If there's anything to worry about, I'll give you a call."

Edgerton was on my heels. He reached out and put a hand on my shoulder. I shrugged it off and got a couple of steps closer to the door. Edgerton reached out again, grabbing at the sleeve of my jacket. I turned. Skip put a solid hand on Edgerton's shoulder. "Let him go," Skip said. His tone defied argument.

"Why?" Edgerton persisted. "Why can't he wait a damn minute? We could come up with a plan. We could—"

Skip shook his head. "He's gotta go now."

"Why now? Why not wait until—"

Skip glared. "'Cause it's what you do when it's your mom."

Chapter Twenty-five

The sun was still high overhead as I pulled onto 35W and headed south toward Burnsville. A bank of fluffy clouds was stacking up on the horizon—white, but with splotches of gray darkening the interior. I drove calmly, well within the speed limit, telling myself that Mom not answering the phone didn't mean anything. She was probably out somewhere, maybe at Carla Haberman's, checking out the grounds of her new condo. Still, I was acutely aware of the weight of Dad's Magnum pressing against me in the shoulder holster I wore under my jacket.

When I arrived, I glanced at the "For Sale" sign at the edge of the lawn. The notice "Offer Pending" had been added. I wondered exactly how long it had been since Mom had put the house on the market.

There were no cars in the driveway and certainly no sign of Bollok's El Camino. As I pulled in, I began to wonder what I would do if she wasn't home. I couldn't remember if there was still a key to the house on my ring. I couldn't remember the last time I'd let myself in.

I got out of the car slowly, still sore, still moving as gently as I could. I shut the car door behind me and stared for a moment at the front door as if willing it to open, my mom standing on the other side. When it didn't, I walked up the front steps.

I knocked, softly at first, but then more insistently.

There was no answer. I knocked again. Then again. I pulled my key ring out of my pocket but didn't appear to have a key to the family home. I had my lock picks in my car, I remembered.

But before breaking in, I decided to do a bit of recon. I made my way around the side of the house and peered in the garage window. It was dark inside, but I could make out my dad's old Buick parked within. Mom was typically suburban. She never walked anywhere. If she'd left, the car would be gone, too.

I slid the Magnum from its holster.

I heard the front door swing open. For as long as I remember, it had made a sweeping sound when it opened. Not harsh or grating, but a light swoosh like the wing of a great bird in flight. I inched toward the sound, both hands wrapped around the big handgun.

I stepped around the corner of the house. The front steps came into view, and with them, the figure of Willard Tousignant. He cradled a shotgun in his arms, not raising it, just letting it lie there like a sleeping python. I smiled an incongruous smile of recognition when I realized that it was my dad's gun. "I guess you better join our little party, friend," he said.

"I appreciate the invitation, Mr. Tousignant," I told him. "But I'm thinking I might do better to just blow your head off where you stand."

Tousignant grinned. That great big clown grin. "Oh, I wouldn't do that," he said. "Janos is inside with your mom. You shoot me, and he's liable to react poorly. I think you'd best just come on in and join us. Your mom's been asking about you." He motioned with his head. "Come on in, now. Let's go see how your mom's getting on."

Tousignant turned and disappeared inside. I kept both hands wrapped around my gun as I followed him meekly through the front door and into the living room.

When you are trying to sell a house, the experts will tell you to remove most of what makes the place yours. Things like photographs and knickknacks you picked up on vacation. Things that tell a personal story. Evidently, Mom was having none of that. The foul ball that Dad caught off the bat of Kent Hrbek during the Twins run to the playoffs back in 1987 still had a prominent place on the bookshelf. Along one wall stood Dad's gun cabinet—the door open, his shotgun conspicuously absent. Along another wall, facing the TV, sat Dad's recliner, a thicket of framed family photographs standing proudly on the nearby side table.

Mom was sitting in Dad's chair. I don't think I'd ever seen her in that chair before. Bollok stood behind her, the barrel of a Beretta M9 trained at the back of her head.

She started to sob when she saw me. "Oh, Lyle," she exclaimed. "Why'd you have to come?"

She started to rise, but Bollok reached out his free hand and viciously pushed her back into the chair. It took preternatural self-control on my part not to shoot him immediately.

"We're getting you out of this," I assured Mom.

Bollok bowed his head slightly. His gun barrel didn't so much as quiver.

"I'm glad to hear you say that, friend," Tousignant said. "You do what I ask, and I'm sure we can find a way to get your mom through this."

Bright sunshine streamed in through the curtains, slicing across the room and forming a barrier between us.

Tousignant stood to my left, near the entrance to the archway that led back into the kitchen. He'd taken that position deliberately. My eyes focused on Bollok, I could only just make Tousignant out at the edge of my peripheral vision.

"You have some kind of proposition, Mr. Tousignant?" I asked.

"I do, now that you mention it. I propose that you help me get my money."

"Now, what money is that?"

Tousignant snorted. "Well, I think you know that's a bit on the complicated side. But I'm here to make it uncomplicated. It don't matter if it's money from poor Donnie. I figure his coward of a daddy owed me big for doing his time for him. And I don't care if it's the money that your pal Fullmer handed over at the mall the other day. Hell, I don't care if it's the money your sweet old mama makes from the sale of this house. Money's money. It's mine, and I'm gonna get it. And I don't care how many of you folks I have to kill to get what's mine."

"It's nice to hear you're so egalitarian about all this, Mr. Tousignant. I mean about the equal opportunity killing and all. But can I ask one question? Why are you so all fired focused on me? I mean, the way I get it is that Mindy was afraid that her partners were going to stiff her on the ransom, so she reached out to you. If you'd done your job, this would be over. You can't hold me responsible for your failures."

"So, you've talked with the Fullmer girl, have you?" Tousignant asked. "That's fine. You let me know where she is, and I'll leave you to it. After all, she promised me a cut. Just tell me where she is, and I'll let you live." He paused. "You and your mom."

I shook my head. "Can't do it, Mr. Tousignant."

I kept my eyes centered on Bollok, but I could make out enough of Tousignant to know that he'd shifted his position. Then I heard the sharp *click, click* of a shotgun shell being chambered.

"Have it your way, fella," he said.

Mom took a deep breath, closed her eyes, and lowered her head.

"Sorry I got you into this, Mom," I told her.

She sobbed again, but when she raised her head, her eyes were full of determination. "You didn't get me into this," she said, her voice surprisingly steady. "Your dad asked you to find out about Donnie. That's why we're here."

"You shoulda known better," Tousignant interrupted. "It's never a good idea to go trying to pay off somebody else's debts." He chuckled. "I guess you'd say it's really kinda ironic. Your dad gets you into this mess. Donnie got into this on account of his old man, too. I'm guessing Donnie told you about him killing his daddy. Told me, too. Unburdening himself, I guess you'd call it. Told me about your daddy letting him get by with it as well. And now we're looking at you letting your mommy get killed. Helluva world, ain't it?"

I caught movement from Tousignant out of the corner of my eye. Time's up, I thought.

I held the Magnum steady, the barrel sighted directly at Bollok's head. Slow pressure on the trigger, I reminded myself. Like they teach you at the range. No margin for error. My aim had to be true.

A loud crack sounded from the back of the house. For an instant, I wondered if it had come from my gun. Bollok's head snapped up at the noise, his eyes darting to where Tousignant had been standing. I never took my eyes off him.

Instead, I squeezed the trigger.

Bollok's head exploded—a violent splatter of blood and bone spraying a ghastly pattern on the living room wall.

As Bollok crumbled to the floor, I glanced over at Tousignant. He was on his knees, the shotgun on the ground before him, the top of his head split wide open. His eyes wide but glazed and unseeing, he slowly collapsed onto the living room carpet.

Mom stood, strangely silent and dappled with blood spatter. She stared first at me, then at each of the two dead men, and finally at Skip as he came out of the kitchen, a nine-millimeter Glock in his hand. Skip crossed the room slowly, first approaching Bollok, then Tousignant, nudging their weapons further from their prostrate bodies. "Can't be too careful," he said.

"I…um…I…" I mumbled.

"Save it," Skip said. "Take care of your mom."

I slipped the Magnum back into its holster and went to her, taking her in my arms.

After several seconds, Skip said, "We got a problem. The cops will be here any minute. I can't be here for that."

I nodded. "That piece registered to you?"

Skip smiled. "You know better."

I reached out a hand. "I'll take it. It's best to leave it here. Better if the cops find it on the premises."

He handed me the gun. "I gotta go. Edgerton's waiting for me in my car. He insisted on coming."

"I owe you," I told him. "Big time."

"Don't mention it," he said. Turning to Mom, he

added, "Seriously. Don't mention it. Ever." He then disappeared into the kitchen and out the back door.

I sat Mom back into Dad's recliner and took Skip's gun into the kitchen, where I found a towel and wiped it clean of any fingerprints. As I re-entered the living room, I heard the sound of approaching sirens.

Mom rose, surveying the room, her eyes sweeping the bodies of the dead men, their blood spreading slowly into her carpet. She turned to look at me. "Give me his gun."

"What? Why would I—"

"Give me his gun," she repeated.

I handed her Skip's gun.

Mom walked over to Tousignant's body, careful not to sully her pumps with his blood. She grasped the gun firmly by the handle and slipped her index finger around the trigger. She sighted it at the corpse, her finger tightening. Before the gun went off, she loosened her grip and tiptoed back to where I was standing.

She handed me back the gun. "They'll think I killed him," she told me. "I wish I had."

Chapter Twenty-six

We managed to get all of Mom's stuff into one truckload. It helped that she'd held several yard sales after insisting that Chuck and I look through everything she'd labeled as dispensable prior to the move. Chuck took a bunch of stuff. He had a big house with plenty of storage and a well-developed sense of nostalgia. I had the Magnum and Dad's old service revolver.

Mom had wanted to hire a moving crew. I'd insisted that we rent a small truck and do it ourselves. I'd enlisted both the Milkman and Edgerton to help with the move—the Milkman, unsurprisingly, turning out to be much the better worker. While he and I hauled box after box from the house to the truck, Edgerton mostly regaled Mom with stories about the dogs, his recent promotion at work, and the adventures of the Drealth—the bug-like alien race that populated the graphic novel he'd been working on for the past couple of years.

The truth is that it was the Milkman who did the lion's share of the work. I was still pretty sore from the travails of recent weeks and couldn't really lift anything much heavier than a throw pillow. But we'd got an early start and had the truck loaded by early afternoon.

I stood with Mom on the front steps, staring into the living room one last time before we locked up and left the house forever.

We'd hired a couple of out-of-work neighborhood

guys who knew something about construction to clean up the living room after the shootings. The drywall repair was actually pretty inexpensive, but replacing the carpet cost a lot more than I would have figured. Still, the place looked pretty good, and Mom insisted that her insurance was going to cover it.

As we stood on the front steps looking into the living room, I was suddenly struck by how much had changed. It wasn't just the lack of furniture. It ran far deeper. Back when I lived there, even when my dad was out on patrol, even when I knew full well that he was nowhere near home, I always felt him in the house. I'd stop what I was doing, even turn the TV down, and listen, wondering if I heard his foot on the stairs. It struck me forcefully—sad and certain—that now it really was no more than an empty house.

"Your dad loved this place."

I reached out and took her hand. "I know. It meant a lot to him that he had a place of his own. A family to call his. A place to center himself."

"He loved you and Chuck," Mom said. "More than anything."

"I guess."

Mom frowned. "After all we've been through, you can't doubt that?"

I smiled. "Dad was always a cypher. It was clear how much he cared about his family, but the truth is he treated me pretty badly. I could never please him, and he made damn sure that I knew it."

"He was just trying to help you be the best you could possibly be. That's all. He just wanted the best for you. Especially since…" she paused.

"Especially since I didn't turn out at all like he'd

hoped," I said.

Mom patted me on the arm. "Both you and your Dad always had to do things your own way. It's no surprise you didn't always see eye to eye."

She sighed and pulled the door toward her, closing it with a definitive click.

We walked down the driveway to the waiting truck. I'd been pretty disappointed when I'd picked it up and found that it was not an automatic. I hadn't driven a manual transmission in many years, and there had been much grinding and cursing on the drive from the U-Haul to my mom's house. That and it was far larger than anything I was used to driving. After several failed attempts, I'd had to ask the Milkman to back it into my mom's driveway. But even though the Milkman had offered, I'd insisted that I drive the load from the house in Burnsville to Mom's new condo. I wanted her to know that I was solidly behind her in her new, more independent life. Still, I vowed that this would be the last time I ever willingly drove one of those rigs again.

The Milkman and Edgerton drove my car to the condo. I helped Mom climb into the passenger seat of the truck and slowly pulled out of the driveway, silently thanking the gods that the Baileys who lived next door had moved the car they'd had parked on the street and which I'd nearly crushed trying to pull the truck into the driveway earlier in the day. I drove carefully and quietly until I reached the freeway and felt relaxed enough to reengage in conversation.

"You doing okay, Mom?" I asked. "Pretty tough few weeks."

"I'm okay, honey. I'm excited to be moving into the new place and sad at the same time. Change has never come easy for me, but I will say that I'm glad to be letting go of a few things."

"Like what?"

She smiled. "Like I'm actually glad to get out of the old neighborhood. Don't get me wrong, when your father was still with us, I was thrilled to be there. But with him gone, I'm glad to be finding a place of my own."

"You guys had lots of friends there. You'll miss them."

Mom shook her head. "Not really, Lyle. They were Ray's friends. I have a few, I guess. But I'll make more now between the crowd at the new condo and at church. And they won't all be cops or cops' wives." She paused. "By the way, what do you hear from Johnny Fullmer?"

"Mindy came home," I told her. "She's living with Knuck and Phyllis. They say it's just till she gets on her feet. Didn't say when they expect that will be."

"I thought she was living with Donnie. They don't have to hide now that…that those two men are gone."

"No, Mindy's not with Donnie anymore."

"Why not?"

"Wasn't meant to be."

Mom paused. "And Naomi?"

I shook my head. "That wasn't meant to be either."

"I'm sorry, honey."

We fell silent looking out the window as we crossed the Minnesota River. In the distance loomed the six-hundred-eighty-foot concrete smokestack of the old Northern States Power Black Dog plant—long since rechristened the Xcel Energy Black Dog plant. Although I still cringed at the name change, I had to applaud the fact that the old girl no longer burned coal. Word was that the company was on track to get more than half of its power from carbon-free sources by 2030. I wondered where I'd be by 2030. I wondered where any of us would be.

"Too bad about Donnie," Mom said. "Him losing Mindy and all."

"Uh-huh," I agreed.

"He's lost so much."

"Uh-huh," I repeated.

I should have left it at that, but somehow I couldn't. "Did you know that Dad let Donnie kill his father?"

Although I didn't turn to face her, I could feel her looking at me. "I'm not sure I'd put it that way."

"I know, but…But I guess I would. Put it that way, I mean. Vernon Murdoch is begging Donnie to put him out of his misery, and Dad conveniently places a gun within reach. Then he walks away. Hard to put any other way."

"Your Dad didn't know that Donnie was going to do that. There's no way that—"

"He knew," I said. "He either knew or at least thought it likely. Either way, it's a helluva burden to place on a high school kid."

"We all have burdens, Lyle. And they're not all placed on us. Some we take up on our own."

I thought about that. About what Donnie felt he owed his dad. About what his dad had asked of him. I thought about what parents owed their kids and what kids owed them in return. Finally, I thought about the shadows of the past, how they encroach upon the present, and how, together, they shape what's to come.

Then I smiled at my mom and drove her to her new home.

## A word about the author…

Brian Anderson is a graduate of the University of Minnesota whose Dinkytown neighborhood provides the setting for his mystery series featuring private investigator Lyle Dahms. The Dahms novels spring from his lifelong love of mystery fiction, especially the works of Dashiell Hammett and Raymond Chandler, as well as more contemporary masters like Robert B. Parker and G. M. Ford. He is a three-time finalist in the Pacific Northwest Writers Association mystery and suspense contest, and his debut novel, The Shiver in Her Eyes, was a finalist in their Nancy Pearl Contest for published fiction.

In 2024, he released his standalone novel Yule Tide, which features a fallen angel turned private investigator who fights to wrest Christmas from the dark forces who have taken control and twisted it to their evil ends.

Brian spent much of his professional career working to alleviate domestic hunger serving as the operations director of the Emergency Feeding Program of Seattle & King County as well as the manager of the Pike Market Food Bank in downtown Seattle. Married with three beautiful daughters, he now lives and writes in Ocean Shores, a small city on the Washington coast.

www.brianandersonmysteries.com